D0376388

NA

ARENA

John
Jakes

OLMSTEAD
PRESS
An [e-*reads*] Book

Copyright © 1963, 2001 by John Jakes

This is a work of fiction.
All the characters and events portrayed in this book are fictitious, and any resemblance to real people or events is purely coincidental.

All rights reserved.
Except for the quotation of short passages for the purposes of criticism and review, no part of this publication may be reproduced in whole or in part in any form.

Published in 2001 by Olmstead Press: Chicago, Illinois
e-reads: New York, New York

Previously published in 1963 by Ace Books, Inc.: New York

Cover designed by Hope Forstenzer

Text designed and typeset by
Syllables, Hartwick, New York, USA

Printed and bound in the USA by
Rose Printing, Tallahassee, Florida

ISBN: 1-58754-117-3

Publisher's Cataloging In Publication Data
(Prepared by Donohue Group, Inc.)

Jakes, John, 1932-
    Arena / John Jakes.
    p. ; cm.
    ISBN: 1-587-54117-3
    1. Animal trainers—Rome—Fiction. 2. Rome—Fiction. 3. Historical fiction. 4. Adventure stories. I. Title.
PS3560.A37 A7 2001
813/.54

Editorial Sales Rights and Permission Inquiries should be addressed to:
Olmstead Press, 22 Broad Street, Suite 34, Milford, CT 06460
Email: Editor@lpcgroup.com

Manufactured in the United States of America
1 3 5 7 9 10 8 6 4 2

Substantial discounts on bulk quantities of Olmstead Press books are available to corporations, professional associations and other organizations. If you are in the USA or Canada, contact LPC Group, Attn: Special Sales Department, 1-800-626-4330, fax 1-800-334-3892, or email: sales@lpcgroup.com.

Author's Introduction to the New Olmstead Press/e-reads Edition

In the 1960's, the pseudonymous Jay Scotland wrote six mass market paperback historical novels, four for Ace Books, two for Avon. These represent my first ventures in a field that had provided me with enthralling reading for years. At the time, I never imagined the success that would come to me when I returned to historicals with *The Bastard*, the first of *The Kent Family Chronicles*, in the 1970's.

Of the six novels that preceded my later work, *Arena*, the fifth, remains my favorite. Ancient Rome was always a subject that fascinated me. Consequently much more research went into *Arena* than went into the other novels of the 60's. The first one, a pirate novel commissioned by the late Don Wollheim of Ace Books, contained almost none, I am chagrined to say. I wrote *Strike the Black Flag* much as the old pulp magazine hacks churned out their monthly novels: in a hurry, for money, with precious little concern about the accuracy of the content.

Arena was different; I worked to unearth and include authentic background and detail. That may be why I like the book more than the others, even though I see plenty of passages that make me wince after nearly four decades. I was tempted to revise the text but did not; I hope you'll enjoy the novel but judge it gently, as early work.

The author of the published novel was "Jay Scotland" because, for the pirate novel, Don Wollheim had asked for a pseudonym. He didn't think my name sufficiently romantic for historicals. Never one to stint on acerbic observations about his writers, Don wrote that, to him, John Jakes sounded like "faulty plumbing."

In less than an hour I came up with an alternate. I recalled that the great crime writer Cornell Woolrich, asked to supply a pseudonym, invented "William Irish" out of a family name and the first country that came to mind. I took Jay from my initials, opened the atlas, found Scotland near Ireland, and there you are.

I'm delighted to see this favorite of mine return in a new print edition and in the new formats of this startling new age of electronic publishing. I thank Richard Curtis and his colleagues at e-reads for making it possible.

John Jakes
Hilton Head Island, South Carolina
January 2001

Author's Note

This novel deals with Imperial Rome under the last of the Julian Caesars, L. Domitius Ahenobarbus, better known as Nero. His world has been rightly described by the scholar Grant as "unique, terrible, and rich in allurements and astonishments." Even so, the author feels obliged to point out that certain elements in the story are not wild imagination but historical reality.

First the characters. Some of the following are well known, others not. All were real people: the blond courtesan Poppaea; Agrippina and Octavia, Nero's mother and wife, respectively; Serenus, the commander of the night watch; Burrus, Prefect of the Praetorians; the scheming Sicilian horse breeder Tigellinus; the evil sailor Anicetus; the two men whose philosophies were so different, yet so strikingly alike—the millionaire savant Seneca and the apostle Paul; and the young prostitute Acte and the beautiful poisoner Locusta.

The other characters, including the beast-man Cassius whose chronicle this is, are fictitious. The Bestiarii School, however, was an actual training ground for animal handlers and hunters. The erotic cult of Cybele was widespread in Rome. The great fire of 64 did begin in the Circus Maximus (though nobody today knows how). The method of "manufacturing" unicorns, Agrippina's death, and the fear of the Vestal Virgins are all matters of record.

Lastly, a word about proper names. Those of citizens were in three parts, full of confusing duplication. Both Seneca and Serenus, for example, carried the same nomen, or second name, Annaeus. Because this is a tale of adventure, not an instructional tome, the author has simplified many triple names to a double or even a single one.

J.S

Book I

57–59 A.D.
THE BEAST MEN OF NERO IMPERATOR

CHAPTER I

—————◦———◦◦———

Not for several moments did we guess we had been tricked into dying.

The lanista's helpers grunted and hauled ropes. The trainer himself, scarred and white-locked Fabius, threw a whip to me and one to the Egyptian. I caught the butt and waited, wondering why Fabius retired so quickly to the stands. He sat among the students who had been allowed to watch. Strangely, he neither met my stare nor issued any last words of instruction.

Ropes squealed on pulleys. In the niches around the wall of the little amphitheater the fronts of the log cages slid up out of sight. The Egyptian Horus, an arrogant coppery giant, tested his lash. He snapped it so hard the three leaden balls at the ends of the triple thong sang and whistled. I scuffed a sandal in the imported sand. This sparkling Egyptian stuff was not ordinarily laid down in the school arena. Usually the yellow clay was flooring enough for our lessons. I began then to suspect.

The first leopard padded from its cage. It sniffed the morning air. It was soon joined by the second, longer, leaner, hissing gently over wet fangs.

Horus never lifted his eyes from them, saying in a whisper so as not to arouse the animals, "Cassius, we must help each other. They're man-eaters."

"Help yourself," I said. "You've never acted so comradely before."

He cursed in his own tongue. With careful steps he walked to the shadows on the amphitheater's far side. A cloud skated across the sun. Above the stands rose the jumble of golden houses on the Palatine where the Emperor lived out his days. Over the walls drifted the shrilling of fruit hawkers in the arches beneath the Circus Maximus. A chill seized me even though the hot sun of Latium warmed all my body. In the manner of a student, I was naked except for a codpiece.

The leopards sniffed the wind. A hush gripped the stands. I picked out faces from my eye's corner: Fabius, staring into space as though overcome with guilt; the foxy new student Syrax with the gold hoop in his ear; the thick-nosed and powerful Xenophon. Well, none of them would mourn my death. I had no friends among the slaves and the criminals and the auctorati who were pupils here.

A few nobles were present too, including a Sicilian with a long jaw who wore the toga of an eques, or knight. Beside him sat a Praetorian in glittering armor. This pair seemed to enjoy the spectacle of two victims waiting in the muggy Tiber breeze for the leopards to cease their padding back and forth, their hissing and purring, and rip us.

The whip was almost useless. I thought of my father's trick. Would it help me? I had never tried it before. The Sicilian in the stands called; "Stay alive, there, Horus, and we'll recommend you to the Emperor!"

"Don't forget we've placed side bets," added the Praetorian. "I'd hate to lose my sesterces because Fabius trained you poorly."

"A little action, a little action!" The Sicilian pounded his knee.

From somewhere the soldier produced a pebble and flung it at the nearer leopard. Stung on the flank, the beast uncoiled and leaped, flying across the sun with its claws after my throat.

I cracked the whip as I'd been taught, striking the leopard in the snout. Twisting and spitting in mid-air, the beast came down with claws raking my shoulder. One of the lead-tipped thongs wound around its foreleg.

I tried to free the lash with savage jerks. The leopard snapped. I tore the whip loose, retreated three paces and sucked air. The leopard crouched again, not yet fully provoked.

In the year and a half I had been bound to the Bestiarii School I had never faced a man-eater. Now I understood why old hands like Xenophon said they must be trained to strike a human being, and why, once trained, a lioness was soft and kittenish compared to them. Tame leopards I had killed in plenty at small circuses in outlying districts, but never one that had been coached to savor human blood by devouring crippled slaves with chunks of meat tied to their broken arms and legs. I knew the reason for the special sand, too. The animals had been taught that when there was sand underfoot, they were expected to claim a life.

Fabius had said nothing of this. He was offering Horus and me as dumb sacrifices, for what reason I didn't know. I waited for the first leopard's next lunge, watching the second one, too. I was standing in full sunlight, my scent blowing down the wind. Horus was still as a statue in the purple shadow beneath the amphitheater wall.

The first leopard licked his foreleg, turned baleful eyes upward to me and gathered his muscles for the spring. The second hovered close behind. Instantly I knew the Egyptian's game. Let one leopard, or both, turn on me, and he had the better chance to live. Well, I'd lived only twenty-one years and I had too many more waiting ahead to surrender to such treachery.

The smell of my own sweat was sour. I rubbed the blade of my right hand against my left palm, testing its horniness. Horus grinned, safe in the shadows. I threw away the whip.

Fabius leaped up. "Cassius, have you lost your wits? Pick it up before—"

Both leopards sprang at once.

Too eager, the first jumped wide of the mark and skidded around on the sand. The second struck my chest. Its stinking weight carried me down with a crash. Great yellow eyes loomed and my cheeks ran with the slime of its fangs. I dug my fingers into the neck to hold off the powerful jaws an instant longer. The bloodied claw marks on my left shoulder maddened the beast even more. Behind me I heard the second leopard growl. Rolling under the cat's weight, I thrust my right hand between its fore and back legs and cracked hard across its loins.

With a howl of pain the beast fell away. I scrambled up and dived for the whip. My father had said a single blow, strongly delivered to the vitals, would immobilize a man-eater like a thunderbolt. For the first time I had found out he was right.

The leopard writhed on its side and struggled to stand. I raised the whip and brought it down. The lead balls cracked the skullcase. On the fourth blow brains and blood spilled out and the killer died.

Salty sweat streamed down my chest. I gulped for breath and thought dully of the second leopard. A shrill scream told me.

The spotted devil was after Horus, deciding to exercise its new taste for human blood on someone less hazardous than I had proven to be. Horus had been smiling cockily a moment ago. Now he cowered against the amphitheater wall, laying feebly back and forth with his whip as the leopard bit pieces from his thighs. Shouting rocked the stands. I paid no attention, watching the Egyptian shed his arrogance and batter helplessly at the beast clawing his guts open.

I never moved. He had abandoned me to die. He could suffer the same fate. It was not long in coming. The leopard was too aroused to be hurt by the flicks of the whip. A leap, a sinking of fangs, and hot blood squirted from the Egyptian's throat, then fountained out of his mouth as he fell. When the leopard started to make a meal of his face, I turned away.

Thronging out of the stands, the students clamored around me. They slapped my back and offered congratulations. Syrax thrust a cup of posca into my hand. The sharp vinegar and water mixture helped wash the taste of death from my mouth. The big Greek Xenophon was the only one who had no favorable word. His glance was dark and envious.

"Stand back," I said at last. "There comes the man I want."

Across the sand strode Fabius, his aging body still hard and flat as bronze above his leather kilt. His arms and legs bore the proud whitened scars of his years in the Circus Maximus before he won the wooden sword. Astonished, I saw that he was not the least apologetic. He was furious.

"The Egyptian was one of my strongest men, Cassius. It was a cold-blooded thing to let him die."

"Look who talks of cold blood! First you trick us by saying we're going against a couple of toothless bitches for the sake of learning style with the whip. Then Horus stands like a rock in the shadows so the killers will take me first. Well, master Fabius, I can play the game of putting myself first as well as the next. You ought to know that by now."

A student cried, "That's it, Cassius, tell him! He wants to break you because you're always the loner."

Fabius glared. "A few more remarks of that kind and the Tiber'll turn clear before any of you get a chance in a big hunt in the Circus. Cassius, that hand trick—"

"Mine. Don't ask to see it again."

"From your tone one would think you were the master of the school instead of an inmate," he grumbled.

"And one would think you were a treacherous back stabber instead of a brave man who fought honorably in the arena for years."

That cut him hard. His leathery features wrenched but he only muttered, "Watch your tongue."

"No, Fabius. I'm not one of your slaves or your thieves like Xenophon, sentenced here as fodder for the lions. I'm a citizen, the son of a freedman. I became auctorati, bound myself to your school for three years to learn the trade of the bestiarius so I could earn wealth. Are you becoming like the rest of the mob? Screaming for the sight of blood and to hell with the skill of hunting and handling the animals?"

A flush darkened his cheeks. "You know better. I despise the way they cry for senseless killing. The profession of bestiarius is honorable."

"Except when you find it necessary to ring in a couple of man-eaters by surprise. Who were you trying to impress? That eques and his Praetorian friend scowling up there in the stands? What are they, emissaries of Jupiter Stator, himself?"

Nervously Fabius took my arm. He drew me away from the students. They drifted to the Egyptian's corpse and stood examining it with unfeeling curiosity. The sated leopard, still licking its chops lazily, had slunk off to doze, no longer remotely interested in fighting. Several handlers with goads prodded it back into its cage and the log front dropped.

Fabius said, "You're too free in your mockery of the gods, Cassius. Not to mention everything else respected in Rome. Speak softly of that pair. Gaius Julius is the tribune of the Praetorian cohort stationed at the palace on Palatine Hill. The eques with the thin purple stripe on his toga is a good friend of the Emperor. His name is Ofonius Tigellinus."

I gazed in astonishment at the Sicilian. He was talking heatedly with several seedy wager takers. "That's Tigellinus, the horse breeder? He was born no better than I."

"But he has the Emperor's ear. And from the looks of it, he lost a pretty sum betting on the Egyptian you let die."

Filled with wonder, I stared at the Sicilian's long, paunched body. A breath of renewed ambition whispered in me. "He was banished by Claudius for shady dealings, wasn't he?" I asked.

"Aye," Fabius nodded. "The young Emperor brought him back because he raises fine chariot horses. Somehow they always manage to win whenever the Emperor races them in the Circus."

The old warrior's face showed disgust. The Emperor's urge to drive had shocked and scandalized the Senate almost as much as his appearances as a harper in public poetical contests. Again I sensed the winds of change blowing in Rome these days, bringing fresh opportunities for a man with wits. Forgotten was the blood trickling down my arm. Almost forgotten too the trick of switching leopards. I was overwhelmed by the simple fact that a peasant like Tigellinus had risen to a position of eminence, and gained membership in the equites, the noble class second only to the senators.

"There's an odd look on your face, Cassius."

"I'm thinking that if the Princeps can raise one man to eques, he can raise another."

"That's fool's talk."

"Is it? Why?"

"For one thing, you still have a year and a half to serve this school."

I stared coldly. "Not that you're making it any easier for me to fill out the term."

Had I not served him well in the past, learned my lessons with the bears and the wild dogs and brought some small honor to the school at provincial games, I would never have dared to speak so. But I had come to the school freely and knew with coldness, not conceit, that I was an apt pupil. Further, he was shamed out of his usual blustery by the fakery with the leopards.

"All right, I'll admit it was a foul piece of business, Cassius. But the school hasn't prospered lately. The owners are unhappy. The Emperor displays little taste for beast shows. He prefers to hire gladiators from the Dacian or Gallic schools. All of us here, as you well know, depend on the patronage of persons giving the games for the livelihood. Tigellinus grows more influential at the court every day. Further, he has a liking for the bestiarii. Since the Emperor just forced his mother Agrippina out of the palace and dismissed her honor guard, he must do something to placate the mob. He's scheduled lavish games in the Circus Maximus. I'd hoped, through the influence of Tigellinus, to provide a large contingent for the Emperor's show. And don't forget that the Emperor is building his own circus across the Tiber."

"That still doesn't explain why you sent us against man-eaters without swords."

He cast more anxious glances at Tigellinus and the Praetorian Julius. They were still engaged in noisy argument with the wager takers. He said, "Your hot temper will be your undoing, Cassius.

I admit I deceived you deliberately. I heard rumors among the students about your trick with the hand."

"That'll teach me to talk too much."

"Talk any less and you'll be a block of marble. Knowing you, your foolish pride and aloofness—it's not good these days, lad, not when all the world bows before a twenty-year-old boy— I realized we'd never see the trick unless you were forced to use it. If you proved yourself worthy, I hoped to put you in the Circus Maximus."

His last statement calmed me somewhat. "The trick's not so difficult. It's partly knowing where to strike, partly having a tough hand. When I was a boy my father made me stand for an hour a day striking the edge of my palm against a pillar."

"Understand my position, Cassius. I wanted to gain some attention for the school. You and Horus were the best prospects. The rest of the students are cattle, except Xenophon and perhaps that Syrax, though he's too new and too shifty to tell for certain. Criminals who are so clumsy they get caught stealing some citizen's grain dole ticket will bring no fame to us."

"I bound over to help myself, not the school."

His glance sharpened. "A man can't live all his life without a hand from others."

"No? That dead Egyptian thought so."

A flurry in the stands caught our attention. "Ah, Gods! If we haven't had trouble enough today! We've gained attention, but all the wrong kind. Here comes more. Tigellinus and his friend look black as thunderclouds."

The clammy crawling on my spine warned me that the pair stamping across the reddened sand came on no errand of friendship. At closer range Tigellinus was a man of weak physical appearance despite his impressive ivory toga bearing the narrow purple stripe of his rank. Deep in his glance glittered the craftiness of one who had plotted well. That ability I could respect, but not the weak petulance of his mouth nor the arrogance of his slightly bulbous eyes as they raked me.

His companion, the officer Julius, was resplendent in brazen armor that winked in the sun. His features were aristocratic, befitting a Praetorian tribune. Yet they still displayed a certain coarseness, especially in the thickness of his curling lips. Fabius gigged me. I saluted with the customary gesture, vowing I'd make no other obeisance. The old trainer's fear of royal disfavor was apparent in the way he seemed to lose stature, changing from a brave man to a fawning toady. A curious silence fell on the amphitheater. Even the wager takers in the stands ceased their clacking. Grouped together, the other students watched us. The eyes of the olive-skinned Syrax shone attentively. Those of big Xenophon were bright with jealousy and malice.

"What's this fellow's name?" Tigellinus asked Fabius, ignoring me.

"Cassius, sir. One of the best fighters. If the Emperor should choose to hire him—"

The tribune Julius snorted. "Why would Nero hire a lout who cost two of his friends a handsome sum today?" He pulled his flat sword and gouged me under the chin. The point hurt not half so much as my own mounting anger. "Listen, beast man. Tigellinus and I were the special patrons of Horus who lies dead yonder. We don't take it lightly that you abandoned him to the cats."

"He abandoned me first, Tribune. He deserved what he got."

Tigellinus colored. "An insolent one, Fabius. What's his origin?"

"He was raised in the streets around the Circus Maximus, sir. His father trained bears for the arena when Tiberius reigned. Don't think too badly of him. His tongue is a mite free from time to time, but he's a talented boy. You saw that yourself. He's not like most of my jailbirds. He's auctorati, bound over by his own choice."

One of Tigellinus' eyebrows hooked upwards. "Bound over? Why is that, lout?"

"To make something of myself." I stared at him. "As others born no better have done."

Fabius gasped. The tribune clenched his hand on the pommel of his sword while Tigellinus bit his lip. The Sicilian checked his anger in time to say with a mocking smile, "So he has ambition too, Fabius. Perhaps he even hopes one day to wear a toga like this?" He preened himself, fingering the thin purple stripe.

Too much death and anger had unbalanced me. I blurted out, "Yes, I'll wear the eques toga the same as you. If the Emperor can confer the honor on a horse breeder, he can do the same for a bestiarius who—"

Tigellinus struck my cheek. "You gutter slime! Fabius, you're an idiot if you think I'll recommend your school for the Maximus games when you allow a wretch like this to insult your patrons. Of course," he added with a narrow smile, "Julius and I might reconsider if he were properly punished. Scourged."

Fabius stammered, angry with me and somehow sorry for me as well. I rejected his pity. I watched my two newfound enemies, recalling what I'd said a moment ago. I hadn't really meant to speak out. Yet in one instant the vow became reality. I knew with a queer torment that I would never rest until I held the same rank as this soft, cunning Sicilian whose courage rested in a Praetorian's sword.

Fabius spoke slowly. "Sirs, what if he apologized for his words? Could we overlook the scourging? It's harmful to a man's spirit, being humiliated before his mates."

Tigellinus shook his head. Julius said, "We'd enjoy listening to him howl a little, Fabius. Otherwise you'll see nothing but gladiators in the next games, of that you may be positive."

"Do it," I told Fabius. "But they'll hear no yells for mercy."

Throwing his hands into the air, Fabius ordered out the wooden scourging stand. I knelt before it, resting my neck at the junction of the two posts forming the V. Fabius sought someone to lay on the whip, as was customary. Xenophon was only too happy to volunteer. Strangely, I felt like laughing as the first stroke flayed by back.

At last, after aimless years, I had a destination. Chosen by chance, perhaps, and by anger, yet how many men who proclaim that they ordered their lives in a pattern from the beginning were actually victims of fate's whims? The vow I'd made to be an eques was burned into me for life by each cut of the lash.

Fabius walked off, pale. Xenophon's arm rose and fell rhythmically, drawing blood. The pain numbed by mind. Once the Praetorian dragged my head up by the hair.

"Cry out for my friend Tigellinus. Cry out, you dung!"

I gathered spit in my mouth and sprayed it on his legs. Tigellinus howled with anger, seized the whip and finished the job, lashing me until the lights in my skull went out.

But I never screamed.

CHAPTER II

———⟩●⟨———

CARTS RUMBLED and thunder from an impending storm, somewhere south in Campania. Night must have fallen. The vegetable wagons were never allowed through the city gates by daylight.

I groaned and opened my eyes. Beneath my belly I felt the tangled wool of the blanket on my cell's stone bed. A golden flame, tallow in a pottery bowl, wavered and leaped. All along my backbone pain roamed.

Dismal shadows flittered on the cubicle's rock walls. The darkness was thickest in the empty niche above my head. I tried to rise, fell back and floated off in hazy dreams of the past.

Through drifting mists shone the face of my father, a scarred and bearded fighter. He said he found me as a bundle in a hollow alongside the great Via Cassia leading down to Rome from the country of the legendary Etruscans. He was convinced I was a child of more than base blood. Wealthy fathers often decided they did not wish to burden their pocketbooks with additional offspring. They exercised the right of paterfamilias and left the unwanted young at roadsides on stormy nights. The poor seemed to love their boys and girls too much for such cruel separations, he told me once.

My father Cassius Flamma was a widower long past his prime when he picked me up that night, a year before the current Emperor was born. Cassius Flamma was a lonely man. He cared for me as well as he could, considering that his sole income was derived from running a fly-by-night animal show in the Field of Mars. The performance featured a couple of Mossolian hounds and two toothless mothy lions. He would wrestle the old lions, parade the dogs around on their hind legs and collect a few coppers from the crowd before the watch came along to send him and his rickety cage carts packing.

He died when I was twelve, but he had taught me how to write and read the native tongue by then, as well as the universal language of commerce, Greek. And he'd left me a share of memories.

Tales of how he'd won the wooden sword in the Circus before Tiberius himself. How he'd become a freedman before that, and was therefore able to confer Roman citizenship on his son. He showed me the trick with the hand, maintaining he'd learned it from a Numidian gladiator and put it to use on animals. And he initiated me into the hidden lore of the arches under the Circus, those dark, secret mazes where men diced and planned robberies and pimped for Cappodocian girls who performed lewd dances between acts of games.

Lying with my back torn half open, I remembered him saying that the path to fame, though dangerous, lay straight and sure in the Circus. I'd waited a long time to follow that path.

From my twelfth year to my nineteenth I had worked at various jobs, selling sausages on a tripod in the streets or unloading wheat from Africa at the Tiber wharves or sweating at the kilns of the Afer brick works. Then, only then, had it struck me that I was no longer a boy but a grown man who must make his way. To enter the arena it was not necessary to be a slave or a criminal. I could promise myself for three years to any of the training schools. I chose the Bestiarii School because of my father.

The time was ripe for success. Never before had public spectacles been of such importance to a ruler.

True, the Emperor favored gladiatorial contests, but some said he might be persuaded to enjoy animal exhibitions provided they were sufficiently base and bloody. Once I saw Nero Caesar Augustus at a great distance, when he was passing through the Forum, but the facts of his nature I knew only by hearsay, for I was busy in small outlying circuses where Fabius sent me to practice baiting bears with a veil and sword or to chase deer with a spear from ponyback.

Gossip held that the Emperor was an unbalanced creature whose policy of favoring the nobles at the expense of the liberty of the people was held in check only by the activities of his advisers. He had three—the learned and wealthy writer Seneca, the Praetorian Prefect Burrus, and his mother Agrippina. Already, though, Nero was beginning to exert his authority. And why not, some asked, springing as he did from rotten stock?

It was widely believed that his own mother had poisoned her husband the Emperor Claudius with a dish of mushrooms. She had obtained the poison from an equally beautiful and infamous noble's widow named Locusta. That was three years ago. Since then, the boy and his mother had ruled as co-regents. During that time, Claudius' own son Brittanicus—Nero was Agrippina's boy by a previous marriage to one Ahenobarbus—had also fallen victim to poison. The Emperor then cast out his mother's favorite official, the imperial financial secretary Pallus. The most recent to go was Agrippina herself. She had retired to her great private house, stripped of her guard of honor.

The Emperor further scandalized the Senators by learning the harp and racing his chariot like a commoner. The mob loved him for the games he gave, though. So did the Praetorians. The Emperor was shrewd. The more circuses for the people, the less time they had to dwell on his countless infidelities to his wife Octavia and his liking for roaming the streets at night with noble friends, attacking helpless citizens for sport.

Fragments and snatches of all this floated in my head as I lay in my cell after the whipping. Perhaps the winds of change that blew down the Tiber were not healthy, tainted as they were by the boy Emperor's own mad breath, but they were strong enough to make me think dizzily that I must wake up and begin to move again or I would die no better than my father. I knew somehow that tonight I was a changed man, and would make my vow to become an eques come true or die doing it.

Then I heard a voice.

"Cassius? Here's a sponge of wine and a handful of parched peas. Wake up!"

I rolled over. I blinked. A wily young face, deeply olive, and a golden ear hoop blurred, then sharpened. He extended the dripping sponge. I knocked it aside.

"Leave me alone, Syrax. I need no one's help."

He chuckled. His small, dark eyes gleamed. He juggled the peas and from the folds of his sleeveless tunic produced a small bowl containing a messy yellow paste. He put the bowl on my couch.

"I'm well aware you won't ordinarily accept a hand when it's offered. But never let it be said that a Syrian provincial doesn't recognize his duty when he sees it. Smear some of that hideous stuff on your shoulders. It's meant to soothe the pain and heal flesh. The school physician's drunk somewhere. That's why I brought it myself. They gave you quite a hiding, didn't they? You bore it well, though. Stop scowling! I'm your friend. I was at some pains to steal that bowl from the physician's rooms."

"How did you have time, talking so much?"

"I'm glad to see you can smile, even though it's a sour one. I came to ask—hold on!"

Hastily he threw himself into the corner of the cell where the shadows were deep. I gave several loud snorts to show I was still breathing. The guard paused outside the curtain, then passed on. The corridors were patrolled at night to prevent men from killing themselves in despair over being sentenced to train for the arena.

When quiet fell again, Syrax scuttled back to the couch. He stared down at me with interest. Was he one of those types enamored of Greek love? His interest had other motives, as it turned out.

"When you killed the leopard with your hand, Cassius, I knew you were the sort I needed for a partner."

I raised myself on my elbows and gaped. "Partner? In what?"

"Why, in the beast school you and I will found and operate once we're granted wooden swords." He seized my arm, his narrow foreign eyes glowing with the scheme. "Hear me out, Cassius. The Emperor may not have much taste for beast shows yet, but I'll wager that within a year or more, the animal business will double. Triple, even."

"You're hasty, Syrax. You've only been here a few months. The term is a full three years."

He waved the quibble aside. "The mob or the Emperor or both can grant the wooden sword any time they want. You know that. It could happen the first time we hunt in the Circus Maximus. I'm not promising it will, mind you, but it's possible. So are many things. A large villa. Riches. Rank. Fine food. The caresses of fine ladies instead of the gigglers they ship in once a week. I know a great deal about you, Cassius, though you've never bothered to do more than nod to me. I know you seldom have a woman in this cell, for instance. And not because you favor the Grecian style, either. Because you stand alone, needing no one. I admire you, my friend."

"I do stand alone, Syrax. That means I don't need you."

I said it seriously, though I was amused by his nerve. His bold, bright speech wiped out awareness of the pain in my back. I studied him critically, both fascinated and repelled by the naked, laughing greed on his thin Southern face. Some inner sense whispered that for all his clever talk and quick grins, I would be safer to stay clear of him. He was a man driven by an ambition as furious as mine. But I was curious too.

"Since I admit I travel my own way, asking no favors, what convinces you I need your assistance?"

He raised both palms in the manner of a Levantine trader. "Our school."

"Oh? How do you propose we build it? Even granting we manage to stay alive, win freedom with the wooden sword and find ourselves at liberty? Will the Emperor donate the land? Will he furnish us the money to build dormitories, import beasts and hire whores for the students?"

"That's my part," he grinned back. "I may look like nothing to you since I'm a foreigner. But I know Rome. I was shipped here with my parents when I was small. They died in an insulae fire, the miserable creatures. Since then I've managed to ingratiate myself with quite a few equites and senators. I am also a man of wide business experience."

He ticked off on his fingers an astonishing collection of occupations including notice writer, oracle, fortuneteller, physician and professional actor at important Senatorial funerals, where he impersonated, as was the custom, the dead man in the burial parade. He concluded in a tone that reminded me of the upstart Tigellinus, "My last position was one of considerable authority. I served a wealthy landowner as his chief steward."

I laughed. "Then why are you here?"

Unsubtle anger blazed in his eyes. "A little matter of using the master's signet ring on some documents. The damned magistrate called it forgery. He offered me a choice. Leave Rome or bind myself to one of the schools."

"Naturally you couldn't leave Rome when there are so many fortunes awaiting a clever man."

His fingers were hard on my arm. "Don't joke, Cassius. That is, unless you enjoyed the whipping you got today. I heard your promise to Tigellinus. That you'd wear the eques toga. Did you mean it? Or are you like the rest in this miserable place? A braggart, full of nothing except wind?"

For that I would have struck him, except that I felt again the humiliating bite of the thongs on my back. A dark sense of fate swallowed me as I said, "What I told Tigellinus will come true. I swear it. I'll let nothing stand in my way. Does that answer you?"

"Not quite. When you say nothing can stop you, have you the will to back it up?"

My resolve was suddenly hard and cold as marble. "Yes."

He threw back his head and laughed, the ringlets of his hair shining. From the faraway plain rolled the boom of the thunderstorm, like nameless fate sealing our bargain. With surprising skill, and another reminder that he had practiced for six months as a physician, since the law required no examinations or even any training for doctors, he shoved me over on my belly and began to apply the messy unguent. The stuff stung cruelly at first, but soon produced a soothing numbness. I fell into a drowsy state while he prattled on.

Syrax elaborated on how we would found a successful competing school as the beast games increased in popularity; how his numerous contacts among the upper classes would help us locate the required financing; how I, by virtue of my size and strength, would be the lanista while he tended to the commercial side of our affairs. He was an accomplished improviser.

"Who knows," he said, finishing with the ointment and wiping his hands on his tunic, "perhaps we might even uncover a few real unicorns to increase our fame, not those clumsy rhinos they pass off in the Circus while the mob hoots in derision. Or we might learn the secret of training a beast to mount a woman."

"What?" I said angrily.

"It's never been done before, and I understand things like that appeal to Nero."

"If that sort of depravity is to be our stock in trade, I'll have none of it."

"I thought you said you'd do anything—"

"Except the unthinkable."

Quickly he put on a sympathetic smile. "Sorry, Cassius. A joke only."

"That's better," I growled. "What you suggest is an insult to a man's nature, and our profession as well, low as it may be. At least on that point I agree with master Fabius."

"Fabius is behind the times," he said under his breath. "Still, we can worry about it when we—What's all that racket?"

He peered out the curtain into the darkened hallway, then turned back, grinning. He extended his hand to clasp mine.

"Best I hurry to my cell. They're carting in the ladies for the weekly health session. I intend to indulge. Why don't you? By way of celebration?"

I felt nothing but an overpowering urge to sleep. "Celebration of what?"

"Our pact, my friend. The only reason you've played your lone game this long is because you've never encountered a man with wits to match yours. Now you have. The two of us together—we'll force Tigellinus and his kind to bow to us, one day."

He said it with such quiet force that I wondered what poverties and indignities had been his lot as a child. He was nakedly hungry behind his light, grinning manner. Thunder drummed across the Capitoline and the foundations of the building shook. With a laugh and a salute Syrax sped out the door.

He carried a greeting to the women trooping into the vestibule at the hall's end. I turned my face to the wall, pretending to sleep. I was amused by what he had proposed, yet intrigued by it too. Master of the second beast school in Rome. Rich. Welcomed in the homes of the wealthy. It was a dream worth pondering. And who could foresee the strange turnings destiny might take in the years ahead?

I was dozing off amid the squeals and gigglings of the women when a noisy altercation outside roused me again.

"What's wrong with a Greek?" a man was saying angrily.

"Nothing, except that they stink and have rough hands!" came a feminine reply.

"Fine talk for a whore," the man grumbled.

"Acte!" another woman chided. "Xenophon is already a famous fighter. Treat him with respect."

"Respect? His manners are crude as a hog's. Look, he's already torn my gown. I'll take any other man in the school tonight, but not Xenophon."

The Greek's reply was curt. "You'll take me if I force you, dove."

Perverse anger pushed me to the door. The women brought in from the brothels along the Tiber were clustered in the stone corridor. They smelled warmly of Parthian musk and jingled with bangles and trinkets of copper. Talk stopped when I appeared, including the bawdy remarks of the students lounging in various stages of undress at the cubicle doors.

Xenophon's thick fingers circled the wrist of a girl in a white gown and sky-blue shawl. Seeing me, he released her. I enjoyed his look of dismay when I said, "I'm glad you turned her loose, Xenophon, because she's the one I chose for tonight."

His black brows thrust together. "Then choose again."

"No, I won't. You've already had your sport today at my expense. Now I'll have mine at yours." I paused. "Unless you care to settle the dispute with fists."

Growls from the other inmates stayed the Greek's hand. Loud complaints that he'd used me unfairly upset him, for he enjoyed and even needed the admiration of his fellows to sustain him. I did not. I was ready to tell them to mind their own affairs when I realized that none of them, except perhaps Syrax, cared a whit about me. Xenophon was a bully and they enjoyed watching him squirm.

The Greek thought over my invitation. Then he moved forward a step. I doubled my hands, ready to fight. A lash cracked as Fabius appeared.

"Into your cells, into your cells! You'll bring the watch with your racket. We have trouble enough smuggling these women through the streets. Xenophon, what's wrong with you? You look as though you swallowed poison."

"Nothing, master Fabius. Nothing we won't settle later."

He caught the waist of a plump Phoenician wench and shambled off to his cubicle. There being more than enough women, Syrax managed to procure two for himself. The last I saw, he was entertaining them with anecdotes of his intimacy with many famous persons in Rome. Fabius snapped the whip again and threatened loudly, but he threw me a grudging glance of approval when he noticed the girl had wandered unbidden into my cell.

Turning, I saw the tallow light glow through the cheap cloth of her tunic, limning the slenderness of her thighs and the round high peaks of her breasts. At the hall's end guards marched in, depositing at each sill the night's ration of wine. I waited outside until the men passed with mine. The jar was chilled. Or perhaps the flesh of my palm was hot.

The girl waited. I stepped into the cell and drew the curtain, surprised to discover that I hardly felt the hurting of my back; that an immense loneliness filled me suddenly; and that the girl was very beautiful.

CHAPTER III

—————

"**D**O YOU PLAN to stand there all night holding that wine jug?" she asked, laughing.

Embarrassed, I thrust it to her. "Help yourself."

"Oh, I don't care for any right now, thanks." She sat on the couch and removed her sandals one by one. "I only wanted to see whether you had manners. Not many in this place do."

She indicated the tear in her tunic made by Xenophon. Her red mouth formed a professional smile. Her hair, brown and lustrous, was piled and piled upon her head in a profusion of coils and ringlets, after the current fashion. She was plainly arrayed except for the whore's kohl blackening her eyelids. A spiced scent of perfume hung around her. She seemed hardly older than I, but was fully developed, with a woman's breasts and long legs.

While I helped myself to a draught from the jar, thunder boomed again. Somewhere in the darkened maze of cells a girl shrieked in a frenzied way. I had a peculiar impulse to pull down a rag from a wall peg and scrub this girl's face clean.

"My name's Acte. Or did you hear that?" Her voice was pleasant, less shrill that those of her sisters. "Who are you? Perhaps you prefer to remain nameless."

"Cassius. And that's a strange remark. Don't you have any stomach for the work?"

"Would I be here if I didn't? I've visited the school several times in the past two months. So you're Cassius. I've heard about you. They call you Cassius the Cur."

A tightness filled my throat "Who does?"

"Oh, men here. They say you growl whenever you speak."

"Fools. They imagine soft words and friendliness will make them rich."

"Is that why you're a slave to the school? For riches?"

"Can you suggest a better reason? But I'm no slave. I bound myself voluntarily."

Changing the subject, she glanced about the cell and noticed the empty niche. "Where's your god? The rest have one."

"Tell me which of the gods is most reliable and I'll put his statue there."

A curious light, a mixture of amusement and pity, filled her dark eyes. "Then the stories are true after all. You're quite as strange and bitter as they make out."

I hauled back the curtain on the dark, whispering hall. "Get out, no rule requires me to endure lectures from a whore."

I spoke harshly because, for a moment, I'd found myself wanting her, and it hurt to discover she was an imperious bitch free with opinions about everyone's state except her own. She did not stir. She reached for the wine jar and drank a little, with surprising grace.

"Did you hear me, woman? I said leave."

She shook her head.

"You refuse?"

"I refuse. Perhaps I deserve your contempt for selling my body. But I'm also a human being. I mean to be civilly treated."

I laughed in spite of myself. "Acte, the world doesn't turn on civility, but on copper coins and the whims of the boy on the Palatine."

She leaped up. "I don't believe that. The gods will protect and help any who appeal to them."

"No doubt they help you pull up your hem several times every night."

She leaped at me across the dim cell, cattish and quick. Her nails tore a trail down my cheek. I seized her wrists and held her, laughing. She spewed out a string of street oaths surprising even from one of her profession. Soon her anger turned to tears. I couldn't help puzzling. One instant, she behaved like the lowest harridan, the next like a girl-child barely old enough to know the difference between men and women.

Fighting her off, I said, "I repeat, Acte, you're free to leave. I picked you only because Xenophon laid these marks on my back. I'm in no mood for sermons on the gods. Cassius the Cur, as you call him, can only growl."

"Certainly I'll go," she said acidly. "I expect you're a Greek at heart anyway. Outwardly you're dark and mannish, but secretly you probably prefer plump little boys who—"

With a knotted fist I struck her, spun her onto the stone couch where she lay gasping. Her gown tangled around her hips. Her breasts rose in sharp thrusts under the material.

"I'll show you who's Greek and who's not, whore!"

I flung off my waistcloth, dropped and pinned her hands on the blanket. Though she was agile and strong, it was not enough. I hurt her at first. She beat her fists against my shoulders and cried out.

Suddenly her tinted mouth was very close, breathing out a sweet scent. I lost my stomach for such coward's work. The rest of it was gentle enough, but neither of us took any pleasure. At the end, when I went for the wine jar, she sat up wearily, her breasts gleaming like rubies at the ends, a moment before she covered them. She set about adjusting a boxwood comb that had come loose from her dark hair. Dumbly I offered the wine. She drank, then searched my face.

"Thank you, Cassius. They have no right to call you names."

"Oh? Am I a more tender lover than you're accustomed to in your trade?"

"Don't say it with such a sneer."

"Answer, my question."

With a sad look she murmured, "Yes, you are."

Glowering at the empty niche where no god was worth to stand, I wondered what had stopped me when I wanted to hurt her. The touch of her flanks had been painfully sweet. Abruptly I recalled Syrax and our wild scheme. It seemed wild no longer.

"The rest of them, any of them," Acte said at last, "would have finished it roughly. The way you began it. Even that Syrian provincial with the ring in his ear—" A shudder rippled her shoulders. "He's the worst of the lot."

"Syrax? He's harmless."

"Have you ever looked closely in his eyes? Seen what he wants and how far he means to go to get it? And he forces his smiles. At least," she added with a toss of her hair, "I needn't feel ashamed on that score. I never pretend feelings that aren't real."

"Most of your sisters do."

"I am what I am, Cassius."

I sat beside her. "Then you'll have a short and unhappy career in the brothels."

"That's the kind I want. If I told you why I put myself in Sulla's house in the first place, no doubt you'd make sport of my story. But I'll say this. It wasn't because I liked it, or had much choice."

She sat quite close, her legs warm as down near mine. She held the gown to her breasts and stared beyond the stone wall to some unhappy past. Through the gloomy labyrinth of the school echoed laughter and other, less genteel sounds. Someone plucked a hand harp against the rumble of the storm-swollen night sky.

The story she told, plainly and without excuse, was simple enough. Her father and her four brothers and sisters had originally been slaves. They were freed when she was young. Her father's master, a Senator, had been instrumental in obtaining for him a modest position in the Imperial Treasury under Claudius. When that ruler swallowed Agrippina's poisoned mushrooms and Nero was hailed to the throne, first by the Praetorians, then by the Senate, Acte's father was among several hundred losing jobs in the Treasury. Nero replaced the quaestors of Claudius, as well as the whole staff the two treasurers employed, with his own appointees. Rome swarmed with thousands of similar victims of the change in power, poorly trained for any job but one. The older ones, like Acte's father, were out of luck. Places like the Afer brick works gave preference to young men.

So her father earned a few coppers operating a wretched public barber stand, clipping locks over a tripod while the family crowded together in one of the insulae, teetering wood tenements that contained innumerable foul apartments, not to mention pestilence and death. Barbering was not profitable enough to feed six mouths. Unknown to her father, the girl had looked for work, finding nothing that would pay half so well as a place at Sulla's. The brothel was located along the great bend of the Tiber on the far side of the Field of Mars, close by many others. She had been there a little over two months.

She finished her story by saying, "As soon as my brothers are old enough to work decently, I'll walk out of Sulla's and never look back. The gods will help me, too. They favor honest people who don't mock them."

Our glances held a moment. Abruptly I was afraid of her. Of what she might do to me.

"In that way we're alike, Acte. Both inmates of establishments we care little about. Are you being honest, though? Will you stop? I won't."

"Or even give it a thought? The arena is dangerous."

"I mean to make a mark in Rome. One that stands out as clearly as these stripes they put on my back. And I'll do it alone."

"To forsake the gods brings disaster, Cassius. Even a whore ought to pray."

"The only gods I recognize are a full belly, a full purse and a respected name."

"That may be so. Yet you're not as hard as you pretend. It's a long time since I was treated with any gentleness. Oh yes, you did, for all your growling and ranting to the contrary. I wouldn't—lecture you, as you call it, if I felt—well, that you were another Xenophon or Syrax or worse."

What in the name of the nameless powers was she doing to me?

Staring at her, so soft and lovely despite her black-painted eyes, I felt my will melt and my heart go out. I wanted her again. The tallow burned low, throwing off acrid smoke. Back in Sulla's house, would she chortle with her sisters over making a fool of Cassius the Cur? No, she wasn't the kind—

Dangerous nonsense. I had made a vow. Listening to her talk of gentleness and gods would weaken me. I moved stiffly to the curtain.

"This time, Acte, when I say leave, you must."

"Must I? We have until morning. Only then will the real world come back."

"This is the real world. This cheap little room."

"Looking at things only with your eyes, Cassius, brings death creeping inside you."

"A few more months romping with Sulla's guests and you'll change your mind."

She shook her head. "No, Cassius. Not since I came here."

"What do you want, Acte? To glorify yourself by saving me? I don't need saving."

She walked toward me slowly, the gown fallen. Her nakedness was warm and incredibly desirable. "You need it very much, Cassius. We all need it. Rome needs it. The old gods and the decent things they stood for are being killed. Killed under chariot wheels in the Circus. Killed by cruelty and our believing that gods are no more than men who can be bribed at an altar."

She touched my face. "Your eyes are black and hard but the greed in them isn't quite real. Not yet, anyway." Her palm stole up my cheek. "Don't let it become real, Cassius. Fight if you must, but hold back part of yourself. The way I have. Until now."

Her hair floated near my face as I whispered, "Acte, when the sun comes up, they'll fetch you out of here. Why spend a night making ourselves miserable with talk? If you want to take pleasure—"

Her mouth stopped mine with a kiss. She clung naked against me. "Not pleasure, Cassius. All Rome hunts that, night and day. Say love instead. Even if you don't mean it, say it. This night only, love."

"All right, Acte. Love."

She offered the wine-spiced sweetness of her mouth, gently parting, almost like a maid's. My hands crept down her white back and held her. Then we lay on the couch, her hair unbound, her laugh eager, her breasts sweet as pomegranates to my lips.

She knew all the arts of Venus the Purifier. Her caresses were expert and ardent. Yet I believed, as the tallow smoldered down and went out, that what she said was true. A part of her had been held back, a part she gave now with joyous abandon. I wanted to tell her I was committed by the vow before Tigellinus and the crazy pact with the Syrian. My mouth was silenced with her warm flesh. We loved all night long, as though both of us were truly free.

In the hour of dawn, as the last cart rumbled out of the city and the rain drummed at last on the slate roof, sleepy Fabius came by with a lamp, knocking his whip against the outer wall.

"Time's up, ladies, time's up."

Acte folded the sky-blue shawl around her dark hair and leaned against my shoulder.

"A week seems like forever, Cassius. I may not get back even then. Sometimes Sulla sends another crop of girls."

I held her hand tightly. "Then I'll come to Sulla's. One night soon."

Her eyes flew wide. "From here? If you're caught—"

"Too late to worry about that now, Acte. One night too late."

And she was in my arms again, saying things no woman had ever spoken to me. I spoke them also, words I thought only the poets wrote in their silver Latin. A rowdy commotion began outside as the whores trooped away, no more serious or sober than they had been at nightfall. Only Acte and I, caught in one of those strange convulsions that shake the world from time to time, had changed.

"I want you to come, Cassius. I want it terribly. But not if they'll punish you."

"Worse punishment to stay away. Kiss me a last time."

Willingly she did, until Fabius raised such a row that she had to go. The lanista threw me another oblique glance as if to say he was pleased that I'd behaved normally for at least one night. I laughed silently. What would he think if he understood how my whole life had been torn apart?

I was in love with her, and already doubting whether I wanted to stake my future in the arena.

Little stands out in the routine of the school during the next three days, except that my thoughts were constantly full of her. The third night another drenching rain broke over the seven hills. Blue lightning played around the Capitoline. When the school had dozed to silence, and even the vestibule guard was nodding on his stool, witless with too much wine, I threw on a dark cloak and crept by him in the dim torchlight.

Gaining the door, I ran across the court to the outer wall. Cold rain beat my face as I leaped high and caught the wall's edge. Ready to throw a leg over, I heard a voice.

"Cassius! Stop!"

A blue sword of fire sliced the sky in half, followed by a deafening thunderclap. My fingers slipped. I tumbled into the court mud, expecting the thrust of a guard's spear any instant.

CHAPTER IV

BUT INSTEAD OF a death-dealing spear head, the figure hulking over me shot out a hand to seize mine, and jerk me upright.

"In the name of both our futures, Cassius, back inside. Quickly!"

Angrily I flung off the grip. "Syrax! What the devil are you doing out here?"

A brief burst of faraway lightning lit his rain-drenched forehead and the jiggling hoop in his ear. "Watching out for you. Obviously you don't have enough sense to do the job for yourself. Now hurry, Cassius. Come with me before the guards see— oh-oh. That's done it. Down!"

He hurled himself against me and slapped a palm across my mouth to stifle any outcry. A dull yellow light bobbed on the far side of the courtyard, then seemed to pause and float in mid-air.

Rain plopped in little pools. The wind blew eerily. Presently the guard with the lantern sauntered on.

Enraged by Syrax's effrontery, I ripped his hand away. He sighed despairingly.

"Cassius, Cassius, my friend. Don't peril yourself over such foolishness."

"Foolishness? What makes you say that?"

"Well, it's all too clear that you're worked up over that tawdry whore you bedded a few nights back, and you're risking your life to see her."

Once again I was struck by the man's devious ways. "You seem very well informed about my affairs."

"Naturally. I keep my eyes open. You've walked around in a fog ever since the night the women visited. Even old fool Fabius has mentioned the peculiar change in your behavior. When he notices, don't you think it must be doubly plain to someone with my wits? In fact I've been expecting a ridiculous stunt like this. So I've kept track of you."

"Then stop keeping track, Syrian. I do what I wish."

I prepared to jump the wall a second time. He danced around in front of me, seizing my shoulders. "Cassius, remember the pact we made. We are sworn partners. When you endanger yourself, you endanger me also. Satisfying lust is one thing, but completely losing your head over a woman can wreck your future."

"That jabber about partners was a joke," I snarled. "Stand out of my way."

Syrax cocked his head. "A joke, eh? Truly you've become a love-struck lunatic. All right, then. If there's nothing I can do to talk you out of this nonsense, I have only one alternative." He gathered his light, frayed cloak about him and indicated the wall. "You go first."

I gaped. "I don't intend to take you along, you ridiculous leech."

His chuckle carried a cold determination. "Try again, Cassius. Experts have cursed me. I can't be stopped. Words mean nothing so long as I can protect my most valuable asset—which is your talent with the beasts. Therefore I appoint myself your bodyguard. The streets of Rome are dangerous at night. Also, I know the shortest and safest route to Sulla's. Coming?"

With that he leaped for the top of the wall, kicked up a leg and dropped to the other side.

Clearly no amount of argument was going to shake my self-appointed partner's stubbornness. I shook my head in amazement and followed.

In the sour alley beyond the wall, Syrax drew me left when I would have started out to the right. Before long we were twisting and turning through wretched little thoroughfares dark beyond belief.

We spent the best part of an hour slipping along the shop porticos at the edge of the Field of Mars. Several times we were obliged to hide while parties of vigiles, Rome's fire officers who doubled as night watchmen, passed in the distance. Their tallow lanterns danced as they went hunting thieves and malefactors.

The rain slacked off. A slim rind of moon appeared as we neared the great bend of the Tiber. Across the river, gleaming like an omen or a promise, were piled countless huge blocks of marble for building the Emperor's own Circus. Along the near shore crowded small and large houses bright with lamplight. Muffled up in our cloaks, we skulked toward the most imposing, a sprawling place protected by a high wall. An old doorkeeper dozed on a stool at the gate. In the dark opposite him, Syrax hesitated, listening. He indicated the brothel.

"Business is brisk even on such a foul night."

True enough. All the draped windows glowed, crossed now and again by the limber shadows of revelers. A lute hummed. Women laughed shrilly. Drunken male voices rose in a bawdy ballad. My belly tightened when I thought of what Acte might be doing this moment. I tried to remind myself that love would in no way remove her need to earn her keep.

I crossed the street and shook the doorkeeper.

"What do you want?" he said querulously. "Only gentlemen are received at Sulla's."

"Take a message inside to the lady Acte."

The doorkeeper's eyes narrowed in rheumy mirth. "From the looks of that patched cloak, you couldn't afford the price of Acte's toe, let alone all of her. Be off, or I'll shout for the vigiles."

I seized his wrist, turning my head so light from the gate lamp shone across my face. "You'll take the message in, as I ask. Is that plain?"

He nodded nervously. "Oh, very well. But I warn you, stranger. There are illustrious personages in the house tonight. They won't take kindly to—all right, all right! Don't double your fists and glare like a wolf. I'm going. What's the message?"

Gazing up at the lighted windows, I said, "Tell her there's a cur waiting for her outside."

The old fellow made the sign against evil eye. "A dog?" he repeated uncertainly.

"A cur. She'll understand."

Muttering, he tottered away and vanished through a doorway decorated with the green boughs hung on every brothel lintel. I became aware of Syrax standing at my side. Beneath his cloak he jingled a few coins.

"As long as I'm here, Cassius, I see no reason why I shouldn't avail myself of Sulla's choice wares. Do you mind?"

"I'm not your keeper. But where did you get money to buy a woman?"

The Syrian laughed. "Fabius donated it. Unwittingly. But I'm sure he'd consider carelessness with his purse an act of mercy. Keeping up the spirits of a promising student and all that. I'll see what I can do to locate the girl if the old clown has no luck. You keep quiet out here. Don't make any scenes."

He hurried inside, ear hoop flashing. I huddled under the gate out of the bite of the damp Tiber wind. Halloos of the watch drifted from the Field of Mars. An eques in an ornamented chair was carried by, linkboys running ahead and behind. For no very clear reason, I began to worry that something had happened to Acte.

The roistering inside the brothel continued unchecked. Presently the doorkeeper emerged. The reason for his delay was evident in the reek of posca on his breath.

"The lady, as you call her, received your message. She's unable to come out now."

Saying the words turned my stomach. "Was she—occupied?"

"Not at all. She's singing and dancing for the gentlemen. Having quite a merry time. She told me to say she couldn't possibly speak with you until the nobles departed." He leaned forward, his watering eyes strangely awed. "Show some sense, fellow. Get out of here without starting a row. Tonight of all nights."

"No," I said. "I'll wait. Yonder—under the arch across the way."

Still grumbling, he took his seat on the stool. I wrapped myself in my cloak, crossed the street and crouched down to wait. My spirits were heavy.

The message Acte sent back did not jibe with the impassioned words we'd spoken that shattering night at the school.

Or did it?

A new suspicion troubled my mind. Had I made a dismal fool of myself by coming here?

The chill of the night deepened. The singing and shouting in Sulla's continued. The stars that had followed the rain paled. Morning approached, bringing with it the risky task of returning to the Bestiarii School.

The brothel became quiet. The fine gentlemen inside were at the night's true business. And my bitterness was complete. Acte had spoken falsely when she mouthed her words of love. Probably she and some young fop were tittering over the incident this moment, while they rested between sports on the couch. Disgusted and ashamed, I stared at the lightening heavens. I stood up. My bones creaked. Let Syrax take care of himself, wherever he was. I'd remain no longer.

I took but a few dispirited steps in the direction of the Field of Mars before a commotion started in Sulla's courtyard. I dodged back to my hiding place. The night's celebration was done. Half a dozen nobles, heavily cloaked so their Senatorial and equite togas would not be visible, spilled outside, together with linkboys and attendants. The doorkeeper woke, blinking.

"What a dismal, stinking failure of a night," one of the nobles complained. "Lacking something, something. I wonder what?"

He smiled in a rather nasty way. The others grouped about him, waiting. I saw with surprise that the speaker was no more than a youth, some spoiled Senator's son, no doubt. He was thoroughly drunk. He had a round face, ugly popping eyes and a slack mouth. His voice was shrill as he went on.

"No one here has been genuinely impressed with our station, friends. Let's do something about that, eh?"

The young noble tottered forward, eyeing the doorkeeper who sat clutching his hands together, gaze downcast. The other sycophants applauded the young man's move. One, however, stepped quickly to his friend's side. He was older, grizzled, and had a craggy, intense face that seemed out of place among the crowd of loose-lipped weaklings. The older man implored his friend, "Domitius, the wine has overcome us all. Let's not cause any scandal by—"

"Scandal, scandal!" the youth jeered. I puzzled over the oddly familiarity of his flushed face. "Serenus, you're duller than a magistrate. No, I take that back. You're duller than my wife at the height of passion." His companions broke into appropriately fawning guffaws. The youth roared at his own jest. Then he turned to the doorkeeper, advancing on him, words slurring together drunkenly.

"Old man, when we arrived earlier, I detected a distinct gleam of arrogance in your eye."

The poor wretch was barely able to speak. "No, sir. It must have been a mistake."

"Mistakes are things I never make," his antagonist screeched, delivering a vicious box to the old man's ear. The doorkeeper reeled against the wall and fell.

The young noble lifted one exquisite sandal and kicked the old man in the side of the head.

"More respect is what gentlemen require from cattle like you! More respect in the posture! The speech! The glance!"

Each word was emphasized with another brutal kick. Sickened and furious, I watched from behind a pillar. I knew I had no part in this quarrel. Yet I hated these men with a fearful hate, for they were the ones who had taken pleasure with Acte all night, keeping me skulking outside like an animal. The older, grizzled noble was the sole member of the party who was not enjoying the senseless sport.

He cried sharply, "Must we take pleasure from bullying the helpless? I beg you, Domitius, let him alone."

The youth spun, poutish lips spitting the words, "We'll take pleasure where I say and when I say, Serenus. Now if the rest of you spineless japes are friends of mine, let's see you join me in teaching this lump of dung a lesson in respectful posture. He's not respectful enough yet. Not nearly. A few more kicks will do it, though."

And the youth fell on the prone doorkeeper, battering him with heels and fists.

All the nobles except Serenus swarmed forward. My throat grew scalding hot. The grizzled man shouted vain warnings about the watch. His words were greeted with hoots of derision as the gentlemen rained blows on the doorkeeper, whose protesting pleas turned to reedy screams of pain.

Meantime the moon-faced youth had worked himself into a frenzy. "He's not respectful enough! Strike harder!"

I could bear it no more. I plunged across the street.

The first noble I seized by the shoulder squeaked in fright when I struck him in the face and sent him staggering.

The man Serenus rushed to my side. "Get away, whoever you are! Don't meddle in this."

But I had already meddled, and the pack of perfumed dogs was snapping all around, grabbing at my arms, aiming fists at my head and chest. The round-faced noble was the worst of the lot, spewing obscene oaths as he darted under a comrade's arm to kick me between the legs.

I cursed, swinging wildly. My balled hand connected with his chin. His eyes popped in amazement as he hurled back against two of his companions, then spilled on the ground.

People appeared in Sulla's doorway. There was too much confusion for me to notice them clearly. The round-faced youth climbed to his feet, pointing at me with a shaking hand.

"Who is that? Who *is* that filth? Where are your swords? Kill him! *Castrate him!*"

The friends and servants seemed too dazed to move. The doorkeeper huddled against the wall, mumbling incoherently. Hands dipped beneath cloaks. Short swords and daggers appeared. A ring of men closed in on me.

One of the nobles charged, iron blade ready to rip my belly open. Serenus grasped the man's arm, diverting his attack. I leaped for another of the bullies, tearing his sword out of his fingers. I whacked him hard with the flat across his skull. He dropped, moaning.

A sharp gasp of pain went up behind me. I fended the next assailant, dumped him bodily over my shoulder and turned, panting.

Serenus was clutching his side in surprise. He had been accidentally wounded. The man whose sword Serenus had knocked down gazed at the gory point in shock and chagrin.

A linkboy ran in the gate. "The watch! Blocks away, but coming fast."

Distant halloos broke the stillness. I wiped sweat from my eyes, still surrounded. The puff-cheeked youth gnawed his lip. All at once, with a hateful glare at me, he gathered the hem of his cloak in his hands and scuttled for the gate, crying. "Leave them! I prefer not to wrangle with policemen."

Someone shouted a question about Serenus. The grizzled noble was leaning against the wall, drawing heavy breaths. The youth paused in the gateway. He waved a beringed hand.

"He can fend for himself. After all, they're his men."

Like chaff scattering on a wind, the party of nobles and servants vanished. Serenus took a few shambling steps in my direction.

"Please, young man. Your arm. I can't seem to walk well."

Before I could reply, a voice said softly behind me, "Cassius?"

Acte thrust forward through the chattering crowd of kohl-painted prostitutes who had spilled out of the brothel. She ran to my side. I drew back, sickened at the sight of her.

She wore a pure white stola of Milesian wool. The garment was far too expensive to have been purchased with her own meager funds. Her hair was adorned with intricate inlaid combs. Rings and chains and brooches of onyx and sard and amethyst and agate winked on her fingers, arms and breasts. She'd been well rewarded for her night's work, the traces of which still reddened her face to a deep hue.

She saw me staring at her flushed, roughened cheeks. A sapphire on her hand mockingly blazed back the light of the false dawn as she hid one cheek.

"Cassius, I would have come out sooner—"

"Except that what you told me at the school was a lie. A lie to amuse your friends," I finished.

"I beg you, Cassius, listen a moment. Let me tell you why—"

I struck her full in the face.

She fell back, gasping. "I know why, Acte. Because you're a whore, and whores give out false words as easily and cheaply as they give their bodies."

Suddenly Syrax bolted from the brothel doorway. He rubbed his eyes furiously. He spotted the wounded Serenus, who was staring into the street, hunting for signs of the watch. Instantly Syrax turned pale. He pushed Acte aside, hissing in my ear, "I drowse off a while and what happens? You brainless lout, do you know the identity of that wounded man? Annaeus Serenus himself, Prefect of the Vigiles."

"And so? His friends, the fine, noble gentlemen visiting this sweet and pure lady attacked the old man."

"Ah, gods, how I wish I'd stayed awake!" For the first time Syrax looked unsure of himself. "You didn't—lay hands on them? Or anything so rash as that?"

"What if I did? I struck one snot-cheeked boy who started the baiting."

"Brainless clod!" Syrax practically screamed. "That snot-cheeked boy was the Emperor!"

"The *Emperor!*"

The word boiled my guts with fear. Now I recollected exactly why his weak and pudgy-lipped countenance had seemed so familiar. I had gazed on it many times before, struck into the metal of Imperial coins.

"I wanted to come out to you, Cassius," Acte was saying. "But the Imperator wanted his nightly revel and—"

"And whether he's a beast or not, you flatter him with lies, the same way you did me."

"Cassius, what I said at the school—"

"Never mind!" I shouted. "The cur won't trouble you again."

A hand closed on my forearm. Serenus stood there, weaving. His skin was pale, and the greasy swathe of blood on his cloak shone in the day's brightening gleam. He indicated the gate.

"Stranger, whoever you are, you seem to have your wits about you." His deep voice was broken by pained breaths. "I am Serenus, as that man told you. We have only a few moment's grace. The watch turned off to chase some of the Emperor's friends. Futile. They'll be down on us next. It would be highly embarrassing for their commander to be caught disturbing the peace. Help me out through the rear gate. I'm not sure I can walk alone. I'll pay well."

In a sense I felt responsible for his injury. But I hedged. "My friend and I must return to—"

I stopped. There was little point in worrying about Syrax. He had put the salvation of his own hide uppermost, and melted out of sight. I noted the narrow purple stripe of Serenus' toga, just visible beneath an opening in his cloak. I might as well reap some sort of profit from this dismal night, like everyone else.

"All right, I'll help you. Lean on me and direct me to the gate."

Drawing breaths with difficulty, Serenus supported himself on my shoulder. We started toward the rear of the building. Sulla himself, a fat, bald eunuch, was herding his girls back inside. Even the doorkeeper had crawled off to hide. Feet hammered in the street, converging from several directions.

At the building's corner, Serenus stumbled, cried out and nearly fell. Catching him, I happened to turn in such a way that the courtyard was still in plain view. In its center stood Acte, watching us.

The grayish light rippled and shone on the gems she'd won for her night's work. "I meant what I told you, Cassius," she called. "I meant it all."

Propping up Serenus as best I could, I spat on the ground and turned my back.

We had barely reached a low gate in the rear wall when a cry went up in the courtyard. "Ho! Everyone stay where you are!"

"Down here, quickly," Serenus panted. He indicated a thick clump of shrubs adjoining the gate. "They'll make only a cursory search of the grounds. As soon as they're inside, we can leave."

Search they did, but not overly hard, as he'd predicted. One vigile tramped by swinging his tallow lantern. Then stern male voices clamored inside the brothel. Serenus stood up with a groan and I helped him toward the gate.

A bad night's work. The love I'd foolishly imagined Acte felt was false, I'd struck the Emperor himself, and by now I was probably being hunted by Fabius as a fugitive, my life forfeit if I was caught.

CHAPTER V

BY A DEVIOUS route we at last reached the entrance of a splendid house of soft black tufa stone enriched with golden travertine. The house sat almost at the apex of the Esquiline Hill. The view was breathtaking.

Not only the thoroughfares below, the Flavia Victoria and the other squalid streets roundabout, already swarming, but the other six hills and even the distant blue mountains could be seen across the plain. Guiding my companion when he faltered, I had long since abandoned worry over punishment at the school. I was far too late to creep back unobserved. What would come, would come. Instead of fretting, I relished the sharper, sweeter air of these heights crowded with elegant homes. Up here one day I too would dwell, I told myself. I would be a rich eques. But how close I'd come to turning aside from that shining goal because of the false words of Acte!

"Sir," I said, "you have a magnificent house. I assume there are servants on the premises to tend your wound."

"There had better be," Serenus grumbled, whey-faced. "The house is not mine, though. It's Seneca's."

"The philosopher? The Imperial adviser?"

"The same. We'd go to my home, but it's further away. Knock loudly. And hurry. I seem to have struggled this far with a pit in my side only to die bleeding while you talk and goggle."

I rapped at the entrance as he bade. Momentarily a slave
arrived. The man's expression of surliness changed to one of
deference as soon as Serenus threw back the cloak with which
he'd concealed his features during our journey down back al-
leys.

"Wine and bread and linen!" Serenus yelled, shoving inside.
"And tell your master to meet us in the tablinium. Young man,
give me your arm again."

We passed between elegant columns of Luna marble into
the atrium, which was richly furnished. Serenus limped badly,
clutching his side. At each step his wound rained bright droplets of blood onto the tiles.

Brazen tritons sprayed water into the atrium pool. A magpie
chattered in a cage. The air was fragrant with the smell of green
plants floating on the water's surface.

A moment later we entered the tablinium, a sparsely furnished room at the atrium's rear. In this room of the house the
master customarily received his clients. Slaves bustled in and
out fetching basins and ewers and jars of ointment. Clumsily
Serenus settled onto a bench and lifted away the bloodied mess
of his cloak and toga, revealing a long gash running parallel
with his pale ribs. To me the wound looked more gory than
deep.

Serenus gulped a mug of wine and swatted at a slave's head.
"Not so hard, not so hard! Apply the dressing if you must, but
don't tear me apart doing it." He twisted his head in my direction. "Have you never been inside a residence like this, young
man? You gawk like a yokel. Why worry about offending? You've
struck the Princeps himself. You can hardly do anything worse."

He spoke not in reproof but with a sort of weary mirth. He
was a spare, sturdy man in his late forties, with a noble nose,
thrusting jaw and kindly brown eyes. He said by way of finishing, "Stand there if you feel you must, but you have my leave
to sit. That was wretched business at Sulla's. I wonder where
the boy's excesses will bring us. In a way I'm sorry I hadn't the

courage to strike him myself. However, I've always had a certain aversion to poison."

Taking this all in, I was ready to accept his invitation and perch on one of the stone benches when the hangings were swept aside. Into the tablinium stepped a tall, slim noble slightly older than Serenus. He wore a simple woolen robe. His nose was sharp, his eyes intelligent, his cheeks lean, his mouth determined. Outside in the atrium I glimpsed a pretty, silver-haired matron wearing a stola as simple in cut and hue as the man's garment.

The new arrival gestured to the woman. His voice had the rich qualities of a schooled orator's. "Before we talk privately, Serenus, my wife Paulina wishes to inquire after your health."

"Tell Paulina greetings and also that I'll live," Serenus answered wryly.

The tall man turned toward the hangings. His wife, having heard, smiled and glided away. The hangings dropped. Serenus added, "It isn't this gash that frets me. It's the circumstance which produced it. Our young charge grows more reckless every day. He—oh, permit me to present this stranger. I don't even know his name, but he helped me through the streets."

"My name is Cassius, sirs," I said. To the tall man I added, "Ave!"

"Ave," he replied, smiling at the greeting of the streets.

With a clap he dismissed the slaves, who had finished binding Serenus' wound. He settled down to a bench opposite his friend. He poured sweet wine into silver goblets, like a servant rather than a master. He even handed me one. His eyes were tolerant and amused.

"Take it, good Cassius. You've earned it."

"In case you haven't guessed," Serenus said to me, "this is the celebrated L. Annaeus Seneca."

"The celebrated failure," Seneca replied somberly. "In matters of Imperial counsel anyway. Cassius, whatever you hear in this chamber shall go no further."

"Don't worry," Serenus put in. "He won't go running to Nero. He hit him in the face."

Seneca sighed. "The gods preserve us. On what pretext?"

"I didn't know who he was," I said lamely. "But he was abusing an old man."

"Would you have struck had you known his identity?" asked Seneca.

I thought it over, remembering Acte. "I believe so."

The famous philosopher nodded. "Such courage is admirable, though misguided. The Emperor is a dangerous foe. He is circuitous in his hatred. However, Rome could do with a trifle more courage of the kind you displayed. Especially in the Senate."

"I tell you," Serenus blurted hotly, "the Emperor's cruelties will ruin us all! Already the rumors of his antics are the talk of Rome. What if he accidentally murders some poor wretch and we can't hush it up?"

Slowly Seneca stroked his chin with a bony finger. "Worse, Serenus, what if he kills us? Then there would be none to check his excesses. Only yesterday, on the Palatine, Nero was ranting about wanting the status and veneration of a god. When I suggested that deification was reserved for rulers already departed, he took it as a threat, not a comment, the way I intended. He shrieked at me like a spoiled brat. Frankly, I often wish Claudius had been a little firmer in his dislike of the Stoic philosophy. Had he been, I might never have been recalled from exile to tutor Nero, and today I'd be living the kind of life I enjoy, not mixing my hands in politics, at best a dirty business. Well, tell me. What happened, and where?"

Serenus hitched himself nearer the wine. He poured another generous draught, downed it and said, "Sulla's." One more drink and a healthier color returned to his cheeks.

"We have gone there five nights in a row. The Emperor is so enamored of that little whore, I have no choice but to fawn over her and play her lover to divert public suspicion from him. Otherwise his mother Agrippina and his wife Octavia would be stirring up more trouble than they are already. What a fine role for a man my age! Forced to giggle and joke over a prostitute! Although," he added, his features gentling, "other things aside, she's pretty enough, and has a pleasant temper."

From a tray Seneca broke sections of a loaf of bread and ate two. Then he extended the tray to me. I took a piece, knowing again the miracle of being rich. For this was not the cheap, coarse *panis sordidus* of the streets, but the sweet and yeasty *siligineus*, which I had never tasted.

"Perhaps you wonder, Cassius," the philosopher said, "why we speak so frankly about the Emperor."

"It's not my position to say. I can only guess it's because you sympathize with his weaknesses."

Seneca laughed. "And it's clear from your tone you don't. Neither do we. Personally, I would much prefer to live the retired life I mentioned, writing plays and tending to my foreign estates, than capering on the Palatine. By my lights, life is a bad lot at best. It's made bearable only by study and contemplation in solitude. On the other hand, Serenus and I both feel someone must attempt to curb the Emperor's peculiar tastes and temper. We and his other chief adviser, the Prefect of the Praetorian Guard, Sextus Afranius Burrus, deplore his unbridled emotions, his egotism. But we bow and scrape to him because we're fully aware of what the people's lot would be if Nero ruled unchecked. So don't think too harshly of Serenus for the company he keeps. We are, so to speak, watchdogs over a very rowdy and savage animal. How long we'll be allowed to remain watchdogs, no one can say."

Inwardly I felt contempt for the selflessness of these two men. How was it possible to make one's way in Rome while worrying about the welfare of the masses? I said nothing, however.

Serenus grumbled, "Personally, I don't intend to remain the butt of jokes in the Forum much longer. Nor serve as a screen for that mad boy's passion for Acte."

"Acte!" I blurted the word, my palms suddenly cold.

Seneca scrutinized me. "Yes. The young prostitute we mentioned. Do you know her?"

"She's the one I went to Sulla's to visit. Foolishly, it turned out."

"Thus far you've said precious little about yourself, Cassius," Serenus broke in. "Are you a freedman?"

"I was." I decided to risk the truth. "I am auctorati, from the Bestiarii School."

When this had penetrated, Serenus complained, "Oh, splendid. We have a fugitive on our hands."

"How did this happen?" the philosopher asked. "Because of Acte, you ran away from the school?"

"Only for one night. I meant to return. Now it's too late."

With guarded words I told them that Acte and I had become acquainted when she visited the school. I described my nocturnal visit to Sulla's as a lustful lark, rather than the agonizing experience it had turned out to be. At the end Seneca commented, "Certainly the fates weren't kind when you decided on that particular girl. You've involved yourself in a very tangled affair. The Emperor is already experiencing great difficulty with his mother Agrippina because he wishes to divorce his wife and marry his mistress."

At last the dismal truth crushed home. "The Emperor has been seeing Acte a long while?"

"No, only a few weeks," Serenus told me. "She's not the mistress Seneca referred to. That's a little yellow-haired strumpet named Poppaea Sabina. A divorcee who makes a specialty of bathing daily in the milk of young asses. The Emperor's fancy for Acte is merely one more of his temporary passions, of which there seem to be hundreds. He'll use her for what she's worth, then discard her."

And she'll use him in turn, I thought bitterly. Why, I wondered, had she used me?

The gray-haired Prefect of the watch studied my expression, then coughed loudly. I must have appeared embarrassed, for he certainly did. The very fact that he was concerned at all over the feelings of a man of my station warmed me toward him. Rather gruffly, he said, "Truth to tell, Cassius, I like Acte a good deal. It's only the role I'm forced to play that's so damnable. I'm no more of a hot young lover than Seneca. But to prevent scandal it's my duty to cavort like one. If it will assuage your poorly concealed bitterness any, I should report that I've talked with Acte enough to know she cares nothing for the Emperor. She's merely patronizing him, trying to—"

"Please spare me further details, sir," I said miserably. "I know what she's trying to do."

The learned philosopher rose to pace back and forth. He changed the subject. "So you're in training as a bestiarius, eh?

"That's right, sir. I aim to win the wooden sword one day."

Seneca looked dour. "I won't bore you with too many personal opinions of your profession, except to say that there is no sportsmanship left in it. Barbarous punishment of criminals should not be turned into a spectacle. The games have also killed the art of conversation. No one today can talk of anything except the skill of various charioteers, the quality of the teams, or the details of some lewd exhibit held at a private circus."

Waving his wine up, Serenus added, "Nero isn't helping matters any. Have you heard some of his proposals for clever acts? Sheer filth."

After a pause indicating tacit agreement, Seneca said to the Prefect, "I assume we owe this young man an appropriate reward for helping you."

"Definitely," was the reply. I grew tense. "To have been picked up by one of my own vigiles—Well, I'd have been laughed out of Rome."

"And therefore totally useless as a moderating influence upon the Emperor. Cassius? Name your reward."

A wild, unreasonable gamble took shape in my head as he spoke. What had I to lose? This morning—warm, the sun falling into the atrium's light well, sifting through the tablinium hangings—I had tasted the sweet bread of nobility. And only last night I had come dangerously close to forgetting my vow to be an eques.

I said carefully, "Honored gentlemen, any reward I claim would do me no good, since I escaped the school to go on my little errand of the flesh, and can't get back in."

My heart leaped when Serenus waved. "Don't let that concern you. We'll think of some way around that."

I was skirting the edge of a precipice now, and unable to turn back. "Then I ask nothing for the present. I'll take my reward in the future. One day, when I win the wooden sword, I mean to found a second beast school in Rome. One which will restore the good name of the profession. I have the ambition to do it, but certain obstacles block me."

With a gentle smile Seneca said, "You have ambition and a measure of honor both, it appears. Continue."

"No doubt I'm far too presumptuous in asking this. Yet my highest reward would not be money, but words. I know both you gentlemen must be intimate with influential people in the banking world. I'll need funds for the school. An introduction, a helpful word—that would be enough. If you gentlemen could open certain doors that might otherwise be closed to one born as I was, I would be forever grateful."

For a considerable time neither spoke. Distantly through the house rang the voices of the slaves, preparing the morning meal and doing menial chores. The silence of the two men I took to mean refusal, the rejection of an upstart who had asked for too costly a prize.

Then Serenus chuckled.

"This Cassius is a find. There's a certain wolfish greed shining in his eyes. But unlike so many in Rome, he looks like he has the wit and muscle to back up his swaggering air. Further, he has imagination. Or don't you think so, Seneca?"

"Certainly the games are popular," the philosopher agreed, but not happily. "And growing larger and more ostentatious month by month. The games appear to be the only means the Emperor can find to divert the minds of his subjects from his debaucheries. "However," Seneca said, "while I don't agree with your ambition, I agree that you must be rewarded. If my help in securing a loan for a sound business venture is what you wish, you shall have that help at the appropriate time."

So overwhelmed was I by the luck of my thrust, my wild gamble that had suddenly opened the future again, I barely heard the Prefect tell me, "Come to think of it, Cassius, if your scheme is more than sheer talk, I might be interested myself. As a silent partner, of course. Lately I've been so occupied at the Palatine, I've devoted hardly any attention to business. My affairs haven't precisely prospered. I might have another valuable contact for you, in the person of a decurion in the city of Iol Caesaria, in Africa. I met him at a dinner while he was visiting in Rome last summer, and we became fast friends. Ah, but that's the future, isn't it?"

The future, yes, but it quickened my imagination. A decurion—the provincial noble charged with governing an Imperial province overseas—could be of invaluable help in securing unique animals for any school with which he was connected. Seneca broke in on these grandiose visions.

"In the present, however, we're faced with the necessity of secretly returning you to the Bestiarii School. It's almost the second hour already."

I told them that usually, Fabius did not disturb or call us out for practice until the middle of that second hour, preferring his pupils to be well rested when they faced the animals. Serenus and Seneca conferred briefly. They decided the latter was the appropriate person to smuggle me back into the school, though Seneca obviously had no taste for the task. Serenus' appearance when wounded would excite too much attention.

Serenus said thoughtfully, "It may sound odd coming from me, but perhaps I can tell Fabius the Emperor appointed me to look into the hiring of some bestiarii for a future show. Let's try it, anyway. I'll see about a litter."

He strode into the atrium. I reached for a last piece of the sweet siligineus, to fix in my memory its exact taste. That taste mattered more to me now than the flavor of a whore's mouth. When I had finished eating, Serenus clasped my hand.

"Consider our promise of help firm, not fanciful, Cassius. The rewards for a man in Rome these days, even a man who begins low on the rungs, are great. Provided he doesn't trouble his soul overmuch about how he makes his wealth."

"That won't concern me, I assure you, sir."

"The arena is dangerous. More so every day. But I have the feeling that if any can make it, you will be one."

"If desire alone is the standard, then I will."

From the atrium Seneca called that the litter was ready. Serenus said, *"Vale!"* I returned the word, believing that the grizzled Prefect meant his wish for good luck seriously.

Outside the slave entrance at the rear of the house, I crawled into an uncomfortable position at the rear of the large closed litter. Only then did Seneca summon forth his bearers, tall Cappadocians, and his way-clearers, youths with white wands. We set off through the streets. From the increasing babble, it was clear that the usual host of parasitic clients seeking favors from Seneca trailed along behind.

There was a tense moment when the guard at the school gate peered inside, but he jumped back deferentially at sight of the patrician profile of the litter's occupant. The litter bumped to the ground near a shadowy arcade. Seneca clambered out and hurried off to locate Fabius. I slipped out the other side and gained my quarters without detection.

Yet on the ride back my heart had grown heavy again.

Say what I might, I still loved Acte with a helpless passion beyond all reason. Loved her even though she was as scheming, as dishonest, as the basest whore in Rome.

I staggered out of my cell, pretending to have just wakened. I wondered dismally what bad luck such a helpless, hopeless passion would bring me in the days ahead.

CHAPTER VI

—————>>◦<<—————

SEVERAL NIGHTS LATER, Syrax slipped into my cell at the school after dark. He gave a mocking salute, then produced from behind his back a small amphora which he set beside me.

"Taste it," he ordered. His sly olive face shone in the lamp flame. "Though not too deeply just yet. Originally I had two jugs. One went to the clod guarding the end of the hall, to ensure our privacy."

In response I glowered at him. He sighed.

"Well, since you refuse, I'll drink. But you're passing up a good thing. That seems to be your habit. This is Falernian." He tilted the amphora to his lips.

"Oh, certainly, Falernian. It's probably vinegar. Where could you get nobleman's wine?"

Aping the manners of his betters, he wiped his mouth daintily with my couch blanket. "From the same place I received the good news that the school has been hired to supply a large contingent for the forthcoming Imperial games. From the lanista's rooms. Fabius and several guests are sitting around this moment, dead drunk. Naturally Fabius wanted to put on a good show during the haggling over price. He needed several trustworthy fellows with good manners to fetch and carry platters and jugs from the corner shop. In all the confusion, it's only natural that one or two amphorae of excellent wine might be—shall we say—misplaced."

"What's behind this sudden generosity, Syrax? You've hardly said a word the last couple of days."

He chuckled, downing more wine. "Now there's a joke. Cassius the Cur complaining over a lack of conversation. Look here, partner. Don't you understand the forthcoming games may be the first step in our rise to fortune? The scourging you suffered because of Tigellinus and the tribune Julius paid handsome dividends. The school is now in favor, and being hired. As for my silence, I let you alone because I perceived you were nursing a grudge in your usual bad-tempered way."

"Do you blame me?" I snapped back. "I didn't notice you remaining overlong at Sulla's."

His shrug was indifferent. "Preserving my skin comes first. Why should you complain? You returned safely enough. How, I can't guess, but you got back just the same."

"More than safely," I said, one up on him at last. "You're not the only one with high contacts."

"Whatever that means."

The shine in his narrow eyes told me he'd soon find out what it meant. And so he did, after I'd plagued him a while by drinking long and satisfyingly of the sweet Falernian. He could hardly conceal his anger as I strung him along with hints and vague references to Serenus and a certain celebrated Imperial adviser. Syrax was a man who angered easily when not in full command of a situation. Presently, though, the wine relaxed my tongue. I told him the story of my visit in the home of Seneca, and my request for introductions to a banker or two at some time in the future.

The Syrian's expression changed to one of elation. "Brilliant, Cassius! Positively brilliant! Are you certain they weren't making sport of you? Can they be trusted to keep the promise?"

"Yes. They're honorable men."

"Truthfully, I wouldn't have guessed you had the wits to arrange such a splendid deal. Learning you do confirms my opinion of myself in selecting you for a partner."

My head buzzed. Dragging the amphora up again, I saluted him with it. "To our school."

After I drank he seized the jar. "Our school which will prosper, now that the whore's out of your system."

"Yes, she is. How did you guess that?"

"Simple. You've made no mention of her."

Wine fogged my brains more and more, and I found drunken condemnation easy. "Why I became involved with her I'll never know. She's greedy and cheap, like all her sisters."

"Your change of heart makes our escapade at Sulla's doubly profitable. So long as the Emperor doesn't remember your face if he sees it in the arena, that is."

I sobered somewhat on that thought, not only out of fear of Nero, but because Syrax's mask had slipped again. In one hasty, flashing look I'd seen his true coldness, and the certainty that he would abandon me if bad luck brought down the Emperor's wrath. Still, I managed to laugh. He was no more ruthless than I would be from this point on. We simply had no illusions about one another any longer.

"Pass me the wine," I said, trying to stand without success. "I'm not worried about Nero."

"A splendid attitude under the circumstances."

He handed over the amphora. When the prime Falernian dribbled down my chin to my chest, I paid no mind, nor did he. The wine had worked quickly in bellies still growling after a slim night meal.

Syrax waggled a finger. "I'm pleased by your luck with the two gentlemen. I'm even more pleased you've cast that painted wench aside. She'd take your mind off our purpose."

"Exactly," I mumbled. "Another toast to our school."

"Nothing's going to stand in our way, is it, Cassius? Women. Scruples. Nothing."

"Nothing," I repeated dully. Then, more loudly, "Nothing. I vow that to you, Syrax."

With a tipsy chuckle he grabbed the amphora and we drank ourselves to oblivion.

Wine is a debaser of words, rendering them worthless, easily spoken and quickly forgotten. How can I properly explain that what I said to Syrax was the truth and at the same time false?

I fully intended to keep my promise to myself, and to those heartless patricians who baited me that first fateful day. I intended to rise to the eques rank, heedless of the cost. Yet I had not told the strange, devious man fate had chosen as my partner the entire truth. Despite all I knew about her, Acte remained a memory of sweetness and peace, a curious symbol of a life exactly the opposite of the one I now planned for myself.

Was I wrong about her? I doubted it.

Then why did some perverse part of me keep hungering for her? Remembering her? And loving her?

The tempo of our days at the Bestiarii School soon made such gloomy thoughts impossible.

The lanista's whip cracked more and more frequently. We trained from early in the morning until late in the day, drilling until we dropped. Thirty of the school's inmates were to appear in the Imperial games.

One drowsy, heat-muffled afternoon, Fabius was putting us through our paces with a bull and a leopard roped together. A splendid retinue appeared in the stands. I paid little mind, ready to take my turn with the animals.

The object of the lesson was practice in dodging the thrust of the bull's horns. Each student darted in with a sharp wooden goad, jabbed at the bullock and the leopard lashed together until both began to leap and stamp angrily. Then the student rushed between them, avoiding both the leopard's jaws and the bull's tossing horns until Fabius called a halt.

When Fabius ordered me to the center of the training ring, I stepped forward eagerly. After the animals were suitably aroused by my goad, I sprang one way, then another, dodging their clumsy attacks with ease. Dust clogged my throat. Sweat trickled down my forehead. Soon I could see little but the glinting horns and the bared fangs.

I dove under the bullock's barrel to avoid the leopard. Then I lurched up, grasped the horns and leaped over his head, as legend said they'd once trained youths to do on the isle of Crete. The leopard snapped, not eager to kill, merely wanting to show his irritation by eating part of my leg.

As I bound off the bull's back, my left foot struck the earth at a bad angle. My leg buckled. The leopard lunged for my chest.

Over and over I rolled. The leopard jerked up short on the line, spitting and hissing when the bullock stupidly decided to stand his ground. I climbed to my feet.

Fabius trotted up. Behind him, Xenophon glared at me. The scarred lanista surveyed me head to foot:

"All in one piece. Lucky. That was a pretty escape, Cassius. Unfortunately, it was altogether unnecessary. Why do you always do something out of the ordinary when we have important visitors?"

I squinted through the blowing dust. "Who? I see only that matron under the parasol. Roman ladies out to watch a few slaves get mangled aren't strangers here. They enjoy the sport."

"Enough of your impertinence!" he cried. "Mind you do the maneuver more skillfully next time, so I won't be embarrassed. That's a lady of some reputation. Next man!" With an impatient crack of his whip he returned to teaching.

I wandered back to the group of students. They squatted dusty and perspiring in the sun. I watched Xenophon dodge the bull and leopard and privately sneered at his clumsiness. Then I felt a curious prickling on my scalp.

I turned my head. The Roman lady who sat surrounded by eunuchs under her parasol was paying no attention to the burly Greek. She was watching me.

At a distance it was impossible to tell much about her age or features. Her gown was splendid, shimmering like the silk brought from the mythical land of Serica far eastward. It was dyed a rich shade of green. A high pile of curls emphasized the glittering redness of her hair. Her body and breasts looked well-formed and generous.

I grinned to myself. At least I'd fared better than most. Students were constantly plagued by the attentions of fat, lovesick old cows whose husbands had long since stopped touching them, for obvious reasons.

As the afternoon wore on the lady paid little heed to the lesson. I felt her eyes on me almost constantly. When it was once more my turn to bait the animals, I came off well, receiving Fabius' commendation, as well as polite applause from the lady. I bowed to her. Fabius was all smiles.

The sun sank and the day ended. The lady's retinue assembled and she left the stands. Fabius dismissed us. Xenophon walked over, smirking.

"There's a real match for you, Cassius." He indicated the departing woman. "But you might not be so skillful evading her peculiar brand of menace."

"I didn't see anything peculiar about her," I growled. "To the contrary. She plainly has an eye for a man with talent, and feet that aren't made of marble."

He flushed at the reference to his repeated stumbling during the lesson. "One day—" he began. Then he choked off the threat. "Why should I bother with you? Let Locusta get her hands on you, and you'll never trouble me or anyone else again."

I was startled. "Locusta the poisoner? The woman who supposedly helped Agrippina murder her husband Claudius?"

"So they say," replied the Greek. "I hear she has an interest in many things. Business properties. Gladiators who gain the public's fancy for a moment. The cult of the Great Mother of Pessinus, Cybele, of which she's a priestess. People say their rites would make even a satyr's eyes pop. Best of all, she's an expert with deadly roots and herbs." He laughed coarsely. "That's why I congratulate you, Cassius. Good luck on your new friendship."

I returned his laugh. "You'd like nothing better than to have some woman feed me a bowl of poisoned mushrooms, wouldn't you, Greek? Then you'd have no competition in the Imperial games. No one to show you up for the clumsy lump you are."

He lashed at my head. I ducked under the blow and he went purple in the face.

"I'll out-score you in the games, Cassius, and watch you bleed on the Circus Maximus sand when you die!"

A pitiless hate congealed inside me. I'd borne his insufferable conceit and bullying ways too long.

"Want to wager on it, Greek? I doubt if you do. You have nothing better to put up than the hot gas that gushes from your mouth day and night." So saying, I walked off.

Fabius had watched the little scene with evident displeasure. One day there would be a reckoning between Xenophon and me. While he was not an easy enemy, I looked forward to it.

Though none of us from the school was present to see, we could well imagine the clamor around the Circus Maximus as the opening day of the games approached.

In the Vallis Murcia, that long cleft between the Palatine and Aventine hills, the arches around the outside of the great Circus would be jammed by thousands of slaves and freedmen fighting for one of the ivory tokens that would admit them to the wooden upper tiers of the mammoth amphitheater. Day and night the streets roundabout would echo with the croakings of astrologers, the sibilant whispers of child whores, the rumble of cage carts delivering penned and snarling animals to the warrens within the stadium walls.

Thoughts of Acte receded from my mind in all the excitement. Only now and then did I entertain a painful hope that she might turn up on the night of the regular visit of the girls from Sulla's. She did not. I spent the long hours completely alone.

Next day, I went to Fabius. I found him fretting over a broken wheel on a cart loaded with lethargic brown bears. I asked whether by chance I had received any messages.

"None," he said shortly. "Don't bother me with foolish questions, Cassius. The games are only two days hence, and there are a million things still undone."

Plainly I ought to forget her forever, I told myself. Concentrate upon the events of the next few days. I had never fought in Rome before. Much was at stake.

The remaining two days blurred into a confused round of last-minute preparations. Then came the hot, bright morning when Fabius, finely attired, assembled thirty of us for the march to the Circus and the opening of the games of Nero, Princeps and Imperator.

We walked in threes, Fabius at our head. We were clad in loose white smocks and a few cheap glittering amulets. As we neared the looming Circus we passed through cheering crowds. They scattered flowers before us, or occasionally let out a bitter curse if the person cursing happened to favor regular Dacian or Gallic gladiators. The sky rang with the thunder of thousands of voices. The roar seemed to shake the very foundations of Rome.

Side streets were clogged. As we descended toward the tunnels beneath the stands, we passed long queues of citizens with ivory tokens in hand, waiting their turns to be shown their seats by the locarii. The Circus was the great leveler. All Rome's business enterprises shut down during the six days of entertainment. Men were free to cheer, scream or insult each other, as they wished. The only social distinction was maintained by the seats they occupied. Senators and equites took the lower tiers of stone, their boxes draped over with rich cloth pavilions. Freedmen sat higher up on the wooden benches. The slaves were highest of all. How many jammed the great U-shaped structure I could not guess. My father told me once it was more than a hundred thousand.

The arches outside were confusion. Street musicians played. Hawkers shouted. Bettors arranged wagers on the program of events. Praetorians in armor kept watch on the lines, so no thieves would slip back to the empty streets to loot. In the tunnels beneath the stands the confusion was even worse.

From wooden cages first dragged into the arena, then placed in barred niches all around the lower wall below the first tier of seats, animals screamed and clawed and vented their anger at penning. Lions snarled. Elephants trumpeted. Wolves howled. Ostriches made their queer sound.

The Bestiarii dressed with the aid of handlers, in a long, dim passage at the open end of the Circus. Xenophon and I, among others, were given stout spears with round iron disks half way down the shaft. These signified that we were to go against wild boars in the opening animal hunt. Syrax drew a veil and sword for bears.

Fabius was everywhere, now taunting, now encouraging. In the tunnel's cool and dusty dimness, I had no time to fret over the countless angry looks thrown me by Xenophon. Out there beyond that square of sunlight at the tunnel's mouth lay death, multiplied many more times than one. Out there, too, lay fortune. This was the start of a perilous road upward. I meant to make the first steps meaningful ones.

Brazen trumpets signaled the arrival of the Emperor's party. Slaves ran back to inform us that the priests had marched out to erect the altar to Jupiter Latista along the stone Spine which ran down the center of the Circus. Sun glared on the pure white sand strewn with gems, on the spotless robes and red scarves of the priests leading out the sacred white bull and the pair of rams with headdresses of gold.

After suitable chanting and sprinkling of wine, the animals were slain. The priests examined their entrails to see whether the gods wished the games to proceed. With Nero sponsoring, naturally the omens were favorable.

The priests retired. I was sweating. More trumpets blasted. The stone walls reverberated with cheers. A gilt chariot flashed by the tunnel mouth, drawn by black and white striped tiger horses from Africa. I had a fleeting view of the youthful Emperor adorned in his purple toga, a heavy gold wreath on his head, an ivory scepter crested with a golden eagle in his right hand. Behind the chariot marched drummers and pipers and flutists.

The Emperor's chariot circled the arena. There was another lull, followed by fresh trumpeting. The opening parade began.

We marched into the blinding sun. Garlands showered down upon us. The mob screamed praise. Our company was directly behind a host of Dacians attired as Retiarii, the fighters with net and trident. In the parade were all the chariots scheduled to race, and gladiators by the score, and elephants from Ind and Numidia carrying ornamental booths, and girls nude to the waist whose breasts gleamed as red as the rose petals they strewed, and Thracians and criminals—in short, nearly a thousand fighters and entertainers.

Each group marched down the arena along the Spine to the Emperor's box. It was covered over with a canopy attached to four ivory statues fashioned in Nero's image. Walking in a rank with four others from the Bestiarii School, I picked out several familiar faces in the lower stands.

The slippery Tigellinus lolled on a couch with a jug of wine at his elbow. The Praetorian Julius was making a hasty last-minute wager. Serenus too occupied a box, and further down, beneath a parasol, the red-haired Locusta sat. I thought she moved her painted mouth in a smile as I passed, singling me out, but I couldn't be sure.

As we neared the Emperor's box we passed before the six most sacred personages in Rome, the Sisterhood of Vestals. They were simply robed, sitting quietly, secure in the knowledge that theirs was the holiest task in the city—the tending of the immortal fire whose kindling, some said, dated from the time of Romulus and Remus. Of all the thousands present, only those six women of various ages who had vowed to remain chaste all their lives or suffer death, made no vulgar outcry.

At the head of our company, Fabius halted before the Imperial box. From thirty-one throats the traditional cry was shouted.

"Hail, Caesar! We who are about to die salute thee!"

Diffidently the Emperor Nero nodded in return. He had more interest in the next group in line, bare-breasted Greek slave girls with dark mahogany skin. The Emperor's wan, fleshy face looked sweaty in the shade of the canopy. His bulging eyes never once met mine, or even noticed me.

Beside him sat a blonde woman, older, wearing a silken gown so transparent she might have left the gown at home. I took her to be his mistress, Poppaea Sabina. From the way others higher in the stands pointed at her, he was scandalizing the populace by flaunting her openly. No one honestly cared about it, though. This was the time of the games. Madness ruled.

Quickly we completed our circuit of the Spine. We returned to a position near the mouth of the tunnel, from which we had emerged. Slaves removed the bodies of the sacrificial animals. Trumpets rang again. All the bars on the cages set into the lower walls squealed up at once.

A hundred animals poured into the arena. Deer and wild boar with fierce tusks, bears and bulls, antelope and jackals, queer long-legged cranes and hyenas, a few leopards and even some domestic cattle. A moment later a dozen foxes were released, each with a burning firebrand lashed to its tail. The foxes ran yipping among the other animals, driving them to a frenzy.

Fabius' face gleamed with sweat. He gave us a last look.

"For the school, lads. Break ranks! Kill them!"

The mob howled and applauded as we raced down the Spine.

Each man went his own way, picking a quarry. Two bestiarii running beside me dropped back to chase an antelope. I ran on, sighting a promising tangle of three wild boars being harried by a fox further down.

The spear with its round shield weighed in my hand. Because the games usually commenced rather tamely, and only grew bloodier as the days went by, this first animal hunt was designed merely to whet the crowd's appetite. No one could be seriously hurt slaying a dumb cow or a snapping hyena. Only the boars and an occasional bear added the spice of danger. Perhaps this was why Fabius outfitted me for the boars.

A shadow fell across the sand directly ahead. To my right Xenophon appeared.

He was puffing hard, bound on beating me to the trio of boars. They pitched their tusks at the fox circling them while the fox leaped wildly, driven mad by the fire singing its bushy tail. Xenophon grinned and ran harder.

I ran hard as well, straining every muscle. A man stumbled in the sand as we passed. The wild pony he'd chased hoofed his skull into two pieces. The mob cheered wildly.

Drawing ahead, Xenophon flung his spear at one of the boars with all his might.

Instantly the three hairy tuskers swung round. Their small eyes burned with mindless hate. Snorting out of wet snouts, they charged.

Xenophon dodged behind one of the statues decorating the base of the Spine. He left me to fight the trio alone. He was laughing.

The Greek's spear had furrowed a long wound down the backbone of one of the brutes, then skimmed off into the white sand. I took a hard grip on my own spear. I lifted it over my head and lashed down as the first boar neared.

The point went true, into the boar's throat and gut.

Torn to pieces inside, the animal bit down on the shaft. I struggled to wrench it free.

The second boar, bleeding from Xenophon's throw, hurled itself over the first to tusk me. The round shield on the spear met the tusks with a clang. The animal fell back, tumbling over as I pulled the gory point from the throat of the first.

The third boar backed off, pawing the sand for a new charge. Behind me, cheers went up. I paid no attention, intent on Xenophon and the two remaining animals.

The boars lumbered forward side by side. I jumped over them both, racing on to where the Greek's spear had fallen. Cursing, Xenophon broke from his safe nook behind the statue, guessing part of my intent.

The thews in my legs ached as I ran, heedless of the trample and thud of the boars turning back, charging again, tusks aimed at my backside. I snatched up Xenophon's spear, avoided his lunge that carried him by, then pivoted, a spear in each hand.

Two wet snouts loomed, and four tearing tusks. I bit down on my lip and rammed both spears at once.

The one in my right hand pierced the animal's neck. The left one slid into the wounded boar's shoulder and angled back to the ribs. The animal pitched over, kicking.

I let go the right spear so the boar who'd swallowed it could die. Xenophon's shadow grew large as he ran up behind me.

Feigning a move to rip the shaft out of the wounded boar, I worked it back and forth until my shoulders ached. The wood splintered and broke.

Xenophon lurched to a halt. I whirled and handed him the useless shaft.

"Here, Greek. See whether you can out-score me with half a weapon."

Clutching the wood in his hands, he stood with a muscle in his throat leaping, wanting to kill me. Nonchalantly I moved toward the other boar and proceeded to pull out my own spear.

Flower petals rained down from nearby boxes. Xenophon saw the cheering was all for me. He dared risk no open attack. He stalked off, swearing, to find another prey.

Too late. The last of the fire-tailed foxes was being slaughtered. Animal corpses littered the sand. Only one bestiarius, so far as I could see, the man who'd been trampled by the wild pony, was down. Others were wounded, but not seriously.

Syrax limped toward me. He carried his bloodied veil and blade in his right hand, and three severed bear claws in his left. He grinned.

"All with more than two kills will receive a garland from the Emperor, Cassius. Come on, what are you waiting for?"

Apprehensive about going before Nero again, I borrowed his sword and loped off the right forehooves of the three boars. I carried my dripping prizes down the length of the arena toward the ivory-columned box. From the opposite direction a slave named Mercor approached. He held four large crane feet. Apparently we were the only ones who had managed more than a pair of kills. Many times the animals destroyed one another before a bestiarius could reach them.

Syrax smiled broadly as we marched up beneath the Emperor's box. Already wager takers bustled in the stands, pointing to us, marking down our names. Victors enjoyed a certain fame so long as they stayed alive. The more victories, the greater the fame. Truly, this was an auspicious beginning.

The triumph palled somewhat as we presented ourselves to the Emperor. The moon-faced boy peered indifferently over the marble rail.

We flung our gory trophies in the sand before him. Syrax spoke for us. "Emperor, your servants Syrax, Cassius, and Mercor beg your favor."

Nero tossed three vine garlands down and waved us away.

The frantic beating of my heart stilled. Nero turned to fondle the arm of the blonde wench seated beside him. Perhaps the light had been too poor at Sulla's, or the wine too strong. He had not recognized me.

Syrax adjusted his garland with sticky red fingers. We strolled back in the direction of the tunnel. Slaves cleared the arena of dead animals.

To provide amusement between the acts, a company of andabatae, senile old men buck naked except for gladiatorial helmets with no visors, swung blindly at one another with comical bladders. At the far end of the Circus a company of Secutorii, gladiators with greaves and the Gaul fish insignia on their helmets, waited in place to begin hand to hand combat.

"Too bad about Calluris," Syrax said as we marched along under the admiring stares of the crowd. "I had to let him take the fight out of the second bear before I could finish the beast off."

"What happened to Calluris?"

Syrax shrugged. "Oh, the bear ripped his belly open. Poor fellow died."

"I thought only one man got killed. Redarus, with the pony."

Syrax waved. "Calluris and I were on the other side of the Spine. Look, what does it matter? We got the garlands, didn't we? That's what we came for."

I was about to retort that a garland couldn't be fairly won at the expense of another man's life. He gigged me with a bloody elbow.

"There's that stupid Tigellinus talking to Madame Poison. It appears she's more interested in you. Partner, this is a momentous day. In the name of the gods, flash her a smile."

He moved ahead of me with an exhilarated step, exchanging greetings with the crowd in a merry voice, as if it didn't trouble him that he'd won his victory by letting another man die first.

I looked carefully to the left while I walked. Ofonius Tigellinus had moved over to Locusta's box and was now bending at her shoulder, lust so patent and open on his Sicilian face that I wanted to laugh. I didn't because the woman was watching me closely. Her breasts rose and fell like pointed weapons under her gown. Her copper hair shone. Her eyes were greenish, wide, slightly tilted and inscrutable. She seemed in a state of excitement.

Her painted mouth broke into a lazy, sensual smile. She inclined her head in greeting.

I judged her to be forty at least, but her arms, ringed with bangles, looked smooth as a virgin's. There was something cold, passionless, even a little forbidding in her glance, though.

Soon I reached the spot where Fabius was waiting by the tunnel. He was slapping Mercor and Syrax on the back happily. I was thankful Tigellinus had been too intent on making advances to notice me.

Fabius congratulated us on doing well. We trudged back into the tunnel. There we relaxed and joked among ourselves. We would not appear again until the fourth day of the games. Then we would be pitted against lions and leopards trained as man-eaters. It would be far more of a test of skill than this morning's mild slaughter.

I lifted the garland of vine leaves and settled it on my head, then accepted a mug of posca from a handler. I was a fool not to enjoy the victory. Nero hadn't recognized me. I had drawn the notice of a famous lady. And if Fabius didn't concern himself about Syrax winning at the expense of Calluris' life, why should I?

I slopped down the posca. "Here's to another garland three days from now, Syrax." Then I went to dress, untroubled even by the sullen, vengeful stares of the hulking Xenophon.

That evening, in the midst of a drunken celebration Fabius arranged at the school, I was summoned by the lanista himself.

He spoke low in my ear, "Go to your cell, Cassius. There you'll discover a fine new tunic and sandals. Put them on. Wash the wine from your face and climb in the litter waiting in the courtyard."

Wine had made me rash. "Am I to be exhibited again? I earned praise for you once already today."

He refused to be provoked, laughing like a conspirator. "Whether you're—ah—exhibited depends on how you behave yourself, and what transpires between you and the lady who sent her slave here with the request that the bestiarius Cassius join her for dinner. Locusta, you blockhead! It's a great honor for us."

"So I'm allowed out only to enhance the school's reputation even further?"

"I swear by Mars I don't know what makes you so quarrelsome! Fine things can happen to a man who wins the approval of a woman in high position. Certainly it wouldn't be like making up to some fat gray old harpy. If it reaches that point," he added with a lewd glance. "Look, lad. The reputation of our profession is none too good among the so-called righteous elements in the city. So why scruple about Locusta's reputation? What bothers you? The tales of poison?"

"Nothing bothers me," I returned, putting down my foolish hesitation. "I'll go, and gladly."

So I did. In style, too. Fabius had rented a handsome gilt litter with side draperies. Half a dozen of the witless bullies who passed for guards at the school surrounded the conveyance. We jogged through the twisting streets in the light of the sinking sun. Even under guard, the litter and the clean linen against my flanks gave me a sense of freedom and power that was new and startling.

As we neared the Forum I saw, scrawled on a wall, among other greetings and epithets, large charcoal words some girl had written.

Cassius the Bestiarius is the maiden's sigh.

I smiled. Writing such mottoes was a custom in Rome. The sentiment was empty, and the name of the man in the phrase was changed as often as some new gladiator acquired a bit of notoriety in the arena, or an old one died. Yet the fact that it was my name filled me with fresh confidence.

The litter bumped down. I looked out. I discovered we had stopped on the center of the Forum. The guard in charge indicated a number of tall white boards propped against several pillars.

"Might as well enjoy your fame while you can, Cassius. I hear your name's there in the gazette. Stretch a bit and read about it, if you wish."

Eagerly I jumped out. I pushed through the crowd around the *Acta Diurna*, the message boards which served as the dissemination point of Rome's popular gossip, as well as of news of such things as the corn crop in Numidia and the activities of the legions in Gaul. Rapidly I ran my eye down one album, then the next.

Several citizens were commenting on a sensational story about a Greek thief. Condemned to death, he had been escorted to the broad and splendid Forum yesterday, to be stoned to death, only to be spared when the execution party accidentally encountered the six Vestal Virgins in a nearby street. The holy women had been making their morning trip to the Fountain of Egeria near the Coelian Hill. There they drew water used in preparing their sacred cakes. For a condemned man to encounter the Vestals face to face was considered a terrible omen for the city. Such a man was always freed, regardless of his crime.

But I wasn't interested in the antics of criminals. My eye rushed on, locating at last the album devoted to reports of the games. My name was near the top.

Cassius, a bestiarius new to the arena, displayed much promise by slaying three boars during the opening hunt. He killed two with a pair of spears simultaneously. Vale, Cassius!

The other accounts were meaningless. I read mine again and still again. Surely I had taken the first great step upward.

Two of my guards urged me back into the litter. I went at once. Gone were thoughts of Acte. Gone were any doubts about turning into some kind of male whore for the woman with whom I was to dine.

Why should I be the one to question the accepted customs of Rome? What did I care for Locusta's dark reputation? She might very well enhance my career, and provide me some pleasure in the bargain. In this confident state I arrived at the grim and forbidding gate of the Temple of the Earth Mother, Cybele. Within, cymbals clashed and pipes skirled.

"Locusta's house is just behind yon temple," the chief of the guards informed me. He leered good-naturedly. "Our delay in the Forum cost us dear. They're celebrating their rites. No doubt we'll have to camp out here a while."

He scratched his chin, studying the high wall. Its clay was washed an evil scarlet by the sundown. Weird orgiastic yells echoed from inside.

The guard went on, "Although I hear the punishment is losing an arm or leg if you're caught, I'd like to enter that place. Without an invitation like yours, I mean. I hear also the customs of the cult would stand even the hair of our pleasure-loving Emperor on end. Ah, well. No such luck for me. I'm on duty tonight. I suppose we'll have to wait until they summon— Who's that?"

He snatched his dagger from its scabbard. Unseen, a smaller portal in the great gate had opened. A creature glided forth into the shadows beneath the wall.

Creature is the only proper word. It was a man physically. But it was effeminate beyond belief. Smooth cheeks it had, and lips painted with cosmetics, and hair curled into perfumed ringlets. The creature wore a black gown ornamented with cabalistic symbols. I gathered this was one of the cult's Galli, or priests. I knew little of the religion, except that moral people maintained the worship of the Eastern goddess was merely a pretext for the basest of sexual spectacles. Many exalted Senators, equites and their wives, however, participated. Who was I to scruple?

"This is the man Cassius?" the priest inquired in a reedy eunuch's voice. He carried a sistrum, a peculiar bronze rattle which gave off a bizarre clanging sound when he pointed it at my chest. The guard said gruffly that I was indeed Cassius. The priest went on. "The lady Locusta invites him within. You gentlemen remain here. Food and wine will be brought out."

He minced back toward the gate. Inside, the frenzy of yells and sharp cries had increased. The burly guard looked at me balefully.

"On second thought, Cassius, I'm not positive I'd care to go in there at all. Sounds like all the black imps of the world let loose. Shout if you need help."

I did not tell him my own spine was crawling. The priest held open the small portal and I walked in.

CHAPTER VII

O F ALL THE strange foreign cults that enjoyed favor in Rome, that of the Great Mother of Pessinus was by far the oldest. It dated to ancient times, when her temple was first raised in faraway Galatia. In the days when Hannibal of Carthage marched against Rome, the populace, impatient with defeats and eager to enlist the help of any and every deity available, brought from the East a great image of Cybele and erected it in the Temple. While other religions died, this one prospered, though all said its mysteries and rituals contained little of a spiritual nature. In fact, just the opposite. No doubt that accounted for its popularity.

Still, the cult was a part of that wave of popular passion for blood and lewdness which I intended to ride to prosperity. Thus I hardened my heart while the eunuch priest with the jingle rattle led me down a maze of passages into the heart of the building.

Cautioning me to speak no word and remain behind the stone gallery to which he led me, the priest glided away. He emerged moments later on the Temple floor below. It was a great gloomy hall. No outside light leaked in. What illumination there was came from dim lanterns set into niches. At one end rose an immense image of the Earth Mother, taller than three floors of an insula.

Her stone eyes gazed down past gigantic carven breasts to the spectacle taking place before her. The carcasses of several lambs lay on a low altar. To one side, some Galli played flutes and timbrels while others leaped into the air, forming a ring of dancers. They banged together sistra and brass-handled flails. Nearest the stone goddess danced a dozen or more women. They were young and old, bedaubed with blood, hair unkempt and eyes vacantly rolling. Everyone was naked.

They performed a sort of leaping, twisting ritual supplication of the goddess. Their movements perverted every posture and attitude of human love. The pipes skirled. The timbrels thudded. In the flickering light of the lamps I saw that the dancer who leaped higher than the rest, thighs and breasts smeared with blood, hair flying like a copper banner, was Locusta.

The women were the Corybantes, the priestesses of the Earth Mother. Soon they were joined by the Galli. The priests tore off their symbolic robes, revealing their ghastly eunuch's bodies. They sought partners among the women for the completion of the indecent ritual.

Sour bile rose in my throat. The music reached an hysterical pitch. One of the Corybantes, a slim, black-haired girl, leaped onto the altar. She seized a dagger and with an ecstatic shriek plunged it between her own thighs.

Though I am not by nature a prudish man, that was the most I could bear. I rushed from the gallery into a damp, stone-walled corridor where I vomited up what was in my belly.

Coming to my senses, I realized the great Temple was quiet, empty except for the lamb corpses and the ruined body of the dead priestess. The stink of blood swam all around. Great Cybele stared down with unfeeling stone eyes on the welter of gore.

The same priest who'd fetched me to witness the ceremonies appeared on a stair. He beckoned. The reek of my sickness was powerful in the corridor. The eunuch never showed that he noticed. He led me from the Temple into a dark garden. He bade me wait and hurried away.

He returned with a basin and towel with which I washed. Then he conducted me to the entrance of a modest house.

Lamps glowed in the windows. The sight of lights restored my sense of balance. What I had witnessed seemed remote and unreal.

At the entrance to the house the priest departed. I entered the atrium alone. A Thracian girl, barefoot but demurely clad, emerged from the shadows to conduct me to the peristyle. Other lamps on taborets gleamed there. Golden fish swam lazily in a lily pool. On a couch Locusta reclined, fully dressed and composed. Had I not known what she'd recently been doing, she would have seemed an ordinary Roman matron, only lovelier.

She rose and glided to meet me on slippered feet. I noticed with a start that the pupils of the Thracian girl were a blind milky white. Shadows gathering in the peristyle's corners became sinister.

"My lady," I said stiffly, "you do me honor by inviting me to your house."

"It's a modest place," she replied with a graceful bow. Her stole was pale ivory silk. Through it the mature curves of her thighs and round, peaked breasts shone gray. "But there is considerable wealth attached to the role of chief priestess of Cybele. I prefer to put that wealth to work in various trading investments, rather than waste it on ostentation. Come, sit."

I obeyed, feeling more a prize domestic animal than a man. Locusta's face, despite its faint patterning of age wrinkles, was smooth and pale. Her greenish eyes danced.

"Does it make you nervous, bestiarius, coming here for such an obvious purpose?"

"No, my lady. Nothing could bother me after what I saw in your Temple."

"Be sure you keep what you saw to yourself."

"I will. I don't think I could discuss it in public."

Daintily she plucked a moist, freshly shelled crab from a platter. She offered the dish to me. I shook my head, making a bad start at politeness.

"I take it you don't care for the Eastern mysteries, Cassius. I find that view curious. What's worse? Private indulgence of the lust for flesh, or public indulgence of the lust for killing in the arena?"

"In truth, my lady, I suppose one is no worse than the other. But when I enter the arena, I fight by my own rules. Those rules are as honorable as the combat allows."

Irritated, she threw aside the bit of crab and selected a ripe mushroom.

"My lady, my lady," she mimicked. "Is that all I'll hear from you tonight? My name is Locusta. I don't see why we must pretend with one another. That day I happened to drop in at the Beast School, I became convinced there was something about you that marked you as different from the rest of those oafs. Many of whom," she finished archly, "I have entertained in this same peristyle, by the way. Does my frankness offend you?"

Without her leave, I reached for a cup of wine and drank quickly. Later she told me the sweet stuff was Chalybonium, from Damascus, a favorite of the Emperor's. After a jolt of the wine washed the sourness from my mouth and warmed my belly, I answered her.

"No, my—Locusta. Your frankness doesn't offend. It allows me to be equally frank. I accepted your invitation in the hope that your favor might help me gain what I want."

"Oh, you're insolent on top of everything else!" she exclaimed, with a nasty display of white teeth. She walked to the pool's edge and stood gazing down, allowing me the chance to see her splendid body through the thin silk. She smoothed the material once, a quick motion of her hands down her belly, heightening the prominence of her breasts. "So you came here not for an evening's entertainment or a meal, but for something more?"

"Much more. I aim to be free one day. To found my own Beast School and be appointed to the rank of eques."

"The rank of eques! Not really! Do you honestly expect you can climb that high?"

"Others have, with the sufficient influence behind them."

"Ah!" Her jade eyes narrowed. "That's the reason you're here."

"Partly," I agreed. "Also partly because you are a very attractive woman."

"Is that truth, Cassius?" She started toward me. "Or empty flattery?"

"A little of both."

I was sincere. Except for the rather twisted light that flashed in those green eyes now and again, revealing another woman hidden beneath the fashionable exterior, I could enjoy her for what she was—cool, perfumed and lovely.

"How can you possibly hope to become an eques? You're a slave at the school, are you not?"

"No. I was born a freedman. I bound myself over."

I proceeded to tell her a bit of my history. During the time, she sat beside me on the bench, a good five hands' breadths away, but sufficiently close for me to catch the scent of her skin and the subtle warmth of her body. Another jot of wine and I talked more freely still.

The blind Thracian girl slipped in and deposited a platter of steamed fowl. The fare went untasted as I talked on, growing less gruff with every drink. Through the veil of wine the telltale signs of Locusta's age softened. All at once I realized I was gazing at her, but seeing Acte.

Painfully I forced the girl from my mind. But her image returned over and over, strangely sorrowful. I finished my account with difficulty.

"A grim life," Locusta murmured. "But listening to you describe your ambition, I can almost believe you'll realize it someday. You're strong. You have an imposing face. No, don't bother to reply. I am not in a position that requires me to flatter a man like you."

"Of that I'm sure. It's said you have the Emperor's favor."

Once again green devils danced in her eyes. "Yes. I felt we'd get round to that."

"The tales of poison are common gossip in the streets, Locusta. How can you escape them?"

"Why, I don't try," she said merrily. "You, though, Cassius. What do you think of such tales?"

"Whether they're true? I never concerned myself over them before. Should I?"

She touched my face. "That depends on how long our mutual interest lasts. As yet, I've had no indication except from watching you fight. Seeing your body work smoothly and well. How can I be sure either of us will want to see the other again after tonight? Perhaps I won't even know after tonight is over," she finished. Her meaning was unmistakable.

I threw back her stare. "I think you'll know."

She clapped her hands in delight. "Good! I warn you, though, Cassius. I meet many men. Some are fools. Some aren't worthy of the name. The carrion normally found in the arena are good examples of the former. The filthy creatures who guard the Temple are good examples of the second. If it turns out you're either of those types, I might as well send you back to Fabius."

I caught my breath at the way her round breasts strained. "I'm not the second. I'm sure I can prove that to your satisfaction."

"Time enough for that. We were discussing poison."

"What sort of poison? The kind that killed Claudius and his son Brittanicus, Nero's rival?"

"Those kinds will do. Well?"

"I have no opinion on the rumors, Locusta. That's because they are rumors, nothing more."

"What if I confirmed the rumors? Told you that I, a single woman, really do enjoy a considerable amount of favor with that petulant boy who rules us? Would you wonder how on earth I came into such lucky circumstances?"

"Naturally."

"So if I admit I enjoy favors from Nero, do I strengthen your opinion about the rumors?"

Annoyed at her teasing, I shook my head. "Opinions don't matter. If, however, you told me everything yourself—"

"That," she broke in quickly, "a lady of discretion would never do."

There was a kind of hellish joy glittering in her eyes now, a depraved pleasure that ought to have warned me off. For she was admitting with her glance that she had worked with Agrippina and her son Nero, perhaps secured poisons with the aid of agents of her cult in the East. She was admitting she had killed men, and showing amusement over it.

Would she kill again? I wondered with a chill. I supposed she would, if it served a purpose. But I reminded myself that she was comfortably settled, and all she wanted, it seemed, was a lover who suited her. I would be content in that role.

Locusta indicated the impressive array of dishes set out.

"Don't you care for dinner?"

"I was fed at the school." I smiled slowly. "And the stars up there above the roof are moving all the time. Why should I waste one night of freedom on gluttony?"

Suddenly she moved against me. Her firm nakedness burned through the silken gown and the thin cloth of my tunic. Her jade eyes lifted, fired with the same lust that must have smoldered in them when she danced before the Earth Mother. She placed her arms around my neck, teasing my lips with a quick kiss.

"Cassius, there are different sorts of gluttony."

"Yes, Locusta." I gazed down at her thrusting breasts. "Yes, there are."

Again she gave me her moist, painted mouth. But briefly, saying, "Another good sign. You've no idea how long I've searched for a man who combines a little wit with a little strength. An ordinary peasant from the arena wouldn't begin to understand that simple-minded joke I just made. Are you sure you understand—?"

Tired of her teasing, I proved I did, pulling her tight, my arms around her back. She kissed me fiercely, using her open mouth like a weapon to bruise mine. There was a wildness in her caresses that excited me, turned me rough when she drew me to one of the Spartan sleeping rooms off the peristyle.

Dim lamps flickered through the hangings, touching her coppery hair with fire. Greenish eyes wide, she pulled my head down to kiss her full, pink-ended and shaking breasts.

Fiercely her fingers crawled along my back. She dragged me into an embrace that was not gentle but more like an attack, an angry, violent wrenching and straining.

Her back, her thighs moved and trembled with enjoyment as I bedded her there in the whispering dark of the Earth Mother's house. My senses reeled when she bit my lips and moaned, louder and louder, crying strange savage words in Greek until at last, with one piercing cry, she sank her teeth into my shoulder while our bodies shuddered away to quiet.

Little love or joy had gone into the union. I knew it as I lay in the dark with Locusta's hair spread on my shoulder and her mouth murmuring sleepily near my ear about my proficiency as a lover. I felt strangely spent and hollow, as though what we'd done was entirely without significance.

"Cassius, my dear? If I continue to find you appealing, there's almost no limit to the honors I can help you attain. For one, how would you like to be invited to perform not for the rabble but for the Emperor himself?"

"Of course I'd like that."

"Well, as you must know, Nero stages *ludi privati* quite often. To be selected as feature performer at such private games would be a higher step than you might manage for yourself in years of trying. I can—"

The scream came from the peristyle.

"No! You may not enter! My mistress says—"

"What your mistress says is of no damned importance, wench," a rough voice yelled.

"Knock the blind pig out of the way!" another, oddly familiar voice bawled.

Locusta leaped up. She flung her gown around her. There was cold rage on her face, turning her old suddenly. She stormed into the peristyle.

"That sickening voice has sounded in my ear once too often!"

I grabbed my tunic and stumbled after her. I blundered into the peristyle as the blind Thracian girl's screams dwindled to helpless sobs. Three good-sized slaves, all armed with short swords, waited on the far side of the pool. Another was just delivering a vicious kick to the belly of the fallen blind girl. Out in the Temple garden the Galli set up a frightened row in their squeaking voices. Then, from a clot of shadow behind the strange slaves, lurched the Sicilian horse-breeder.

His toga was wine-spotted, his eyes ugly. "I had to thrash a few of those simpering priests to get in here, Locusta," Tigellinus said. "But thrash them I did. I heard you were entertaining a lover tonight. You conniving, red-haired bitch!"

"Horse-breeder, you're drunk. Disgustingly drunk," Locusta exclaimed. But rather than flying at him in anger, she was abruptly calm. She hurried to his side. "Haven't I told you that when the time is right, I'll invite you here in style? Tonight is not the night. I realize I may have led you on a little at the games this afternoon—"

"Led me on!" Tigellinus snorted. "You were far more explicit than that. Yet the moment I try to make any arrangements, you shy away. You—never mind. I didn't come here to argue with you." He brushed her aside, stumbled toward the pool and upset a bench. "Where's your lover? Let's see the kind of man you prefer over me."

Tense and angry, I stepped from the shadow of a colonnade. "Here, Tigellinus."

The Sicilian's eyes focused with difficulty. He swiped a hand across his lips, blinking and muttering to himself. "What's this? A slave, from all appearances. Somehow I'm sure I've seen—Ye gods! The arrogant pup from the Bestiarius School! And he was in the arena today, wasn't he? By heaven, I thought I recognized—" Tigellinus stopped, chuckling. "Well. Well, well. My young friend, I remember how you cost me a lot of money on Horus the Egyptian. I'm sorry to say your career has just come to an inglorious end. No magistrate in Rome will punish me for killing you."

With a skewering motion of his finger he signaled for his quartet of slaves to do their work.

Like inhuman things they all began to walk forward at once. Their short swords shone. Before they had taken five steps, I moved.

I closed my hands on a bronze salver and sailed it through the air. The edge caught the first slave in the side of the head. He stumbled, cursing.

"Attack him!" Tigellinus shrieked. "Attack him, you dung, or I'll flay the hide off you!"

Cold in my belly, I grabbed the next handy object, a wine jar. I threw it square at the head of the second slave. He fended it with a clang of his sword. Locusta grasped Tigellinus' arm with one hand and slapped his cheek smartly with the other.

"That's enough, you ill-tempered fool! I won't tolerate hired assassins in my house! Meddle any further in my affairs, and you'll lose any chance you ever had of getting what you want!"

Over her shoulder the Sicilian glowered at me. The slaves waited. Tigellinus began, "Remember, woman, I have influence—"

"Care to test yours against mine?" Locusta countered.

"You're bluffing," Tigellinus snarled.

"Am I? Shall we go to the Palatine this moment? Waken the Emperor? Have him settle this dispute?"

Tigellinus chewed his lip and changed his tack. "Locusta, I won't stand for being humiliated by a common criminal from the arena!"

"You'll be more than humiliated," I shouted at him, my temper out of bounds. "You'll be killed, bug-eyes."

Locusta whirled on me. "Be quiet! Don't make matters worse."

Tigellinus laughed, or more properly, snorted. The sound broke the tension of the moment.

The slaves picked themselves up. One threw me a half-grin, as if to say it was nothing personal. Locusta treated Tigellinus to a slow, bedazzling smile, the same kind of smile that had gleamed up at me while we made love. Politely, but firmly she tugged the Sicilian's arm.

"Come with me, Tigellinus. Bring your man. This way, into the atrium."

"I don't see why you constantly put me off, Locusta. I am a man of position, wealth—"

"Let's discuss it where there are not so many ears to hear," she wheedled.

My anger quickened again. Her glance at me as she left indicated I was not worth bothering about. Firmly she directed Tigellinus out of the peristyle, coaxing, laughing low. The slaves followed.

Restlessly I paced beside the pool. I swigged more wine. After what seemed an interminable time, the voices in the atrium faded. An outer door slammed. Locusta appeared, looking pleased.

"Why the black glare, Cassius? I got rid of him, didn't I?"

"Do you always make arrangements with your next lover in front of your current one?"

She pressed against me. "Cassius, Cassius! What an idiot you are! Do you really think I could bear to have that overweight frog touch me? I didn't want his men to kill you on the spot. I gave him some vague promises about visiting me later, to persuade him to leave. But I think he means to settle with you," she added gloomily. "Be careful of him, Cassius. He's dangerous, in the way only stupid men can be."

"Why do you flatter such a wretch?" I demanded.

Her expression grew surprised, then cold. "Look here. He's one of the most important men in Rome today."

"According to whom? Himself?"

"No, you simpleton. The Emperor."

"You dared him to go before the Emperor, didn't you?"

"Wild bluff and he knew it. He chose to give in in the hope that I may one day—ah—do the same." Her maliciously triumphant smile faded out. "Frankly, I wouldn't care to match my power against his. I might win, but I might lose. I prefer to use other methods to get my way."

"Like promising yourself to him?"

In exasperation she sat down and pulled me to a place beside her. "One thing you'll have to learn, Cassius, beast-man. That is the location of power in the society you intend to invade. The power lies not with the Senators, for all their impassioned oratory about liberty for the mob. It lies with the army. More specifically, with the Praetorian Guard. Tigellinus' good and faithful friend Gaius Julius—"

"The tribune," I interrupted wearily. "Yes, I've encountered him too."

"So Tigellinus said. Julius commands the most powerful of all the Praetorian cohorts, the one quartered on the Palatine. In theory the Senate raises an Emperor to the throne. But the Palatine Praetorians really hold the key. They can remove an Emperor with the cut of a sword in the night. They can hold the Palatine Hill against all attackers if they wish, until they get a new Princeps who suits them. It's common knowledge that Nero chafes under the restraints placed on him by the current Praetorian Prefect, Burrus. Should the path be suddenly—let's say cleared—Tigellinus and his faction, including the tribune Julius, might become the most powerful men in Rome overnight."

"And that's why you'd take Tigellinus for a lover?"

"Of course. Pleasure with a man is one thing. Maintaining my position is another. Luckily I have one means to reach both ends. I wheedled Tigellinus out of his drunken rage simply because I believe in playing all possible sides against one another to best advantage."

She paused to let this sink in. Then she added, "Isn't that the way you operate, Cassius? Or did I misinterpret what you told me earlier? How you want to be an eques regardless of the price?"

For a moment I tried to search beyond the surfaces of those laughing, old-and-young green eyes. I hunted for the truth of this woman. Was she a witch? The cleverest of goddesses? Or an unholy combination of both? The answer eluded me.

But not the realization that she was infinitely dangerous and devious. The rewards of her favor could be great, and I must never forget that. I would never care to have her as my enemy, though. At length I said, "You heard rightly, Locusta. I'd prefer to kill the Sicilian because he had me scourged. But I suppose I can tolerate him if it serves a purpose."

She stroked my cheek, whispering, "It will, it will. The purpose of keeping you alive, and close to me."

I drew back. "Tell me, Locusta. What advantage do I really represent to you?"

She brought up her mouth for a long, lingering kiss. The moist warmth of her lips lighted fires in my body again.

"The advantage of having a man of strength and wit give me pleasure. A man whose body is strong but whose ambition is even stronger. Pour wine for me, Cassius. I want to drink to our alliance."

Somewhere far off, perhaps in a mean upper room, I heard the abused Thracian girl sobbing in blind pain. Locusta had not seen to her injuries, so far as I knew. But that was not my affair, I reminded myself. I splashed wine into cups and handed her one.

"May the nameless gods preserve me, Locusta, but I'm caught."

Changeable as weather, she lifted the silken gown above her waist and gave a lewd laugh.

"And the prisoner's fairer than any you've ever known. True, Beast-man?"

Fairer than all but one, I thought. I said nothing, fumbling to embrace her.

This time I abandoned myself wholly to the arts she knew so well. The night wagons rumbled on through Rome, and the stars turned around the earth, watching in some mystic way the destinies of us all. Through the night we were drunk on the taste of each other's flesh as much as on wine.

Shortly before dawn she sent me away with a last drowsy, sated kiss. I ached in every joint. Outside the forbidding wall of the Temple the dozing guards shivered and snored in the chill. I jostled them awake.

The guard in command passed off one or two rough jokes about my night. I did not answer him. Somehow, what had transpired in Locusta's house did not seem decent enough to talk about in daylight.

Fourteen of the inmates of the school returned to the Circus Maximus on the afternoon of the fourth day of the games.

Xenophon was not in the company. He lost the privilege because of his poor performance in the first hunt. Naturally this did nothing to lessen his hatred of me.

Today we would go against the man-eaters. We arrived in our tunnel, removed our tunics and amulets and pulled on our codpieces. We took swords from the handlers while a loud ovation shook the stands. Returning from the sunlit tunnel mouth, one of the handlers commented, "The Greens took the chariot race. They're releasing the pigeons with leg ribbons to inform the gamblers on the coast. Guess who was the featured Green driver."

He tapped his knuckle against a charcoal-scrawled board spiked to the wall. The board listed the program for the day. Representing the Green racing corporation was one L. Domitius Ahenobarbus.

That accounted for the extra cheers the winner received. The program also reported that the Green team was composed of prize Arabians bred and trained by O. Tigellinus. In truth, what chance did I stand with an enemy like the Sicilian who pandered to the Emperor's whims and provided him with victorious teams?

The cheering gradually ebbed away. The between-acts performance commenced. According to the program, a simulated boulder was to be wheeled into the arena. To the fake rock a criminal was chained, representing Prometheus. Down the tunnel drifted yells of the rakers and perfume-sprinklers who were freshening the sand to mask the stench of blood left over from the morning's gladiatorial contest, fifty hoplites versus fifty secutores. Suddenly the chaffering of the arena workers was broken by a shrill, unearthly scream of agony.

Syrax, adjusting his codpiece, smiled. "The trained eagles must be making fast work of that criminal's body. Excellent. It'll put the crowd in a bloodthirsty mood. Ready to condemn us if we make a mistake, but ready to reward us if we're victorious."

Laughter from thousands of throats obscured the criminal's cries. I was thankful I did not have to watch the birds claw and break away his entrails. Fabius hurried back from the tunnel mouth. His face was slicked with perspiration.

"The stakes are high today, lads. Nothing less than your lives. I've just seen the animals. Prime killers. Fight well. If not for me, then for yourselves."

There was sadness, almost a regret in his little farewell address, as though he wanted to protest the carefully staged slaughter, and missed the old days when a bestiarius could win the wooden sword with a single skillful toss of a rope loop around the legs of a running ostrich. Killing was what they demanded now, those screaming multitudes who howled their blood lust as the trumpets blared the call to the next event. Even Syrax's sword hand shook a little as he filed out ahead of me into the blazing sunlight.

Perfumed fountains sprayed rainbows into the air along the Spine. Though the sand had been carefully raked, dark stains were still visible beneath the sparkling surface. Sunlight scalded my bare back. My chest ran with salty sweat.

We made our way to the Imperial box and saluted. Young Nero, his lips working wetly at a peach, dismissed us with hardly a glance. We fanned out in a long line as a timber barrier was rolled away from the mouth of another tunnel. Slaves scurried out of the way. Pitchy smoke curled from the black opening.

All at once the lions and leopards burst forth, growling and snapping. Other slaves pursued them down the tunnel, hurling bundles of burning faggots to make them run.

The big males and lionesses scattered, scenting the human flesh to which they'd become accustomed in training. A lioness and a leopard closed on the nearest bestiarius, a slim, shy auctorati. He made a misstep and died almost at once. The lioness' fangs bit through his breastbone.

Dust clouded up. On my left Syrax took a couple of cuts at a racing leopard. He chopped off its left forepaw with a lucky stroke. Meantime, I had my eye on a bushy-maned brute who slowed his run when he saw me.

He stood wrinkling his damp nose, breathing soft through his fangs. Screams rose, followed by the crunch and bump of some man and animal tumbling over and over. The sandy dust grew even thicker.

I watched my lion's throat for the ripple of the growl that would precede the leap. I controlled my shaking sword hand and let my fear work for me by tightening every nerve. Behind me, I heard Syrax cursing as he feinted at his snapping leopard.

The lion unleashed his yellow might, clearing the ground with all four paws to smash me down and kill.

I hacked and ran to the right simultaneously. My sword hewed a bloody channel down the lion's flank as he bolted past. He trumpeted in anger because I was not where I had been a moment before.

He swung his maned head, searching. He saw me and leaped for my legs, eyes hell-yellow with hate. The mob cheered senselessly.

I braced my right leg behind me, intending to stand fast and strike down for his throat. The leg bumped something. Syrax cried out behind me, "Cassius, you fool, don't knock me over when this bitch leopard is—"

His warning turned to a roar of anger. His back collided with mine. The impact bowled me forward so that the point of my sword burrowed into the sand as the lion hurled through the air. I pulled the sword loose just as the lion was on me, knocking me flat.

The snapping jaws grazed my arm. The beast writhed on top of me. I had a distorted view of Syrax prone on his back, one hand at his leopard's throat while the other rammed the sword in and out through its ribs. My lion kicked, its claws opening bad wounds on my thighs and chest.

In a space of a breath I swung my sword arm over, blade foremost. I struck the lion's neck from above. The slash, not anywhere fatal, made it leap again, claws digging long channels in my leg. But I managed to roll from under and totter up.

The lion turned and came racing at me again, gore streaking its mane and gushing from the deep cut in its neck. Maddened with the hurt, it bunched on its haunches, a yellow streak that lifted from the ground. For an instant its underbelly was exposed.

I dropped the sword and wrenched my palm around hard edge foremost. The hand whipped over to my left armpit, then flew outward in the killing trick, aimed for the lion's vitals.

With all the force I could muster I smashed my hand between the legs of the beast as he loomed over me, cracking flesh and genitals. The lion seemed to roll over in mid-air. He dropped with a loud thud on the sand.

Back to back with me, Syrax grunted ferociously as he finished the leopard. I heard a lioness growl somewhere in the blowing dust. I paid no heed, snatching up my sword. Blood rivered from claw marks all over me.

I leaped in as the crippled lion floundered. I opened his throat with one stroke.

Moving off again, I wasn't fast enough to avoid the spasmodic lashing of his left foreclaw. The talons snagged in my calf and brought a shriek of pain to my mouth. A great gob of calf muscle remained impaled on the lion's claw as he gave a rough sob and died, his bowels spilling on the sand.

Weakness and nausea overwhelmed me. Slowly, as if in a nightmare, I felt my clawed leg buckle. A thunderous ovation rang from the stands. The faces of spectators were like phantoms behind the roiling dust. I got the breath knocked out of me when I sprawled on the sand.

Dully I blinked into the hazy blue sky. Some vague voice was trying to draw my attention.

"Cassius, the maneless bitch is—Cassius, jump up! *Jump up before she*—"

The lioness hit from behind, leaping over my head and landing full on me. Her head dropped to chew away my hips and crotch. Her weight, her animal stink, brought a whirling sense of death close by. Then, abruptly, her yellow body went rigid.

I summoned the last strength in my arms and heaved upward. Her carcass rolled off, stabbed through from right to left by a sword that burned white in the sunlight. The blade was warm red where the tip had protruded.

Staggering, his body a spiderweb of cuts and clawings, his codpiece hanging by a thread, Syrax jerked and pulled until his sword came free of the dead lioness.

"Never let it be said that your partner failed you, Cassius," he panted.

Choking, I could not reply. After a moment I was able to stand on my own feet. I retrieved my sword and hacked off the forepaw of the killer I'd slain with the hand trick. While I sawed through the bone I became aware of a peculiar tickling on my back.

Bright petals drifted down in the sand before me. I rose with the dripping paw. At last the chant in the stands made sense.

"Cassius! Cassius! Cassius! Cassius!"

I turned, feebly acknowledging the cheers with a nod of my head. Syrax peered toward the boxes. He threw me a disgruntled smile. With a savage motion he chopped off the leopard's paw, then the lioness'.

"You've won favor with that showy hand stunt, it seems, while all I did was save your life." He forced a grin. "Well, I'll just make the best of it. To the box, eh?"

He spun on his heel and trotted off. I hurried after him. Four other bestiarii converged from various parts of the arena.

Syrax was the only one with two kills, but because of the way I'd slain the lion, mine was the name the crowd chanted as I stumbled along in the dust.

I counted human bodies. Fragments of thoughts swirled through my mind. Six alive, eight dead, to provide the mob with gossip and diversion.

"Cassius! Cassius! Cassius!"

A Senator and his mistress fondled one another wildly, gripped by the mass hysteria that frequently transformed arena crowds into mindless exhibitionists.

"Cassius! Cassius! Cassius!"

One rank of legionnaires marched down either side of the Spine, shields locked, spears thrust ahead to form a pointed wall that drove back the lions and leopards still living. Behind the soldiers, handlers with flails waited to catch any beasts breaking through.

The soldiers parted to let me pass. One called, "Brave performance, Cassius! Make the Emperor pay for it!"

I walked on, following Syrax, drowning in the cheers that roared off the walls. Others on the far side of the Spine who could not possibly have seen me fight took up the chant.

"Cassius! Cassius! Cassius!"

A girl bared her breasts and held them out to me. Suddenly, in spite of the redness dripping like a slime from my wounds, I felt drunk. Wildly drunk on the wine of fame, and the breathless release of having lived through such an ordeal. True, Syrax had saved me from the lioness. But I had killed one lion with my bare hand. Why shouldn't I claim the fruits of winning?

I lifted my head, smiling and bowing blearily as I neared the Imperial box. Far up in the stands someone cried, "The wooden sword! Let's have the wooden sword for valiant Cassius!"

More voices picked up the cry. Miracle of miracles—the wave of victory was cresting a second time.

The Emperor was on his feet. He bowed formally to the six of us clustered below his box. His cherry-colored cheeks puckered into an insincere smile as he reached for the garlands.

A petulant frown erased his smile. He heard the mob's roar. "The wooden sword! *The wooden sword for Cassius!*"

So thick were the showering flower petals, I barely saw the Emperor hesitate, then turn to a slave. The dull pine gleam of a carved toy suddenly appeared in his hands.

Before he could throw it down, fingers closed on my arm. Standing close, Syrax stared at me, white teeth broken into a grin but his eyes cold, demanding.

"Ask the sword for me, Cassius. You owe me your life. *"Ask!"*

The risk seemed small, drunk with pain and shock as I was. I flung up my right arm.

The crowd in the vicinity of the Imperial box quieted. The Emperor nodded his chubby head, giving me leave to speak.

"A boon, Emperor! For my companion Syrax who saved my life that I might claim victory from your exalted hand. The wooden sword for Syrax too!"

The cry was picked up by nearby spectators, then passed along the tiers.

"The sword for Syrax the brave!"

"He saved Cassius!"

"Two wooden swords!"

"Two wooden swords!"

My partner basked in the recognition, bowing and posturing. All at once Nero peered at me quizzically. Was he remembering the night at Sulla's?

Then his round eyes misted over with unconcern. He shrugged and flung down two wooden swords and turned to accept the shrieking adulation of the mob.

Nero's sycophants tossed garlands to the other four bestiarii. They had no thought for them, clapping us on the back.

"Good, Cassius!"

"Lucky devils!"

"Clever Syrax!"

"Freedom! Freedom for you both!"

Greedily Syrax snatched up one wooden sword. He threw back his head and laughed wildly.

Down the line of boxes I glimpsed Tigellinus and the Praetorian Julius. They were silent and scowling. But beyond them shimmered a froth of reddish hair beneath a parasol. I dipped the wooden sword in a gesture of acknowledgment. Through the storm of flower petals, gambling tokens, fruit peels and other objects being rained down in praise upon us, I thought I saw Locusta nod and smile in return.

The crowd thundered our name until the heavens shook. Strangely, there were tears in my eyes as I closed my fingers around the rough-hewn wood. A splinter slid into the flesh of my palm, a tiny pain, the sweetest pain on earth.

There in the sunlight and the thunder of voices, I was free of the school forever. Moving upward, steadily upward, to the fame and wealth I'd nearly died to earn.

CHAPTER VIII

O ur companions from the Bestiarius School thronged around us in the tunnel.

They slapped dressings on the worst of our wounds, and bound them with linen. Then they hoisted us to their shoulders, draped flower wreaths about our necks, thrust pots of wine into our hands and carried us along the dim stone passage leading to the outer arches. Even old Fabius was beside himself with joy. Although he was losing two pupils, his reputation could not help but be enhanced as a result of our victory.

Syrax and I shouted jokes at one another. We grew drunker by the minute from the wine we gulped. Outside the tunnel entrance a crowd of several hundred had collected. They broke into cheers as we were borne forth.

I cracked my head on the tunnel ceiling and tumbled to the ground, laughing despite the soreness of my wounds.

"Watch my precious skull, you oxen!" I bawled. "I want to live to enjoy my new freedom. I want—"

Words stuck in my throat. From among many sweated, screeching faces, one leaped into prominence, unsmiling, streaked with tears. Acte's.

She thrust around a quarrelsome orange vendor who thought Syrax or I might be in a mood to scatter some coppers his way. Above the caterwauling of hawkers and the plaudits shouted by a cluster of small boys, she called, "Cassius? Please let me speak to you a moment."

"Our plans?" Syrax was shouting to the mob. "Confidential for the moment. But you'll all be suitably impressed when—"

"Let me through!" I said, pushing. "Let me pass."

A great roar shook the arches as the next event commenced inside the Circus. The sound faded from my mind. So did the pushings and jostlings of our admirers. All I saw was Acte.

She was lovely as ever, high-piled dark hair lustrous in the shadows. She was forced to speak loudly because of the racket, "I owe you an explanation for the night at Sulla's."

"No. None's due, not any more."

I was shoved against her gowned breasts by the heave of the mob. I drew back, remembering how I'd been wounded that night, with a wound far more lasting than any bothering me now. The wine and the wooden sword gave me the cruel desire to injure her the same way.

"I understand perfectly that you had to play up to the Emperor and his rich friends. What happened to us at the school happened because of my boredom and your wish to amuse yourself at my expense."

Tears glimmered at the corners of her dark eyes. "They've hardened you already, haven't they? Made you greedy."

"Gods above! You have the gall to speak of greed!"

She reached out to touch me. "Cassius, I love you. Please hear me out. Many times I've tried to—"

A wiry little Libyan girl, no more than fifteen, thrust herself between us. She was bare to the waist. She began fondling my chest while her painted mouth repeated a catalog of the delights available to any man who'd won the wooden sword. For a price, naturally. Acte looked stunned when I laughed and slipped my arm around the little whore's waist.

"What difference is there between you and this charming creature, Acte? None, so far as I can tell. Oh, you're very adept at pretending otherwise. But your game's too transparent. Now that the Emperor has granted me freedom, I've become a man with a future in your eyes. A man who might be of value to you financially. I'm sorry to say my future doesn't include you. Don't you have enough clients already? I hardly see that you need one more."

"—only a few sesterces," the Libyan girl was cooing. "For a handsome man like the famous Cassius, a few sesterces would buy any and every act he wished to—"

"Enough talk, dove," I said. I turned my back on Acte, fondling the Libyan girl's bare breasts. "Let's see whether the performance is as good as the promise."

I shoved my way back to Syrax and the others. We went reeling off toward an inn a few blocks from the Circus. There we drank the night away with Fabius standing the entire cost and weeping drunken maudlin tears.

Acte was no more than a healed scar now. A memory of a lovely but false face, of untrue words, of one night's deception.

The Libyan girl stuck to my side all night long. Before taking leave of the crowd at the inn to go above stairs with her, I chanced to look closely at the lanista. Fabius appeared winesotted and happy.

What would his reaction be when he discovered Syrax and I intended to out-rival him with another beast school?

Promptly I put this selfless consideration aside. Had I perished in the arena today, his remorse would have been professionally brief. So was mine.

I praised and thanked him. I followed the Libyan girl to some dim chamber where we spent the rest of the night, Acte forgotten.

And Fabius and his coming failure, too.

In the months that followed, many changes were wrought in my life. All, so it seemed, for the better.

Shortly after the end of the Imperial games, Syrax and I left the Bestiarius School and took up quarters at a small hostelry, paying our way with the modest purses presented by the Emperor's treasurers to every winner of a wooden sword. I presented myself at the home of Serenus soon after. He had not forgotten his obligation.

We went together to Seneca, and he accompanied us to the great banking house of the Probi in the Via Sacra. Sextus Probus, the head of the firm, was a wealthy and wily old eques. After considering the guarantees offered by Serenus and the introduction provided by Seneca, not to mention my widespread reputation, he agreed to loan initial funds for the construction of a beast school upon property to be selected.

For help with that selection I turned to Locusta, whom I saw almost nightly. The occult of the Earth Mother had vast interlocking holdings in Roman real estate. Behind their smooth, sexless facades, the eunuch priests were skilled in the ways of the marketplace. In a month Syrax and I had chosen an abandoned tallow works on the Vicus Tuscus, a street in the industrial quarter leading down to the Tiber.

The tallow works was long since bankrupt. But it had a sound wharf on the river that would be convenient for unloading animal barges arriving from Africa via the port of Ostia. When banker Probus examined the property he readily approved the choice and advanced funds for the project.

Within weeks work gangs were smashing down old walls, erecting an amphitheater for training, a barracks, office quarters and a large stonework structure that would eventually be our menagerie. Meantime, the *Acta Diurna* carried daily announcements that the Cassian School would shortly be accepting candidates.

We contracted for our first shipload of leopards and antelope from Serenus' friend, the decurion at Iol Caesaria. Magistrates, learning we were in business, were only to happy to have one additional place to sentence some of the hundreds of criminals who daily passed through their courts. And while criminals made surly students for the most part, they soon felt the sting of my whip as I began turning them into bestiarii who could at least make a respectable showing at outlying circuses.

Perhaps I was a harsh, even a brutal trainer. Yet in the year following the opening of the Cassian School we lost not a single man. Almost weekly one or two stout country lads would appear to swell our barracks by binding themselves over. Our reputation was growing, and well.

I devoted myself almost exclusively to the training amphitheater. Syrax managed the bookwork. He had the head for it. He also traveled widely outside Rome, arranging to supply half a dozen men to this circus or that. Even under the Emperor's new edict forbidding provincial governors from giving circuses or spectacles to win the good will of their subjects—a rule which did not apply to the Emperor, naturally—country nobles standing for election were not restricted from doing this. As a result we prospered. Slowly, but satisfyingly.

Serenus had come in as third partner in the enterprise, albeit a silent one. Being a man well respected in the very best classes, he preferred to keep his name from public association with the school. His participation was known only to Syrax, myself, and certain officials at the House of Probi who had access to the private records of our loans and agreements.

Originally Syrax balked at taking a third partner and thus splintering potential profit. I argued that Serenus' contact in Africa would save us time and cash. As it subsequently did. And Serenus seldom, if ever, visited the school. He was content to collect his profits unseen. My partner therefore appeared content with the arrangement after a while.

Indeed, he seemed content with most everything, being full of laughter and my good friend in all things.

Gradually the Cassian School's reputation began to seriously rival that of the one managed by Fabius. More and more nobles visited us, arranging for larger and larger groups of bestiarii. I was satisfied with our progress, and my life generally. I had moved into a splendid, if small, house near the Garden of Sallust. I wore fine clothes. And I had remained Locusta's lover. Except for occasional haunted dreams, I never thought of Acte at all.

Syrax was the impatient member of our firm. One after-noon be brought up the subject of the future as we sat idling in the caldaria of a public bath in the Field of Mars.

An old Senator dozed on a stone bench nearby. Otherwise we were alone in the chamber, looking at one another through clouds of steam billowing from the hot water in the large por-phyry pool. Lusty shouts rang out as men indulged in a game of toss-the-ball in the more bracing frigidarium adjoining.

"Really, Cassius," Syrax addressed me. "We must put our minds to attracting a better class of patrons."

"I'm satisfied with the ones we have at the moment, thanks. We're doing nicely."

"I won't argue that."

He proceeded to do so, however. The old, conniving gleam returned to his dark eyes. He made a peculiar picture in the blowing steam. His olive face seemed to float, disembodied, while his gold ear hoop gave off a dull glitter.

"Cassius, you know as well as I that most of the really fat commissions are still going to Fabius. Especially when the hiring's done by the Emperor's toadies."

I shrugged. "Chalk that off to the unseen hands of Tigellinus and Julius. The Emperor will come around one day. Why rush matters?"

"Because one copper in my hand begets the desire for ten. You feel the same, or you're not the partner I thought origi-nally." Always the sly taunt, smilingly delivered. He rushed on, "For example, why don't we put our heads to the task of turning up some genuine unicorns?"

"Not that again!"

"Think of the sensation it would cause. Unicorns offered exclusively by the Cassian School!"

"All very nice," I replied. "Except for the fact that unicorns don't exist."

"How do we know? We've never been to Africa."

"True. But I wrote the decurion in Iol Caesaria on the sub-ject, remember? At your request. He said the best he could offer was a rhino or two, at prohibitive cost."

That sobered him only a moment. Shortly he was off again. "Then what about the idea I had a while back? Training some sort of animal to have its way with a woman? No one in Rome seems to know how to do it, but I'm sure if the two of us put our minds to it we could—What's wrong?"

He blinked ingenuously, as if he'd only remarked that the temperature of the steam was rather high. I said harshly, "I have given you my opinion on that matter before, Syrax. A man with a sword, going against a lion, is an honorable thing. What you suggest is not. It's base."

He snorted. "Who cares where the profit comes from? So long as it comes!"

"I care, for one." I stood up. "I believe I'll get dressed. I've had enough of this conversation."

For a moment anger smoldered in his black gaze. Then, as always, he glossed over the quarrel with a quick smile.

"Obviously you aren't alert to the temper of the times, Cassius. I heard just the other day that Nero was definitely interested in seeing that kind of exhibition."

"I don't doubt it for a minute."

"In fact, word runs that he and Fabius had a hot argument because Fabius refused to even think about the possibilities of putting on such an act. Not even for Nero's private parties. Stupid, eh?"

"No. Fabius and I are of like mind there. The thought's sickening. Forget it."

"Very well." Syrax sighed, then studied me shrewdly. "We will forget it where it concerns the Cassian School. What I do with my free hours is my own affair, however. Right now I think I'll swim."

So saying, he plunged with a savage dive into the smoking-hot pool. He lashed about with violent strokes to work off his concealed rage. I quickly went to dress, my belly uneasy at the very thought of his scheme. I trusted he'd spoken rashly, and would eventually abandon the disgusting idea. Insistence upon it would surely provoke serious trouble between us.

Luckily he soon seemed his old self. No more was said about the idea. Doubtless he saw that we did not need to lower ourselves to providing audiences with sexual spectacles in order to reap profits. Our fortunes increased modestly day by day. Our contingents to the circuses grew larger. We felt confident that upon the occasion of the next Imperial games, the Cassian School would be well represented.

Public gossip held that the Emperor would be staging those games in the near future. The political climate made it necessary.

In the year since we'd won our freedom, things had gone from bad to worse on the Palatine. The Princeps became more and more reckless. His public face was righteous enough. Coins were struck bearing the mottoes propounded by Seneca. *Clementia. Concordia.* Clemency and good will, the foundations of stable government. Imperial officials regularly prophesied new and greater eras of happiness and prosperity just ahead for all.

Behind the scenes, however, the Emperor was working to assert himself and override the power of the Senate. When he appropriated large sums to build new retirement colonies for old legionnaires at Antium, Pompeii and Tarentum, the Senators balked. They objected that Nero was merely playing up to the Praetorians to enhance his personal power. To which the Emperor reportedly countered, in a shrill scream, that his power must be preserved because every bit of the liberty and prosperity of Rome was a direct result of his sovereignty, but definitely not an inherent right of the citizens. The Senate gave in.

Rumors circulated that Seneca, Serenus and the Praetorian Prefect Burrus were having poor luck counteracting the fanatic personal cult the Emperor was building. As an Imperial adviser, his mother Agrippina's status had been reduced to nil. She was seldom seen outside her fine house. She took the side of Octavia, Nero's colorless wife, in the debate over whether blonde Poppaea Sabina would one day be his Empress.

Mercifully, I was far removed from all this haggling and intrigue. I heard it only second- and third-hand from nobles visiting the school on business. I was satisfied to enjoy my growing status, my modest house, my three slaves, and Locusta.

But one night the politics of the Palatine intruded into my life.

A warm, muggy summer's dusk had fallen over Rome. I had invited Serenus and Syrax to dine. We had completed our meal, and the hot and cold wine had been passed around. My friends were relaxing on their couches. After taking a drink, Serenus asked me, "Cassius, what's become of that girl? The one from Sulla's? I've bean meaning to ask you for some time."

"Acte?" The name still made queer music on my tongue. "Why don't you ask one of the Emperor's intimates instead?"

He waved. "Oh, Nero got over his infatuation for her soon enough."

"Well, I really couldn't tell you what's become of her, Serenus."

The gold hoop in Syrax's ear bobbled furiously. He had choked on the wine. I looked at him, curious. He returned the glance with a bright, innocent smile and immediately began drinking again. He seemed to squirm on the couch, even though he sat stock still. I was puzzling over this peculiar behavior when Serenus interrupted my thoughts to remark wryly, "I realize you're a very busy man, Cassius, what with your great devotion to the teachings of the cult of Cybele. Still, I wondered whether you'd ever seen Acte again."

"Not once. I was finished with her long ago. The last time we met was the day Syrax and I won the swords. She was a greedy little beast. I thought I was in love with her. I found out I'd made a bad mistake." I waved my goblet at him. "A man can't have both a soft heart and a fat purse, you know."

He shook his grizzled head. "Too bad you lost track of her."

"Listen to him!" Syrax said, very nearly sneering. "He talks like a lovesick swain!"

Serenus scowled. They never got along well. He said, "I fail to see the humor in my question, Syrax. I merely inquired about her. I thought her quite a charming girl. Besides, my foxy friend, I'm not so old that I couldn't make some young maiden a good husband, in return for a little companionship. A stone sleeping couch grows damned cold at night."

"Better to have an empty couch than one occupied by a cheat like Acte," I told him.

He shrugged and subsided into sentimental silence. There was a loud knocking at the street gate. One of my servants rushed in to summon me. Moments later I entered the atrium to find Locusta waiting.

"Wonderful news, Cassius! I came at once to tell you. At the Festival of Quinquatrus, in three weeks' time, the Emperor is giving a splendid fete at his villa on the Bay of Baiae. There will be private games. I've arranged for you to perform. In person."

Quick excitement overcame me. I kissed her violently.

"Clever woman! You promised me this honor once, didn't you? But how did you pull it off? Did you talk to the Emperor yourself?"

"Why, no." She gave me a brittle smile. "Nothing so direct as that. I spent a few hours with Tigellinus. The way he's been begging me to do for months. In return, he interceded with Nero to—"

Jealous wrath brought my hand slashing across her face, knocking her backwards. There was fury to match mine in her jade eyes as she spat, "Have you become a complete ass, Cassius? Isn't success what you *want*? I'm disgusted with you."

"And I with you!" I choked. "To sleep with that slimy creature just to make a bargain—"

"Where did you acquire your scruples so suddenly?" she shrilled. "Have you all at once rejected our plan to win the rank of eques for you? Rejected your vow that came first?"

Seething out the words, she faced me, tense and almost ugly. Outside the open door of the house, torches glittered around her chair, highlighting her fiery curls and the malice in her jade eyes.

I heard my guests laughing together, drinking my fine wine. Abruptly my anger seemed ridiculous. What Locusta had done was no worse than what countless married Roman women did every night, from lust rather than worthy ambition. I hardened my heart and took her in my arms.

"Locusta, I'm sorry. I'm delighted with the news."

"That's better." Her pink tongue caressed my lips. "For a moment I thought you'd turned into a weakling."

"No," I said firmly. "That will never happen. Come inside. Let's tell the others of my good fortune."

CHAPTER IX

—————⇒⊳●⊲⇐—————

DURING THE next three weeks I worked myself into a state of high excitement and apprehension. All, as it turned out, for nothing. The performance at the Emperor's villa on the coast went off without a hitch.

Nearly a thousand illustrious persons packed the small indoor amphitheater. Seated in the largest box was the boy himself—I still thought of him thus, for he was barely past twenty, although his puffed cheeks, affected ringlets and sullen, swollen eyes lent him the look of a debauched man far older. At his side was the blonde strumpet Poppaea. She wore a gown of the sheer kind that had once cause Seneca to remark that such dresses neither afforded protection to the body nor concealment to modesty.

Modesty, however, didn't seem to concern Nero. He paid more attention to Poppaea's ruby breasts snuggling against his ribs than to the show I staged down on the sand.

Indeed, he paid no attention to his wife either. Octavia sat in an adjoining box. She was a pretty but frail creature, and she watched the show with obviously feigned interest. Next to Octavia, like a conspirator, was another, older woman, rather lean, with a thin and haunted face and dark hair in which dye could not conceal premature gray streaks. Nero's mother Agrippina.

Frequently she cast disgusted glances at her son. Nero returned them with the blandest of smiles, free of all guile, even as he continued to openly fondle Poppaea's most private parts.

By and large the notables assembled gave my performance a good reception, even though their jaded appetites were not particularly satisfied by my exhibition of catching bear and deer with ropes. When I loosed half a dozen savagely yipping foxes and went against them alone with a sword, picking up a few wicked bites before I killed them all, the Senators and equites and their wives cheered. They liked blood.

Not all, however. Seneca was in the gallery. So was the stubby Praetorian Prefect Burrus. Both watched glumly, disapproving of the gory entertainment. I also spied the tribune Julius in his glittering armor. He had nothing for me but unfriendly scowls.

Ofonius Tigellinus was present too, occupying the box next to Locusta's. Tigellinus hardly gave an eye to the animal show. He fretted and fussed and exchanged sly smiles and remarks with my red-haired woman. Locusta was stunning in greenish silk that matched the color of her eyes.

At the exhibition's end I accepted a garland and a purse from the Emperor. Gone were all fears of his recognizing me. Even now he hardly gave me a second glance. Meantime, Tigellinus was clutching Locusta's arm across the rail, and whispering earnestly.

The audience broke up to return to the main part of the villa for the evening's banquet. I thought again of how Locusta had arranged for my appearance. How many hours had she spent doing it?

While I was bathing prior to taking my place at dinner, one of Nero's masters of revels informed me that the name of the Cassian School would be high on the list when attractions were picked for the next Imperial games a few months hence. With that news I found I didn't care how much time Locusta had spent with the Sicilian. I would play the cuckold to hear such good tidings any day.

I hurried across the grounds to the white villa. The night was warm but blustery, promising a squall. Barges and other pleasure craft were moored at the wharf in the Bay of Baiae. Across the wind-chopped water gleamed the far lights of fine summer homes in Antium. Flushed with satisfaction, I was escorted to the great hall, where the feast was already in progress.

Locusta had reserved a couch adjoining hers, much to the anger of Tigellinus. He was seated on a higher tier, immediately below the Emperor. The sovereign lolled in a purple chair, eating sloppily and directing all his attentions to Poppaea. Agrippina and Octavia sat on his other hand, rigid with humiliation. Neither touched the food heaped before them.

Musicians drummed and piped. Laughter racketed off the walls. A hundred nude male and female slaves ran among the couches with solid silver winejars and trays overflowing with succulent foods. Locusta and I gorged ourselves on wine and fare like tiny hummingbird's breasts stuffed with a delicate spicy dough mixture.

The party grew rowdier and rowdier. Since there was nothing shameful in open lovemaking, Locusta and I were indulging in a bit of it when there was a sudden fearful crash of pottery and metal. Heads swiveled. Eyed lifted. Tongues stopped.

Agrippina was on her feet on the dais. She gazed down at her son, furious.

"All evening I've watched your disgusting behavior. I'll bear no more. To run your hand up that creature's gown while your own wife watches—have you no shame left?"

Poppaea sneered. Nero lurched up, stepping over the jars and platters Agrippina had upset. He seized her arm. His voice was wheedling and his smile looked false.

"Mother, pray don't embarrass us tonight."

"Me embarrass you! Your actions disgrace the title of Imperator, cover it with dung and—"

"Mother! Return to your place." He still smiled in a kindly way, guiding her elbow.

Agrippina pulled back. "Let go. The touch of your lecher's hand sickens me."

Nero laughed, lips slack and moist. He continued to hold her arm. Agrippina's mouth turned white at the corners. I knew he was hurting her, but his tone remained gentleness itself.

"Mother, I insist you compose yourself in front of our guests. None of us here is without some stain."

A flush spread from Agrippina's throat to her cheeks. With a ragged word or two none could hear, she turned away and sat down. The oblique reference to her husband Claudius and the fabled way he died had broken her defiance.

I reached for a cluster of fat grapes and swallowed a handful. I said to Locusta, "That's a nasty situation. I don't see why the Emperor should fear her, though. He's pushed her so far into the background, she couldn't possibly intervene in his affairs. She has no household troops."

With this rather drunken pronouncement, I swallowed more grapes, untroubled by the purple juice trickling down my chin and staining the white stripeless toga I'd purchased for tonight.

Conversation was slow to resume after the altercation on the dais. The musicians were refreshing themselves with wine. As a result, the hall was momentarily quiet. Locusta weaved slightly when she reached for the wine cup. She was drunker than I by far. When she spoke, it was thoughtlessly, and in a loud voice that carried, "The Emperor needs to be wary of anyone with secrets, Cassius, dear. There was the death of his rival Brittanicus, which very few can explain. Very few," she repeated, her green eyes glazed with mirth.

Our tier was but three removed from Nero's. He heard the remark. While I pretended to stare at a Senator's wife who was busy exposing her breasts for her husband's hand, I said in a low hiss, "Be careful what you say. They're watching."

Drunken confidence flashed in her eyes. "Let them! Let the mother and the son keep in mind that Locusta is still available, in case either needs expert advice on how to—"

"Have something to eat," I interrupted, literally forcing a bunch of grapes between her lips.

Locusta sputtered, fumed and swallowed. The sight might have made me laugh, as it did others at nearby couches, had I not been painfully aware of the displeased stare of Agrippina, and the even angrier glance of the Emperor.

Conversation commenced, forced and loud. The musicians
started up again. Lamps guttered while the wind from the bay
blew harder. Hangings at the windows flapped. Locusta lapsed
into silence and grew drowsy, for which I was thankful. Only
once was I forced to use more grapes to stifle the beginning of
a loud reminiscence about Claudius, full of veiled references
to her alleged role in his undoing. I put the wine out of the way,
where she could not reach it, and she gradually grew sober.

As a result of her shrill boasts I found myself without hunger or thirst. The Emperor had clearly heard. From time to
time he turned aside from Poppaea to stare thoughtfully at
Locusta's nodding coppery head.

Presently Locusta grew bored with my company. She excused herself to talk with a group of friends. Men and women
drifted off in pairs. One couple even performed the act on the
floor beside their couch, to the raucous amusement of those
nearby. All at once the music seemed too loud, the food too
rich. My belly was heavy and uneasy. I left the hall.

As I proceeded up the wide marble staircase I heard the
Emperor's voice. He had strolled to one of the small balconies
opening off the chamber, and now he was returning to
Agrippina, speaking loudly as if to demonstrate his good feelings.

"Rough water on the bay, Mother. Perhaps since you planned
to return to your villa anyway, it would be wise to assemble
your crew and sail before the storm. You see I'm concerned
about your welfare after all."

Bowing, he planted a dutiful kiss on her cheek. A crowd
around applauded. Agrippina remained stiff. Octavia gazed
blankly at her husband. Shrugging, I went on my way, glad to
taste the fresh, windy air.

What the Emperor had said was true. Barges tied at the wharf
rose and fell heavily on the swells. Ominous dark clouds obscured the stars. Lanterns bobbed on the vessels where skel-
eton crews looked to the mooring lines.

A moment later I felt I was being watched. I turned. A female figure glided from the shadows.

"I thought no one was out here. I needed air. It's so warm in there, so stifling and—oh. The bestiarius."

I made a clumsy salute. "Yes, my lady. I will retire if the Emperor's mother wishes."

Agrippina moved to the rail beside me. Her dark eyes were empty, mournful as she gazed out over the choppy Bay of Baiae. She shook her head in a sad way.

"Stay. I would enjoy the company of a plain, undevious man for a change."

Without thinking, she turned her face to the light. She must have been no more than forty-four or five, but her features were shrunken, looking almost ancient now. Her fine gown and jewels only heightened the sickly pallor of her flesh. "What is your name?"

I answered respectfully.

"I enjoyed your performance in my son's arena."

"Thank you my lady. I trust the Emperor was pleased with it also."

Her mouth wrenched. "All he cares about is the body of that slut Poppaea." She sighed, then gave me such a queer smile I wondered whether she was entirely sane. "I admire a man with a strong body, a man who uses that body skillfully. Once I too had certain skills. In statecraft. Now I have none. The only thing for which the rabble gives me credit is skill in preparing a meal." Her eyes were accusing, daring me to reply. "A meal of mushrooms."

I said nothing. From her half-mad stare, it was clear she'd paid her price for the crimes charged to her. She shuddered violently, indicating the black, foaming bay.

"My son thinks I should sail home before the storm breaks. Perhaps that's wise. I cause nothing but trouble here. But it's a wild night, and lonely. I have only stupid oarsmen for company." She hesitated, then went on like a pleading child, "You are a strong man. Would you like to earn a generous purse? Can you borrow a sword somewhere?"

"To what purpose, my lady?"

"To provide me company on the trip to my villa. It lies just there, over the water. That cluster of lights above Antium. I want company tonight. Even my barge is strange. My son had it built for me three months ago. The oarsmen are foreigners. Perhaps it's the wind, or the wine, but I'd feel better sailing with one able-bodied man who wasn't a total stranger. I'll pay you handsomely." Her mouth grew wry. "I'll even order you, bestiarius, if you refuse the first offer."

I no longer doubted that she was a madwoman, with a madwoman's foolish fear of a blowing sea. Why should I scruple, though? She would reward me. And while she had no influence in the government any longer, she was still a person of station. In my trade every contact might eventually prove useful. A short sail across the bay and back, an hour's work, and I would have spent my night more profitably than I would lolling inside, watching public fornication and other depravities.

"I will be glad to go with you, my lady," I said politely.

Agrippina smiled at that. We made rapid arrangements to meet on the wharf within minutes.

Then I returned to the hall. I was unable to find Locusta or the friends to whom she'd been talking. Stifling a pang of jealousy, I went outside again. After some haggling and the distribution of some coins from the purse the Emperor had given me, I obtained a short sword from a slave. I wrapped this in my cloak and slipped down to the wharf.

Agrippina's barge was long and splendidly painted. All sails were furled because of the ruthless wind. The craft heaved up and down on the slapping waves. There was a kind of hot, stale smell in the night air, the odor that precedes a violent storm. I spied Agrippina already on board, seated beneath an awning in the stern.

I leaped the rail, ignoring the surly stares of the oarsmen. There were about two dozen, naked to the waist on the benches,

unpleasant-looking to a man. The hortator was an even grim-
mer specimen, a big Greek with a twisting white scar on his
jaw. As I took my place beside Agrippina, feeling totally super-
fluous, the lines were cast off. The prow of the barge swung
out to open water.

"Pull!" the hortator cried. He rapped his gavel on a wood
block to set the stroke. "Pull! Pull! Pull!"

The barge creaked and groaned. Agrippina whispered, "We
shouldn't have come. I should have remained the night. The
water's too rough—"

"We'll make it all right, my lady," I said. "See, we're well
away from shore already."

So we were. The lamps of Nero's villa were mere yellow blurs,
receding. The Antium shore seemed far distant, though.

The creakings and crackings of the barge timbers grew
louder.

"This is a splendid craft, my lady. Didn't you tell me the
Emperor presented it to you?"

Agrippina nodded. Her eyes were lost on the black water.
"His own artisans designed it for me."

I immediately concluded that his artisans should be promptly
dismissed. The wretched hulk was pitching and rolling like a
toy boat. No barge built by men who knew their business would
have suffered so.

Agrippina sat like one in a trance as we plowed on. The
waves roared, lashing us with spray as the wind rose. The
hortator's gavel seemed to lose the stroke now and then, falter.
A dark suspicion entered my mind. The waters of Baiae were
infamous for bands of marauding smugglers and pirates. Could
such a band be in league with the hortator or some of the
oarsmen? Perhaps Agrippina's fears were not so farfetched at
that. Persons of importance had been seized on these waters
before, held prisoner until a handsome ransom was paid.

I unwrapped the sword from the cloak. "Excuse me while I
talk to the hortator. I know very little about sailing but it seems
to me we're no longer making headway."

"Cassius, stay with me. I'm afraid. All this pitching and lurching—Cassius, please—*watch out!*"

Her words became a scream as the barge heeled over. With a snap the tall mast broke.

The mast crashed into the oar benches. Men shrieked, crushed to death. Others leaped over the rail. At once the barge swung broadside to the waves, smacked and smacked again.

The hortator dove over the side. I struggled to stay afoot on the tilting deck, battered by cresting waves.

"Cassius, help me!" Agrippina shrieked. "Where are you? Take my hand—"

"Here, lady," I shouted, grappling for her. All around, nightmare crackings and snappings preceded the breakup of the barge. The deck tilted even more. I seized her thin body tightly as we fell into space.

My hands slipped and Agrippina was gone. The last thought I had before we struck the water was that the hortator had indeed been in league with pirates. No vessel broke up that quickly, shaking itself apart, unless the timbers had been deliberately weakened first. Then, among, flailing, howling oarsmen, the water covered me.

My lungs were tortured to bursting by the time I regained the surface. Water smashed over my head. I heard a feeble feminine cry and swam toward it. Agrippina was choking, going down.

I threw one arm around her torso, squinted through the wavetroughs to locate lights, and started swimming with all my strength.

An eternity later, choken and sodden and aching, I dragged Agrippina up on the damp beach at the foot of the wall of her villa.

While I vomited salty water out of my guts, servants rushed down to assist the Emperor's mother. She was sobbing from shock, her clothes in tatters. Of the barge there was no trace. The oarsmen were gone too, apparently deeming it unwise to swim for Agrippina's stretch of shore.

I wiped my brow and trudged after the servants to the wall gate. Every muscle in my body hurt from the arduous swim with the woman clinging to me like a millstone, howling demented words of fright in my ear. The villa appeared to be nearly the size of Nero's, but there were only a few servants on the premises. Their sandaled feet whispered eerily in the vaulted hall to which Agrippina was carried.

Her cheeks and lips were blue. In a trembling voice she dispatched a runner around the shore to inform the Emperor of what had happened, and to assure him she had survived. Slaves fetched in spiced wine and a butt of meat. I was on the point of telling her that I was convinced the hortator had plotted with pirates to wreck the craft when she rose and stumbled out, saying in a dazed way.

"Wait, Cassius. Wait until I find a new gown. I'll have your purse for you."

Leaning on two slaves, she vanished in the gloom. I grew uneasy. The pirates might be lurking nearby. Even if I told her that I feared for her safety in this dim, empty house, I doubted very much whether she would pay attention. Her eyes shone too vacantly as she left.

I was gnawing on a hunk of the cold meat when halloos and shouts rang from the beach.

Dread clutched me. I ran through echoing rooms into a broad court bounded by the bay wall. Already a dozen men had smashed the gate, with a dozen more pouring after them. They were muffled in cloaks. Daggers winked by wind-tossed lantern light.

Through the gate I saw a host of small craft bobbing on the shingle. The pirate plan had not failed after all.

Yellow from a lantern spilled over me. In its backwash I saw an emaciated pirate whom I took to be the leader. His right eye was puckered into a scarry slit, and a single pearl hung glimmering in his pierced left ear. He pointed at me.

"Here's the first of her slaves. Kill him and do the same for the rest. We want no witnesses."

They swarmed on me, blows and blades raining down. I fought back but the long swim had left me weak. I went down, groaning when a boot nearly caved in my ribs.

The shadow-shapes of the marauders fluttered by, hurrying into the villa. My cry of pain must have led them to think I was mortally wounded, for they paid no more attention to me. The courtyard grew dark. I tried to rise and fell down dizzily.

I heard a faraway shriek of horror, and then nothing more.

When I awoke, I was still lying in the court. The storm had passed. Rosy pink daylight streaked the villa's walls.

I clambered to my feet. Through the wrecked gate I saw the lapping beach, all empty of vessels. I shouted.

My voice rang back again, then again. With an unsteady step I returned to the house.

In the ghostly rooms that smelled all too freshly of blood, one after another I found the slaves slain, twisted in postures of struggle. My gorge rose but I hurried on.

Gulls cried on the distant beach. In the lavish chamber where she had retired to change gowns, Agrippina lay sprawled, her blood brown where it had drained on the alabaster floor. Her guilt had been expunged at last.

I turned away, too sickened to retch, but I carried forever the memory of the mother of the Emperor hacked to death.

CHAPTER X

———≈≈●≈≈———

I WASTED no time searching the villa to discover the extent of the looting. I was sure the pirates had taken whatever treasure was hidden in the house. Eager to be free of the smell of stale blood in those empty rooms, I rushed out through the beach gate. At a small dock a few tiny pleasure craft were anchored. Fishing vessels were already making from the bay into the sea, sails bright against the rising sun. I unfastened the lines of the smallest boat, climbed in and began paddling across the placid water toward the glimmer of Nero's villa on the far shore.

My head ached and felt curiously light, both from physical weariness and the shock of the bestial slaughter. Certainly the Emperor would want to repay the pirates with the cruelest possible punishment. I remembered the leader clearly—a crooked-lidded right eye, a pearl in his left ear.

Long before my weary arms dragged the little boat to the Emperor's wharf I saw the sun shining on coppery hair. Alone on the deserted quay, Locusta waited, pacing.

She was sober now. A black cloak concealed her body. As I hauled myself up beside her she exclaimed, "Do you have any idea how long I've been waiting for you here? People said you went with Agrippina. I didn't believe them." Her nails dug into my arm. "What fool's business have you gotten into, Cassius? Just remember, whatever you've done, my reputation is at stake along with yours. I brought you here."

"Take your hands off me!" I shouted. "The Emperor's mother is dead."

Locusta went white. "You bungler. You infernal idiot. To mix in court intrigues—"

"Be quiet, damn you! This was no intrigue, but a plot by pirates to loot her villa. She died in the struggle. I was the only one left alive." I started up the wharf. "Come along or stay, as you wish. But I must find the Emperor and tell him what's happened."

Locusta hurried after me. "The messenger arrived near dawn. He said the barge had gone down but that Agrippina was safe."

"The pirates had a fleet ready in case the barge trick failed," I replied, approaching two Praetorians who crossed their spears to bar my way. "My name is Cassius. I was a guest at this villa last night. The Emperor's mother is dead. Murdered by sea brigands. I must go to him at once and report."

The Praetorians deliberated. One said, "Take him inside, Marcus. He must be telling the truth, because I know this woman with him."

A few moments later I followed the armored figure through the entrance of the great hall. A lute sang softly. More than a hundred Senators, equites and their women lounged around in various stages of undress. The hall was a shambles of broken couches and stale, strewn food. One of those present was Tigellinus.

He gazed at me with hateful distaste as I presented myself at the foot of the dais and saluted. The Emperor paid no attention.

Nero Augustus Caesar was thoroughly drunk. His toga was filthy with gobs of food. His head garland was awry. He was practicing a difficult passage on his lute and botching it, while an old dodderer I took to be his teacher, the famed harpist Terpnus, vainly tried to correct his fingering.

Locusta gave me a curious glance whose meaning I did not understand. Plagued by fatigue and worry, I blurted out, "Emperor! I beg your attention!"

My outburst spoiled his chord even more. Jarring, discordant notes hummed away to silence. The guests ceased their tittering and drinking, shocked at my rudeness. There was mean wrath in Nero's eyes as he leaned over and deliberately spat at my feet.

"That's for your attention, dolt. Get out of here! Don't interrupt my lesson or I'll have you sliced up and served for luncheon."

Woodenly I stood my ground. "Emperor, your mother—"

"My mother? What about my mother? A fine woman. But forward. Much too forward."

He leaped down from the dais. He seized my arm, his face puffy and drunken.

"Don't you agree she's much too forward? I recognize your face now, from last night. You're the one she dragged with her on the barge. Well, the barge is safe and so is she. I think you fail to realize you have upset me coming here, whining—"

I fairly screamed into his malicious face, "She's *dead*!"

His hand dropped. He staggered back a step. His lips jerked, surely in a grimace of pain rather than a smile.

"What's this lout's name?" he asked.

Tigellinus immediately told him, with obvious relish.

"Well, Cassius, let me inform you that I kill men for making far milder jokes at my expense."

"Emperor, it's the truth! She's lying dead this moment in her villa, slaughtered by the pirates who conspired to wreck the barge."

I spilled out the details of the attack. A measure of sobriety returned to his flushed young face. When he laid his fleshy hand on my shoulder again, I wanted to shudder. He peered into my eyes and asked in a quiet voice whether it really was the truth.

"Yes, Emperor. I tried my best to stop them but there were too many."

Nero returned to the dais. He sank down and stared out from under his brows. His face had turned a sickly white color in the pale morning sunshine.

"I am sorry," he said tonelessly. "Let the gods be witness and Jupiter Stator attend my statement. I, the Emperor, am sorry that my beloved mother is dead."

In my tired and befogged state I believe his soft-spoken grief was genuine. He crooked a finger heavy with two sapphire rings.

"Draw a little closer, Cassius. Sit here at my feet and tell me the whole story once more."

As I approached to obey, I caught a glimpse of Locusta's face, still strained, still anxious. Perhaps I was in more danger than I knew. I might anger Nero with a wrong word, but my body ached so fiercely and my mind was so weary, I cared little. I dropped down on the marble and the round face bent closer to listen.

Slowly I related how Agrippina had been fearful of the stormy water; how the barge had broken apart, doubtless weakened by men on board in league with the pirates; how I had fallen, fighting, in the courtyard. Nero's face became grave.

"Cassius, I believe you. I believe you served my mother as best you could. The men who perpetrated this evil act will be punished. But first, we must find them." He seized a gem-crusted wine cup, draining it. His gaze became oblique. "Who were they, Cassius? Did you recognize them? Have you ever seen any of them before?"

"No, Emperor, to my everlasting regret. I did catch sight of the leader, though."

"The leader?" Nero's voice was flat. "How do you know he was the leader?"

"He issued the orders. Told the pirates to kill all the slaves, leaving no witnesses."

"And his face? Did you recognize it?"

"I did not."

"Was it an ordinary face?"

"No, Emperor. Extraordinary. He was thin. He wore a pearl in his left ear, like mariners do. And his right eyelid drooped, as though it had been cut once, perhaps in a brawl."

Behind me I heard a gasp. When I looked, Locusta was staring at me and trembling. I understood neither her look nor
the shocked, blank expression of the stock-still guests on their
couches.

"An interesting description," Nero murmured. "An unfamil-
iar one to me, however." Eyelids drooping, he gazed around
the ring of faces. "Is it familiar to anyone here?"

Murmurs and head-shakings said no. The Emperor sighed.
He leaned back in his purple chair.

"As my faithful servant, Cassius, you deserve a reward from
your sovereign. Let me confer a payment upon you so that you
may retire from my chambers, and I also, to bear privately the
grief of my heart's loss."

I was so tired and addled I was unable for an instant to com-
prehend what he'd offered. A shadow fell across the marble
between us. With a rude shove Tigellinus thrust me out of the
way and presented himself before Nero.

"A word, Emperor."

Nero nodded. He signaled for me to take myself off. I turned
around, chilled and alert. The intrusion of the Sicilian horse-
breeder meant no good.

I walked the few paces to where Locusta waited, grim-lipped.
I would have spoken, asked her the reason for her anger, but I
feared to break the silence of the hall. The other men and
women, clothes rumpled and stained with the signs of their
debauchery, hung their heads and avoided my glance.

Presently I heard a low chuckle. The Emperor's? He called
my name and I turned back.

"It has come to my attention, Cassius, that you have a certain desire I alone may satisfy."

I was wary now, watching Tigellinus absently pick at a spot
on his toga.

"I am afraid what the Emperor is saying is not clear to me,"
I answered.

Nero smiled, without humor. "Isn't it true you wish to be
raised to the rank of eques?"

Perhaps my mouth fell open in dismay and surprise. I only recall I stood there a great while until the fear of a trap began to unfold me. The only way Nero could have learned of my vow was from the man who heard it first, Tigellinus. I could not conceive of him doing me any favors at all.

At last I stammered: "A wish only, Emperor. Probably an idle one. Far too high a reward for my meager service of last night. I failed your mother when she needed me."

The Emperor waved. "No matter. My sadness makes me tolerant. In a mood to be generous to a fault. It is within my purview to grant the eques rank. I'm told you are now a man of property, and can support the rank's obligations. In return I ask one additional service. A service a man in your profession is well qualified to perform."

"Anything I can do to serve the sovereignty of Rome, I will do," I said, badly worried.

Nero's protruding eyes slid across my shoulder. He continued, "Legend maintains that when poison is placed in a cup made from a unicorn's horn, the poison boils up, foments, revealing its presence and thereby preventing death. For a long time I have wanted to own such a miraculous cup. And only an Emperor has the resources to command that such a cup be sought for him. Since my own family seems to be plagued with murderers, with poisoners—" He was staring at me intently, but I knew now that he had been looking at Locusta a moment ago, and was speaking to her as well as me. "—since my reign, I say, seems to be ridden with dangers, I need such a cup."

He rested one elbow on his knee, ringlets sparkling in the sunlight. He asked in a confidential way, "Cassius, would you take ship to Africa and search out and bring back a unicorn's horn? Say yes, and when you return, the eques rank is yours."

Instead of the wild triumph I should have experienced, I felt only that some kind of trap was closing. But where? And what kind? Tigellinus stared into space.

Could the Emperor be serious? Most sensible people regarded the legend of the unicorn cup as humbug. Fakery. An old wives' tale. I thought over my answer before giving it, "I would go and find a horn, Emperor. But I don't know whether it would work."

"Bring it," Nero replied quickly. "That is all I ask. If it fails, you won't be blamed."

Watching the Sicilian from the corner of my eye, I saw his heavy-lidded glance shift to Locusta. That was it! A plot to get me out of Rome on the thinnest of pretexts, so that Tigellinus might have a free hand with my woman. Suddenly my mind became sharp and swift, discarding choices, picking others.

Had I ever really loved Locusta? No. A year spent in Africa rounding up rhinos—the only unicorns available outside of Ultima Thule, so far as I knew—might be highly profitable for the Cassian School. I could bring back other animals, too. Let Syrax hire another lanista and run the business. At the end of my journey I would be granted the rank I'd vowed to win.

Exultation flooded me. Nero sat drumming his perfumed fingertips.

"You seem a long time deciding, Cassius. Is an answer so difficult to give?"

"No, Emperor. I will go, and gladly."

"Excellent, excellent." He stood up to clap me on the shoulder, his grief mysteriously vanished. "And because Africa is a hot, lonely place, far from the gentle civilizing benefits of our beloved city of Rome, I want you to have companionship." A new, stonier edge was in his voice. "The lady Locusta shall go with you. You may both return when you have the unicorn's horn, and not before."

Locusta moaned then, somewhere behind me. Tigellinus went purple and blustered forward. "Emperor! I thought—" He stopped, trapped.

Nero whirled on him, baring his teeth. "Your thoughts, horse-breeder, concern me no more than that!" He snapped his fingers. Then he bowed in Locusta's direction. "The esteemed lady is said to be an expert on certain exotic potions found in other lands. Perhaps she can help you test the efficacy of the magic cup, Cassius. At any rate I think she'll be of greater value to you in Africa than she would be at my court."

Nero smiled sweetly. Beneath that smile lurked malice and treachery and fear. Only last night Locusta had boasted too openly of her power and her secrets. In Africa she would never be a threat, nor a source of information about poisons to any conspirators who might want to topple Nero off the throne.

But the Emperor's security had been won at the price of infuriating Tigellinus. The Sicilian advanced to the dais with unsteady steps.

"Emperor, I beg you—"

Nero lashed out, leaving a cut on Tigellinus' cheek where his rings struck. His voice was almost a scream.

"Be silent! She goes with him. I'll hear no more."

Tigellinus paled and stepped back. Had there not been so many guests present, I think he would have killed me then and there. The Emperor was trembling, gripped by one of those violent rages for which he was becoming infamous. He snatched up a cup, hurled it at his guests, then another.

"Why are you all still here? Begone! Leave me alone. I'm sick of seeing faces, nothing but faces. Leave me alone to mourn my mother. Leave me alone! *Leave me alone!*"

The guests scurried from the hall. The Emperor slumped back on his throne, his pinkish lips bowed up in a curious smile. Tigellinus stormed past me, bawling for his slaves. Locusta had already gone up the great staircase and out of the hall.

The last I saw of the Emperor, he was sunken into the chair, his lute in his lap. One hand plucked a few sour notes. His head was thrown back. His eyes were vacant. Tears ran down his cheeks. I shuddered and rushed out, because I could not tell whether they were tears of sorrow or of mirth.

Looking about in the antechamber, I failed to see Locusta until she stormed at me from the shadow of a pillar, spitting all sorts of obscene oaths. Tired and unstrung, I gripped both her wrists and shook her.

"One more word, woman, and I'll strike you in the face."

Panting, she wrenched free. "Touch me again, Cassius, and I'll kill you."

"The gods witness if I know what's wrong with you, woman."

"You!" She made the word sound vile. "Your stupidity! Your blindness! To stand there with your imbecilic slave's face—yes, slave! You're no better than that now. To stand there telling Nero how sorry you are about his mother! Weeping crocodile tears with him after you've practically accused him of murder!"

"Murder!" I exclaimed. "Gods! Are you still drunk?"

"Do you know the identity of the leader of the pirates?" she sneered. "Pirates indeed! You worthless wretch! Hasn't it occurred to you that sea-rovers intent on looting a villa wouldn't bother to sink the owner's barge first? They'd simply go ahead and loot. Oh, the Earth Mother consign me to hell for taking up with you!"

She drummed her fists on her flanks, her age showing as her face cracked with rage. I said, "Locusta, I still don't understand—"

"The man with the pearl in his ear and the drooping eyelid! Everyone in that room but you knew his identity! He's the commander of the royal fleet at Misenum. His name is Anicetus. He's a freedman, and one of Nero's closest friends. Now, Cassius. *Now* is there a shaft of light inside that stinking hollow of your head?"

Light there was, and despair that I hadn't seen the truth before: the barge designed by the Emperor's artisans; Agrippina's role as a source of constant irritation to, and restraint upon, her son; the sudden arrival of the hired assassins after the barge sank. It all made evil sense at last.

By sending me to Africa, no doubt at Tigellinus' suggestion, the Emperor had conveniently disposed of the single remaining witness to the crime, as well as another source of danger—Locusta—at a single stroke.

"You've dragged me down," Locusta whispered. "Down into the slime of your own miserable failure!"

I still had foolish hope. "How so? He wants a unicorn's horn. Very well, we'll fetch him the only such horn available—from a rhino. Then we'll be free to return. The Emperor said so himself. By means of a contact in Africa made through Serenus, the task will be easy. We'll soon be back—"

"Jackass!" she cried. "We'll never be back! There's a trap in it. Somewhere, there's a snare waiting to catch us. We'll learn what it is soon enough. That madman in there is clever, the way only madmen can be."

She moved nearer, her painted mouth ugly, the very lines of her body, once so soft, like weapons of her defiance.

"I warn you of one thing, Cassius. I have no choice but to go with you. Arguing with Nero would be folly. I know that from the way he glared at me. But if you've ruined my life—if, because of you, I never see Rome again—" She smiled. "Then, my darling, you'll pay dearly."

Her cloak billowing around her, she vanished across the antechamber. I shook my head, still trying to puzzle out where the trap lay. The humming notes of the lute echoed in the great hall. Echoed and rose and fell, counterpointed by strange, tittering laughter.

CHAPTER XI

—————◦———————

A MONTH later, all my affairs in order, I closed my house, dismissed my slaves and stepped into an elegant litter to be borne to the port of Ostia, down the Tiber on the seacoast.

The sun was high. The breeze smelled fresh. Peasants in the prosperous fields to either side of the great highroad, the Via Ostiensis, saluted as I passed. I expect they thought I was a noble, since I traveled with a dozen porters lugging my baggage in a file behind the chair. I was not a noble yet, but when I traveled this road again, going the other way, I would be.

We descended the green plain. The seven Roman hills were replaced by melon groves, then with the glimmering roofs of the port that served Rome. A field of sails sprang up on the blue Tyrrhenian Sea ahead. My heart grew heavier.

Would the exile really be brief? Or was there yet another snare waiting somewhere?

Near the outskirts of Ostia a group of people had gathered alongside the road to shout my name. "*Vale*, Cassius! Good luck! A safe journey to the famous bestiarius!"

The *Acta Diurna* had carried a lengthy notice about my departure to the African provinces to bring back a menagerie for the Cassian School. Quite a crowd had seen me off in Rome. My spirits rose a little. Perhaps Nero merely wanted me out of Latium for a year or so, until the shock of Agrippina's death passed. The Emperor had retired to his villa at Naples, ostensibly grief-stricken. The populace believed otherwise. I had seen one or two ugly lampoons circulated. The anonymous authors clearly named him the murderer of his mother.

Soon my bearers carried me into the clutter of inns and warehouses beside the great stone Ostia mole. Triremes of the Imperial navy swung at anchor. Also merchantmen out of Egypt with Rome's corn dole. Even a ramshackle trader from distant Albion island. From this last naked stevedores were unloading precious tin ore for transshipment by barge up the Tiber.

The bearers set down the chair. I stepped out, wearing my finest tunic and amulets. Our ship, a Levantine trader with colorful sails, bobbed alongside the quay. As I was seeing to the loading of my things, runners shoved through the idlers loitering on the dock. Another litter was on the way, borne by bald eunuchs. I gathered my cloak around my arm and waited. I had not seen Locusta in many days.

She climbed from her litter and blinked rapidly, unused to the sun. A stevedore accidentally stumbled against her, dropping his bale of Egyptian cotton.

"Clumsy, unwashed pig!" She kicked savagely at the unlucky man's shins. He scuttled away in terror. With a contemptuous glance at the crowd Locusta swept up the ship's plank. Not once did she notice me.

At the rail she paused and stared back across the narrow strip of blue water. I nodded. She did not return the greeting, passing out of sight.

With a sigh I saw to the loading of the last of my belongings. I paid off the porters and the chairmen and wandered a while on the bustling quay. Now and again some child or seaman would point and whisper. The novelty of being a celebrity was beginning to pall.

Under the best of circumstances, a journey into Africa would not be easy. With Locusta in her present frame of mind it might well be unbearable. After one initial meeting, all our arrangements had been handled by agents hired by Syrax, to whom I had bade farewell last night in Rome.

Just as I was about to enter an inn for a last cup of good Roman wine, a chariot came racing down the wharf. People scattered as the driver wheeled up. I went to meet Annaeus Serenus, whom I had been expecting.

My grizzled partner looked older than ever. "A damned broken axle delayed me on the highroad," he informed me. From his cloak he produced a parchment sealed with wax and impressed with a signet. "This is the letter of introduction I promised to Cornelius Publius in Iol Caesaria."

I nodded, tucking the letter safely away. "We've corresponded. I'm sure the decurion will give me every assistance." I added, with a confidence I did not feel, "When I return, our partnership will prosper even more, Serenus. Going to locate a unicorn's horn for the Emperor is only one purpose of this trip."

Serenus shook his head. "Why can't he concern himself with statecraft, instead of with gratifying these bizarre whims?"

I said nothing, By mutual consent Locusta and I had not concealed our reason for going to Africa. We had, however, kept secret the circumstances under which Nero made this request. Only the dimmest rumors of my role in the death of Agrippina had leaked out. To these I had added nothing, for my own sake.

"One last thing I charge you with, friend," I told Serenus. "From time to time, look over the accounts of the Cassian School with the bankers."

"Be assured I will. That Syrax is a good enough fellow, I suppose, but I don't like him and I never have. He strikes me as none too scrupulous about the means he employs to reach a given end."

"With you to keep a discreet watch on him, we have nothing to fear."

Serenus clasped my hand. "A good journey, Cassius. Father Neptune of the Foam smooth your way both going and coming. Let's hope the reckless young man on the Palatine allows Rome to remain standing while you're gone. Have you heard the latest?"

I said I had not. He proceeded to tell me a tale of the Emperor's growing infatuation with things Grecian.

"Word is, he spent one night recently at his Neapolitan villa drawing diagrams of Rome rebuilt on a plan resembling that of ancient Athens. How do you suppose the madman intends to dispose of the Rome we have now? Burn it?"

Before I could reply I saw a certain face in the crowd.

For a moment I was dumb with surprise. My heart broke at the sight of her slim, lovely body beneath a simple pale gray stola that looked rather threadbare. Then I recalled all the anguish of the past, and I hardened my heart.

Acte struggled toward me. Hastily I turned to Serenus, "Excuse me, good friend. I'd better see to my things on board. Farewell."

Taken aback, he had no chance to say anything before I slipped away. But I was unsuccessful in my escape. Acte's hand closed on my arm.

"Cassius? Are you such a hard, selfish man to turn away a second time?"

Facing her was simple enough. Keeping the hardness in my heart was the difficult task. There in the pandemonium of the dock, with the cries and curses of the Levantine sailors rattling in the air and the blue eternity of the sea lapping off to the horizon, she was lovely as she had always been. And painful for me to look upon.

"I suppose you're going to say you walked all the way from Rome to see me off, Acte."

"To tell the truth, I did. The news of your departure was widespread. Oh Cassius, they've made you bitter, haven't they? You look so elegant wearing those amulets and chains, your hair curled and your feet in fine leather boots. But your eyes—"

She crushed against me, weeping. "Cassius, Cassius. Why did you walk out on me that day in the arena?"

Roughly I pushed away, not wanting to remember how I'd loved her. It would only bring woe.

"Acte, if you want to rake up the past, I can do it too. Remember the night at Sulla's when I sent the message in with the doorkeeper? You never came out. You kept me waiting outside like an animal, while you sported with the Emperor so he'd give you a few more pretty presents."

"Presents!" she exclaimed. "Oh, you great fool. In so many ways you're a man. Strong, full of courage. In so many other ways you're blind."

"Don't pretend you weren't flattering Nero to gain some favor."

"Not for me, Cassius. I did it for my father's sake."

"Oh, please. Spare me the cheap little domestic tales."

"Gods, what have they *done* to you? Your lips twist whenever you speak."

"No one has done anything!" I said sharply. "I have made my own way. I will continue to do so. I don't see anything strange in my attitude, Acte. You did the same thing at Sulla's."

"I was trying to get my father reinstated!" We were pushed together as another file of porters passed onto the ship. "Do you think I enjoyed what that puffed-up little boy wanted to do with me? And did? The gods have visited us both with evil luck, Cassius. Yours came as success, mine as failure."

"What you're saying makes no sense, Acte."

"Do you remember I told you how my father lost his position in the treasury when Nero replaced office holders from the old regime with followers of his own?"

I nodded cautiously. Growing within me was a desire to believe in her again; to love her as I once had. She stood with the shadow of the sail of the ship for Africa falling across her face. To love her now would be futile.

She hurried on, describing how the Emperor and his friends had been visiting Sulla's regularly. How she'd seen Nero's interest in her as a heaven-sent opportunity to regain her father's job. Her dark eyes turned ugly with memory.

"Night after night he came to the brothel, promising me every night that my father's case would be reviewed. I knew he didn't actually care for me. He was only indulging his lust. But I believed it when he gave his word. The word of an Emperor. After he stopped visiting Sulla's, my father went to the office of the Imperial quaestors. He was thrown out. Hooted at. Called a stupid old man. That is the sort of Emperor who rules us, Cassius. That's the sort of god to whom you pander. He's not worthy of respect, and neither is the whole rotten hierarchy of Rome!"

"I—I'm sorry about your father." I was weakening in spite of my will. Old memories of that first night of tenderness at the school flooded back. "How is he?"

"Dead," she said softly. "The last rebuff was too much. He stole a razor from a public barber stand one night when he was drunk. He slashed his throat. My brothers and sisters have all left Rome now, to work on farms or at anything they can find. Two were taken in by distant branches of the family. I left Sulla's shortly after that."

"To do what?"

"Oh, this and that." She was nervous, evasive.

"Do you take men from the streets?"

"Yes, if there's no other way to—Cassius, do you have to torture me like this?" She was weeping again, oblivious to the stares of those around us. Over her shoulder I glimpsed Serenus standing in the shadow of an inn wall, watching.

"Cassius, I would have come out that night. But I couldn't, don't you understand?"

"Whether I understand doesn't change the fact that you spouted lofty sentiments when we first met. Then used your body like any other whore to your advantage."

"Yes, I admit that."

"I'm sorry," I said again. "That was cruel. I know you did it for your father. But after Sulla's, you never bothered with me until I won the wooden sword."

Instantly her head came up. "That's not true! I sent half a dozen messages to the school."

"You're lying. I never got one."

She puzzled a moment. "Cassius, this is very strange. A few days after you visited Sulla's, a boy brought a message from your friend. Syrax. He said you were angry with me. But he promised he'd do what he could to mend the situation. Smuggle my letters to you into the school. He maintained they'd never reach you otherwise. I believed what he wrote because I was desperate, Cassius. I sent you letters one after another. Eventually the boy brought them all back with a note from Syrax saying you'd refused even to look at them."

Cold despair froze me. "Syrax wouldn't dare to—"

Looking into her hurt dark eyes, I knew otherwise. He would, to preserve our partnership, keep me free of dangerous entanglements that might hinder our progress. Acte hurried on, "After you won the sword and moved into your house I came to visit you several times. The servants turned me away. They said you'd issued orders. I died then, Cassius. A little at a time I died."

No longer could I stand beside her unmoved. The months of denying vanished in an instant when I took her in my arms. I cursed my own stupidity and held her tight while strangers stared.

"I issued no orders like that, Acte. He must have bribed my servants. He was always afraid of you. Afraid that my interest in you would blunt our drive to success. I said goodbye to him in the city. I'd give my life to have him here for one minute. I'd kill him."

Acte shuddered against me. "Don't, my darling. Don't speak of death. Not when time is so short and—"

Time had all run out. From the prow of the Levantine a wiry sailor leaned over the dock and blew three blasts on a bull's horn. Men scurried on the deck. The captain of the vessel bawled down, "Master Cassius! Hop aboard, if you please!"

"I love you, Acte. I've lied to myself, told myself otherwise. I've slept with other women. But it's you I love."

With a sad smile she answered, "Is that one of the women, Cassius? That red-haired one watching you from the rail? With more hate than I've ever seen on a human being's face?"

Swiftly I spun, catching only a glimpse of coppery curls disappearing over the deck. Ropes creaked. Men cursed each other
in the universal Greek. Idlers shoved along the mole to watch
the departure of the vessel. In seconds I must undo months of
blindness.

"Acte, within a year I'll be back in Rome. I'll have the rank
of eques. Wait for me. I've no right to ask it but—will you
wait?"

Too overcome to speak, she only nodded.

"Master Cassius, we can't delay!"

"A moment more, Captain," I shouted, gathering her in my
arms for one last kiss.

Her love poured out in the heat of her lips and her salt tears.
The Levantine mariners began to lift the plank. Like flesh parting from flesh when a sword cuts deep, I released her hand.

I leaped high, caught the plank line and scrambled aboard.
The men hauled away and the tiller went over. The big sails
caught the wind and the merchantman began to glide past the
dock, sweeping fast toward the harbor mouth.

Face tear-shining, Acte waved. She grew smaller and smaller
still. My mind was a blur of things—the deceitful face of Syrax;
my own ignorant misreading of the facts; my months of loneliness that could have been filled with her warmth and her
tenderness. Had I received a single one of her messages, or
seen her at my house, I might not now be riding this belling-
sailed bird out toward the blue swell of the sea's horizon, and
Africa, and unicorns for a mad Emperor.

I wanted to fix my eyes on her figure on the mole until the
last moment. My attention was distracted. Sunlight glared off
a chariot that must have rumbled onto the dock while I held
her in my arms. The last face I saw, small but recognizable for
one fearful instant, was that of Ofonius Tigellinus, peering over
the shoulder of his charioteer.

Had he been watching long? Had he come down to gloat as
I went into exile, and seen me embrace her? All at once I was

ready to leap the rail and swim back. A hand on my shoulder restrained me.

"Master Cassius?" It was the portly captain. "I was instructed to give this to you after we sailed. I trust you and the lady will have a pleasant crossing. Good day."

He sauntered off, leaving me with the rolled parchment. I grew cold at the sight of the Imperial eagles in the wax.

The letter's first few lines revealed the depth of my own stupidity. The parchment dropped from my hands. At once Locusta was there, picking it up. She scanned it once, then a second time. She was first incredulous, then angry.

"So, Cassius. So, Nero Augustus Caesar had an afterthought which he saw fit to address to you in a letter signed not by himself but by one of his ministers. Now do you see how eminent you are, Cassius, beast-man? How mighty? How clever?"

She brandished the letter at me, growing hysterical. The crewmen stopped working to stare as the canvas cracked and the merchantman leaped toward the harbor mouth. Her voice dripped venom.

"He forgot to tell you he won't accept a rhino horn. He's not like the street rabble who'll believe in anything. You're not to return until you find a true unicorn. The unicorn he knows doesn't exist *anywhere on the face of this earth!*"

She flung the letter in my face and ran.

The sea wind swept over me. I strained to see the Ostia mole again. It was gone, a white smudge behind the butterfly patterns of small fishing skiffs darting among the anchored triremes. I turned my back on the Rome I would never see again.

And the woman I loved who would remain forever lost.

From a cabin somewhere below, I heard shrill laughter peal. I realized then that I was traveling onto the shining sea with a woman who wished me dead.

I turned to the rail once more. I struck my fist against it. Again, then again. Again. *Again,* until the skin broke and blood

came and I wept as the merchantman gathered the wind and
carried me over the Tyrrhenian Sea to Africa.

A worse blow was still to come.

Days later we berthed at the bustling, sunny port of Iol
Caesaria, the capitol of the desert province of Caesariensis, more
commonly called Numidia. The decurion Cornelius Publius
was out of the city touring his forts. Locusta and I took quarters in the city, barely speaking, to await his return.

The hot and alien sun gave our days a strange monotony.
Presently another ship put in from Rome. A letter arrived from
Serenus.

I regret deeply (it ran in part) *that I must deliver this ill news.
But one way or another, Ofonius Tigellinus learned that you were
enamored of the young lady whose name is A.*

My heart went cold. Had he known it before he saw us on
the wharf? No matter. The damage was done. I read on.

*At many public gatherings the Sicilian has been talking openly
of his hatred of you. In this I saw a definite danger to the young
woman. Cassius, do not think badly of me. I am growing old. I
always harbored a certain fondness for her, as you know. Also, the
Emperor's shipboard instructions about the unicorn horn have been
widely circulated, probably on purpose. It must be clear to you, as
it is to those of us here, that you have been exiled from Rome the
rest of your mortal life. Exactly why this happened, perhaps only
you know. Nevertheless, since I am growing old, I yearn for companionship. And I fear for the life of the young woman. When I
explained the circumstances to her, she appeared very sad. But after a week or so, and much persuasion on my part about the good
sense of the move, she relented. We struck a sort of bargain. She
agreed to become my wife.*

From the harbor drifted the chanting of Numidians loading
a galley with sesame oil. The sunlight in my chamber was blinding as death. I struggled to read the close of the letter.

*I beg your forgiveness for my selfishness, Cassius my good friend.
I earnestly hope you will not find it in your heart to quarrel with
my action, which I took not merely for my sake, but also for yours.*

Whatever else happens, A. will be safe with me. Please allow me to remain your obedient—

I could read no more. I could not even weep. Some shocks are beyond pain.

And that is how, on the parched African coast, I faced the total ruin of all my dreams.

Book II

———⟫●⟪———

60–62 A.D.
POISON AND UNICORNS

———⟫●⟪———

CHAPTER XII

——=≈•≈=——

I WILL NOT dwell on the dismal days before the decurion returned to Iol Caesaria, except to say that I lost myself in a state of uncaring despondency from which none could rouse me, neither for food nor bathing nor conversation. None, that is, except the wine seller who visited my chambers regularly, left two fresh skins of cheap, sour stuff and took away the ones I'd emptied.

But a man cannot exist forever in such a state of despair, unless he plans to do away with himself. That was not my intent, I realized, when the effects of my debauch gradually wore off. I began to pay attention to my appearance again, and to the slave who camped on my doorstep.

He reported that the decurion had been awaiting me at his house for five days and nights. So I went, to make the best of my bad situation.

In a cool grove of fig trees on his estate, I met the man who governed the bustling port city. Cornelius Publius was well into middle years, an overweight widower with bright red cheeks that testified to good living. He seemed kindly and thoughtful. He treated me as an equal, and did not question my delay in arriving.

I related as much of my background as I dared, and presented my first letter from Serenus. I had torn the second one to shreds in a rage.

After looking over the scroll, Publius reached for a pale green sliver of Numidian cucumber in a bowl between us, sprinkled it with grainy black cumin and said,

"A hundred stadia or so down in the desert, we maintain a fort. It's one of a string of them set up in the days when Caesar conquered the Gaetulian tribe and raised Juba to the local throne. Game's plentiful nearby. I can furnish guides, transportation and introductions to the commander."

"If you think the fort will serve as a good headquarters, Publius, I accept your word."

"That's more than the Emperor does when I send in my regular reports." Publius clapped for a slave and ordered writing materials. "Since I never receive any answers I assume he never reads them."

Somewhat embarrassed to bring up the subject, I said, "The true nature of my mission—"

He interrupted. "I know. It's been all over town for days. Unicorns."

"The fact that none has even turned up doesn't rule out the chance that they exist. Does it?"

"That's false hope shining in your eyes, Cassius. I judge you to be smart enough to recognize it."

"I am. I have no choice. Nero refuses to accept a rhino's horn."

Applying himself to writing, Publius commented, "Even rhinos are scarce in this part of Africa. You'd have a terrible time journeying far enough south to trap some. I'm not sure you'd make it on your own, let alone with the charming lady who is your mistress."

On that score I said nothing. I didn't wish to tell him that my mistress was drinking practically as heavily as I had been, and never spoke to me except to shrilly denounce my stupidity. Publius finished his letter.

"Actually, Cassius, your presence here makes me wonder what fills the heads of the Emperor and the people of Rome. Do they only worry about finding mythical beasts to gratify their desire for pleasure?" He passed over the scroll. "The liberty in which the Republic was founded can't last long, it seems to me, when no one tends it. But perhaps the Emperor doesn't plan for it to last."

"You may be right. His cult of personal power increases day by day."

Publius indicated the dark green foliage of the fig trees rustling in the humid breeze. "Personally I prefer my isolation here. In my opinion the bloodline of the Julian Caesars bears a distinct bad taint these days. A taint that forecasts its end. On my last visit to Rome it was apparent that the place was becoming a sinkhole of public and private vice."

He cast an oblique glance at me, to test my reaction. When I nodded he laid a gnarled and kindly hand on my arm.

"Your return, I hear, is contingent upon finding the horn of that fictitious animal. Perhaps you'd do well to accept the futility of the search right now. Learn to live content in Africa. The air is sultry, but it's fresher by far than the wind blowing off the Palatine. And much more free."

Remembering Agrippina's hacked body and the disillusionment of Seneca, I said, "I am beginning to believe it, sir. Once I thought Rome was bright and happy. I wanted to be part of it. Lately I've seen some of the tarnish under the brightness." I looked at the sealed letter in my lap. "Still, I am a partner in the Cassian School. I'll go on my hunt, for unicorns as well as more practical quarry, and trust to luck."

Publius rose. "Generally I'm here at all time, except for inspection tours. Feel free to call on me for assistance. Now, about your departure . . ."

Inside the house, he summoned his steward and we made preparations. When I returned to my quarters, I reluctantly went to inform Locusta that we would leave in four days. I found her sitting in a state of dishevelment in her apartment, fanned by a shining-black Numidian girl she had insisted I hire. I could hardly stand to look at her any longer. Her coppery hair showed whitish streaks. Her greenish eyes were dull. Her breasts seemed to sag. She smelled of wine, watching me owlishly while I related my news, concluding, "It makes no difference to me whether you stay or remain, Locusta. If you find the city more comfortable—"

"Comfortable!" she jeered. "A sunbaked wallow for hogs! I'll go with you."

"Why? Obviously you dislike the idea."

"Dislike it? I detest it. I detest you, and all the misery you've brought me."

"Then why in the name of the gods do you continue to hang on me like a leech?" I shouted.

The Numidian girl ceased fanning, biting her lip. Locusta rose, kicking over a cup of wine that ran like blood on the sunlit parquetry. There was devious mirth in her greenish eyes as she advanced on me and flicked my chin with a pointed, painted nail.

"Because, my dear Cassius, it is you who have brought me to this unhappy state. I mean to stay with you, to make certain you bring me out of it again. What you've done, you must undo."

On the point of telling her it was impossible, I hesitated. The gleam in her eyes was unbalanced. She wasn't clinging to me out of passion, or even out of hope, really. She knew the odds against our returning to Rome were monumental. What I saw in her glance—the real reason for her clinging—chilled me through.

I saw hate, deep and devious, feeding and feeding upon itself. One day that hate would be grown so large it would need to devour someone else. I had no doubt about the victim. I had best watch her closely.

She planted a false kiss on my cheek. "I won't ever leave you, Cassius. So long as you live."

And with a tinkling laugh, she returned to her chair. The Numidian girl resumed fanning her with the spray of egret plumes. Locusta appeared to drowse. I hurried out.

Our preparations were completed in the appointed time and we left Iol Caesaria for the south.

Shortly the irrigated farm tracts disappeared, replaced by a sere brown plain where a sirocco blew fitfully and strange antelope bounded on the horizon. Our guide was Egyptian, the bearers black Numidians with sad expressions. They carried our voluminous baggage as if it contained the weight of the world.

The plain rose steadily, a shimmering sandy yellow waste. I took to riding naked in the curtained interior of my creaking four-wheeled ox cart. Sand blew ceaselessly, penetrating the mouth, the ears and the eyelids. When at last we sighted the Roman fort, it looked as beautiful to me as the Emperor's villa once had.

In reality the fort was an ugly, square yellow clay structure with towers at each corner. It was surrounded by a hut village housing the blacks who served the legionnaires. As we passed through the gate I climbed into a tunic to make myself presentable for the first centurion.

I waited in stifling shade while an officer in armor clanked out to meet us. Locusta lifted the curtain of her cart. She was pale and drawn from the heat. The fellow approaching was large-boned, sunburned, rather handsome in a coarse way. He wore only a waist cloth and greaves, as did the other soldiers lounging around the large square courtyard.

Like the appearance of the fort, the salute the officer gave me was slovenly.

"May I present my respects, Centurion Remus?" I said. "And this parchment from the decurion."

He snatched the letter from my hand. "I'm not Remus. My name is Titus Quintus."

"Where is the commander?"

Titus Quintus waved northward. "Taking a holiday on the coast. I'm the second centurion of the first cohort. When the commander chooses to rest for months at a time, I'm the one saddled with the dirty job of running this hellhole." He gave the letter only a cursory glance. "We heard some word of your coming. I take it you're going to bother us for a lot of help."

Bristling at his rudeness, I replied, "Excuse me for correcting you, Quintus. I don't consider asking for help bothering you. Imperial law requires the Legions to render assistance in animal hunts. As you may or may not know, the games are one of the chief industries of the city of Rome."

His smile was acid. "I forgot. I've been sweating my guts out here for three years while the dear citizens sit on their pink butts beside the Tiber, enjoying themselves."

Did the broiling heat affect all the legionnaires in such a fashion? Most of the soldiers round about looked lazy, and many openly scowled their displeasure. I wished the first centurion had not chosen to take a holiday, leaving me at the mercy of this quarrelsome fellow. But since my success depended partly upon him, I strove to be polite.

"I'll try to make only modest demands on you and your men, Quintus."

"Even sleeping takes it out of you in this godforsaken climate."

"I'm sorry. But we are charged by the Emperor—"

"I know, I know. Unicorns." Several of his men exchanged smirks. "Of all the starstruck ideas? Unicorns, on this desert! If you think I'll send my men out searching for animals that don't exist, you have another think coming."

"Quintus, I don't like the reception I'm getting here."

"Oh, you don't; eh?" Quick anger lit his cheaply handsome face. "That's a damn shame. It's the only reception available. And I'm in command. Don't forget that. Now, get your black louts moving. The smell of their unwashed hides makes me sick."

He approached the first of the porters, ordering him forward in pidgin Greek. The other porters shambled after. On various porches of the fort buildings I noticed many naked Numidians going about their tasks. Here and there I saw a head turn or a jaw thrust out and an eye roll with poorly concealed hatred.

One black, taller than the rest and splendidly muscled, was moving across the courtyard with a heavy water jar balanced on each shoulder. A porter stumbled, dumping his bundles on Quintus' head.

"Oxen!" the centurion shouted, flailing around. "Worthless black dung!"

The other porters stopped. The one who'd stumbled mumbled apologies in Greek. Quintus' temper had been roused. He gestured to a nearby legionnaire.

"Arcipor, throw me that snake. Perhaps a few strokes will quick the steps of these shambling idiots."

The soldier sailed him a long lash. Quintus caught it deftly. His arm flashed up. The porter screamed with the lash twined around his thin torso, drawing blood.

Quintus struck again, then again, altogether a dozen times. The miserable porter's flesh was peeled from his spine in ugly strips. He crawled away.

To my horror I saw Locusta watching Quintus from her cart. Her lips were drawn upward in a warm smile and her face shone with admiration.

About to toss aside the lash, Quintus spied the tall black with the water jar studying him. The black's throat muscles throbbed. Otherwise he was still. Quintus wiped his mouth.

"Want a taste of this yourself, Ptolemy? If not, pick up your heels and move on."

The other blacks in the compound waited. The giant called Ptolemy remained frozen a moment. Then he turned and trotted off.

Quintus' mouth wrenched, as if from fear. He sauntered over, dragging the gory whip in the sand.

"A bad lot, all of them. That tall monster's the worst. We have to keep them in line. A few whippings every day and they remember they're animals, not men, as Ptolemy tries to tell them." Quintus executed a mocking bow. "I regret if I offended your sensibilities, master. This is Numidia, not some perfumed bedchamber in Rome."

I checked my anger and allowed him to conduct me toward the stifling main tower. He said apartments had been prepared there for Locusta and myself. As we passed her cart I made introductions. Quintus studied her breasts when they glimmered beneath her sweaty gown. His eyes slid from her breasts up her throat to her face, clotted with lust.

"A pleasure, my lady. I trust you'll be comfortable among round, unlettered soldiers."

She smiled. "A strong whip arm is the guardian of the Empire, centurion. I admire your firmness. I'm sure I'll enjoy my stay."

I was sickened by the vapid courtesan's smile she lavished on the bad-tempered soldier. Before he conducted me inside the tower, he paused, turned and saluted Locusta again. His eyes glittered like a rutting animal's.

At dinner that night, Quintus appeared dressed in his finest armor. He was plainly interested in putting on a display for Locusta. He couldn't do it with the table he set. The food was poor and the wine poorer.

The legionnaires of the first cohort made no attempt to tone down their vulgar remarks because a woman was present. The dismal dining hall with its complement of listless black servants depressed me. One young Numidian girl protested when a soldier slid his callused hand up between her bare legs. This provoked another outburst from Quintus. The girl received three strokes of his whip, while his men applauded.

I remained silent and morose, sloshing down pot after pot of the inferior wine. Locusta, however, praised Quintus for his strength as a disciplinarian. She said hardly a word to me. And neither did he. Quintus was totally ignorant of her background. He was also untroubled by her age, or the streaks of gray shining in her reddish hair. He went ahead pawing over her and offering the crudest kind of flatteries until I went to bed in disgust.

As the days went on, I was virtually ignored by the two of them when we ate together. I had no objection. At least when Locusta fawned over the centurion, she wasn't badgering me about the heat or our wretched existence. One sultry night I heard thick laughter and the unmistakable sounds of passion in her apartment below mine. From then on I slept more easily. I felt no jealousy. I had long since lost any desire whatsoever to touch her.

The first weeks at the fort were occupied with construction of a number of two-wheeled cage carts to hold the beasts we intended to round up. Lumber for these vehicles was shipped in from Iol Caesaria by means of a prior agreement with Publius. Quintus was forced to lend his slaves to work and his soldiers to oversee the labor.

I spent long hours in the sun. Sweat drenched me while I pegged planks together with a mallet. I worked as hard as the Numidians, provoking contemptuous remarks from the legionnaires, who always managed to find the nearest patch of shade. But physical exhaustion helped me forget the past. And Acte.

I'd abandoned any hope of going after unicorns. None existed anywhere in this yellow waste. Upon completion of the carts we were ready to begin trapping less mythical animals. I held several conferences with Quintus. He was barely civil. I kept my temper in rein. We set out at last on our first expedition, after boar.

The company included myself, Quintus, six legionnaires and ten Numidians, with the tall, mahogany-shouldered Ptolemy one of them. Carrying provisions in three cage carts, we rode in three others drawn by oxen. Straight out into the blazing waste we went.

Three days westward from the fort, the land changed from treeless sand to thinly forested slopes leading up to distant blue mountains. In camp at night we heard animals screeching and crashing in the brush. That night again I noticed, as I had before, that the other blacks treated Ptolemy with deference. They paid heed to what he said when they gathered around their own fire at night.

In the morning we scouted a twisting watercourse, long since dried up. At its end we stationed four Numidians with a large and closely woven hemp net. The net stretched from wall to wall in the gully. The remainder of the party journeyed up to the head of the watercourse.

One of the Numidians ranged ahead. He returned to report in labored Greek that he'd sighted a small herd of boars. Stripped to our waists, black and white men alike crept in a loose half-circle through the brush. Each man was armed with a spear, except for Quintus, who also carried his lash tied to the broad belt of his clout.

The black Ptolemy began to smile as we bellied through the undergrowth and peered out at the herd of tusked beasts. Ptolemy was clearly in his element now.

Quintus stood up and parted the brush. He sniffed the wind, then raised his spear.

"Drive them!"

Yelling and screaming, we broke from the brush and charged the boars. Frightened, they stampeded. Their hooves raised clouds of dust as they plunged down the nearest escape route, the watercourse.

Two Numidians followed along the bottom of the gully. The rest of us took the faster way, racing ahead along the high banks. The boars appeared around a bend, tiny eyes fired with fright. The netmen just below us braced their legs for the onslaught. When the first boar struck, it would take great effort to keep the nets from slipping. If we trapped six of the herd, we would do well.

Tusks flashing, the first boar dove into the net. The fury of his charge jerked the strands violently. The other boar piled into the first, squealing, kicking sensing the trap.

All of a sudden Quintus went white. He leaped and skidded down the gully wall.

"Hold on, you black scum! Hold on tighter! They'll slip underneath—"

One of the animals gouged the earth savagely with his tusks. He rammed his head beneath the net and raced through.

Then he wheeled, pawing, ready to charge and kill. A Numidian on the net was thrown off balance by the lunging of the other animals. A large section of the net sagged.

I plunged down the slope after Quintus. He cursed wildly, uncoiling his whip without thinking. "Witless fool!" he screamed, cracking the lash against the spine of the black who'd stumbled.

I pulled at his arm. "We'll lose the whole lot if you persist—"

He flung me off, temper frayed by the heat. His arm rose and fell, rose and fell. Spittle flew from his lips. He bawled senseless words about teaching a lesson. Dust swirled as the other Numidians struggled to hold the net taut and restrain the frantic animals.

We were in real danger now. The boars gored one another, maddened, wanting to escape. The other soldiers and slaves rushed down into the watercourse to help, making an even worse tangle.

The black under Quintus' lash was on his knees. The strands of net had fallen from his hands. One of the legionnaires made the mistake of trying to drive his spear into a boar's withers. He miscalculated, raking the animal lightly. The wound made the beast even more furious. The soldier fled, shrieking. The terrorized Numidians did the same.

A black died when a boar crashed into him from behind, driving tusks through the man's bowels. Trembling, Quintus coiled his lash. Then he began to tremble. Another boar was heading for him.

Though I would sooner have let him die, I dove against him, knocking him out of the way.

Screams of human and animal pain filled the watercourse now. Quintus and I tumbled out of the way as the boar lunged on. But the situation had gotten worse.

Every last animal had broken free of the tangled net, running amok, killing any who got in their path.

CHAPTER XIII

———◦———

QUINTUS STUMBLED to his feet. Another legionnaire pitched over, gored to death on plunging tusks.

"Up the bank!" Quintus shrieked. "Up the bank and save yourselves!"

"We can't let the animals escape—" I began. "Be damned to your animals! I'm out for myself." Quintus ran.

Then I saw he was right. To stay in the watercourse was suicidal. The remaining soldiers and Numidians were scrambling up the slopes. I began climbing after them.

Then I heard a shrill cry. I whirled. The black Ptolemy had stumbled starting up the other wall of the gully. His heels were meshed in the strands of the net. The harder he struggled, the worse he became tangled.

A boar raced by, scented him, stopped. The boar snuffled and grunted. Ptolemy seized a large rock to defend himself. The boar's tusks lowered, flashing in the sunlight. At the same time Ptolemy hurled the rock, and missed.

The boar charged.

It was a long, risky throw. I had no choice but to try. My arm whipped back, then forward. The iron spear head flashed through the air.

The boar leaped up, kicking. The head was imbedded in its neck.

The animal fell a few paces from where Ptolemy lay. A moment later he managed to extricate himself. The boar tumbled over on its back, dead.

From the rim of the watercourse the Numidians were pelting down stones, driving off the stampeding animals. The big black smiled at me across the gully, and dipped his head in a kind of salute. Then he threw off the last clinging strands of hemp and raced up the slope to join his fellows.

Presently the beasts were all gone. We clambered down to reclaim the net and the dead. One black, one white. Quintus would have increased the score, as he told me at the night's campfire.

"You should have let the big one die, Cassius. We'd be better off."

Over his shoulder I saw Ptolemy watching. And listening too? I said, "The others seem to look up to him, and respect him. We might not be able to operate so well without him."

"He's a troublemaker," Quintus muttered. "Doesn't take easily to the Roman yoke and never has. Oh, he's one of the leaders, all right. One day he'll cause us real harm."

"Since you fear him so much," I replied, "why don't you kill him yourself?"

Quintus merely glared.

Next morning he insisted we return to the fort. I took the opposite position. We had a loud argument. At the end of it, I invoked threats of the Emperor's wrath and persuaded him to continue the hunt. And our next attempt to gather the boars fared better.

At the end of three exhausting days we trekked back to the fort with ten savage specimens, plus a dozen monkeys we trapped by putting out bowls of wine at night. The monkeys crept into the darkened camp, drank the wine, fell down in a daze and were thrust into cages.

Upon our return we put the animals in the cage carts outside the walls. I was not happy to be back. Locusta and Quintus whispered together at dinner like long-separated lovers. Once I noted them studying me with contemptuous expressions. For no reason, seeing them with their heads together frightened me.

One night after moonrise I lay dozing in my stifling room. A noise awakened me. I sat up instantly and reached for the dagger I kept beside me at all times. A heavy hand slapped across my lips, cutting off my air. I brought the dagger around to strike at my attacker's backbone. Another hand knocked the blade aside. Then I glimpsed white teeth in the moon, and ebony skin.

"Ptolemy!"

"I am your friend, master. Don't strike at me." He spoke in rumbling Greek.

I gasped for air. "You gave me quite a start."

He hunkered down beside me. "On the hunt, I would have spoken to you except that I don't want to feel the centurion's whip until the proper time. The time when I can turn it back upon him." He paused. "I came to thank you for my life, master."

I wandered to the window, pointing. "How did you get in here? There are soldiers walking the parapets."

"Cattle. Asleep on their feet. I came over the roof." He hesitated again, as if embarrassed. "They talk about your wish to discover a marvelous beast, master. The unicorn."

"Yes. The Emperor Nero wants a cup made from its horn." Briefly I explained the futile mission upon which I had been sent, including the legend of how poison foamed in such a cup. "That's why I'll probably become another Quintus in a few years, Ptolemy. I can't return to Rome unless I have the horns."

Ptolemy pondered. Legionnaires cried the hour on the wall. The black said at last, "I will help, master. I owe you my life."

"A kind thought. But there are no unicorns anywhere on earth."

He smiled slyly. "Not unless a man makes one himself."

"What? You're talking nonsense."

"No, master. I will show you. I will come here again tomorrow, after moonset. We will go. Half a night's march."

"Go where? What's this all about? Ptolemy, come back—"

But he was gone, slipped out the window and disappearing upward, a black wraith. I shook my head and returned to my pallet. He was as addled as the rest.

Ptolemy returned the next night as he had promised. He would say nothing more about what he had in mind, but because I was curious, I went with him. We slipped down through the tower and left the fort with no trouble. Often I spent whole days lounging in my rooms when the sun was too hot for comfort, so I was fairly certain my absence would not arouse suspicion. I followed Ptolemy across the sandy waste, convinced we were both on some kind of idiot's errand.

After a smoldering dawn we reached a stretch of hilly, thinly forested ground that stretched westward for several stadia. Ptolemy led me to the crest of a low hill. On our stomachs we crawled to the edge. There below I saw strange beasts grazing.

They resembled young horses, grayish, and marked all over with black. The bucks sported pairs of long, nearly straight horns of an iridescent grayness. Ptolemy's grin grew wide as he watched me.

"What are they?" I asked.

"Oryx is the Greek name. A kind of antelope. Have they never been seen in Rome?"

"Not to my knowledge. But they have two horns, not one in the center of the head, like a unicorn must have."

"Two horns," he said slowly, "can be made one."

"Explain yourself."

"The horns, master, are soft when the bucks are young. Once, before the Legions took me in chains from my village far from here, I saw a buck whose horns had been twisted somehow, twined and grown together into a single long spike. Perhaps he tangled them in a tree, I do not know. I only thought—"

When I was silent, his face grew sad. "A poor thought, it seems. I am sorry."

"Don't be. I'm thinking."

At first it seemed utter foolishness. But I had known so little hope in such a long time, I was willing to risk anything. I said at last, "We have come this far. What's to prevent us from trying, anyway?"

His face lighted. "Nothing, master."

As the morning advanced we used ropes we had brought from the fort to snare a quartet of the young bucks before the rest of the fleet herd raced away in fright. After tethering the bucks to some scrub branches, we cut strands of rope and bound the soft, porous pairs of horns together tightly. The oryx were gentle when caught. They submitted to the binding with only a few stamps of their hooves and a sad roll of their dull, big eyes.

We cut branches, working until the daylight faded. A bond of silent friendship strengthened between us as we labored side by side. Next morning we scouted the nearby hillsides until we found a steeply walled little valley where a pool of tepid water bubbled from the parched earth. Using the branches we had cut, we built a crude pen around the water, enclosing the four bucks. We stood back to admire our handwork.

"The growing will take many months," Ptolemy informed me. "But if no one comes to disturb them—"

"This place is a wilderness. And we should be able to divert Quintus elsewhere on our forays. He's not very eager as it is. Time—well, that's a commodity of which I have an ample supply. I'll be in Africa the rest of my days if the horns grow separately."

To allay suspicion, we spent the rest of the day locating the wandering oryx herd, cutting from it two handsome, fully grown bucks and a pair of does. We roped the animals on lines and set out for the fort.

At long last my step had a spring to it. I began to see a rough, arid beauty in the sandhills, rather than sheer desolation. Ptolemy chanted under his breath as we moved along, some ancient, crooning melody of the victorious hunter. For all his natural cleverness he was an ingenuous as a child at times, and pleased with my pleasure.

Titus Quintus accepted my account of an impromptu trapping expedition readily enough, though he issued a surly warning that I'd best select another black for a guide. Ptolemy would probably cut my throat one day when I wasn't watching. Inwardly I laughed at Quintus' statement.

Then a thought struck me. How was Quintus different from the man I had been back in Rome? Was I that man still? I found no ready answers in the days ahead.

Those days became months. The months turned into a year filled with marching and searching and trapping. We ranged out far after lions. These we trapped by digging a pit with a high wood fence around it. We roped a lion calf in the pit. Hearing the calf bellow in fear, the lioness would slink out of the dark, jump the fence and tumble into the trap.

We were too far north for elephants or leopards, but the number of cages outside the fort multiplied during the months, until the desert station rang with monkey squeals and boar bellows and lion growls day and night. Quintus professed loudly and repeatedly that he was going out of his mind smelling animal dung.

Now and again he received a letter from the first centurion. Upon learning that matters were going well at his post, the officer had elected to prolong his holiday on the coast indefinitely. When the decurion Publius decided to inspect the fort again, the centurion would return, but not before. Being of lesser rank, Quintus had no choice but to submit to the orders.

About every second month Ptolemy and I made a quick and secret overnight journey to the secluded valley. There, upon the heads of the penned oryx, a miracle was taking place.

Ptolemy bound the thongs tighter at each visit. At the year's end the grown bucks spouted long single spikes, the double horns wrapped round and round each other.

The horns were a mite suspiciously thick and forked at the base when one looked close. But from a distance they were the unicorns of legend come to life. I was gratified that the beasts didn't appear to have suffered greatly. They had waxed fat and healthy.

Through all this Locusta was a virtual stranger. She barely nodded when we met over the night meal. It was no longer a secret in the fort that she was sharing her bed with Quintus. Since I exhibited no sign of jealousy, he probably thought it futile to bait me on the subject. As a result his manner became slightly more cordial.

One night Ptolemy and I were returning from our latest inspection of the false unicorns. The black—whom I had grown to regard as my only friend—paused in our march.

"The fort lies just beyond the next dune, Cassius." He had ceased addressing me as master long ago. "I wish I could let the remainder of our trek pass peacefully. But I cannot."

I sat down to rest in the purple twilight shade of a dune. "What's troubling you? It seems to me Quintus has grown more tractable lately. The whip comes out less often. Locusta keeps him busy."

Ptolemy traced an odd design, much like a skull, in the sun-down-reddened sand. "That is true, Cassius." Slowly his head came up, the great black eyes luminous and sad. "They are plotting against you."

I laughed. "Locusta and the centurion? Plotting to do what?"

"I cannot say. I do not know. But my people, walking silently, hear many things in the fort. A word or a whisper. Be warned."

I had an urge to laugh a second time. Ptolemy's intent expression held me back. I shrugged. "There's little I can do except continue to keep my knife handy."

The black threw down a handful of sand. "I have been told you have some influence with the great Roman in the port city who rules this country. Quintus is a bad man. Cruel. You have seen how he beats my people for nothing. Speak to the great Roman. Write him. Have Quintus taken away."

"I can't do that," I explained. "The laws under which Quintus and the soldiers govern here allow them to whip slaves. I admit Quintus abuses the law, but—"

"Law!" Ptolemy raged. "Evil law, I say."

"Yes, I agree with you. Still, my hands are tied."

Ptolemy stared balefully. "It will not be borne forever, Cassius. My people bow their heads and take the lash, but they know the laws are evil. The Empire too, for allowing such laws. I have some status among my own kind. I hear their evening talk. The bad devils live in them. They are growing rebellious. Since the first centurion left, things have grown worse because of Quintus. One day—or one night—one lash too many may fall. The bad devils would break loose. Then, I could not promise to control my people."

The threat sent a shudder racing through me. "Perhaps I wouldn't blame your people. But giving cruelty in return for cruelty is no answer."

"People who are treated like beasts begin to think as beasts."

"That is so. I only wish there were something I could do. But there isn't."

Then my prompt agreement with his ideas began to puzzle me. I wondered whether my nature had undergone some subtle change. Many months ago in Rome I would have regarded his words as an insult to the Emperor's power.

"There is one thing you can do, Cassius," Ptolemy told me. "I repeat it now. Be warned." He glanced at the darkening sky. "Best that we go now."

The uprising which he prophesied failed to materialize in the next few months. The number of cage carts ranged outside the fort increased every week. I had almost forgotten Ptolemy's obscure warnings by the time a year and a half, reckoned since my departure from Ostia, passed.

I had decided that my menagerie was satisfactory enough for me to begin thinking seriously of a return to Rome. In connection with this, I went by myself one day to check upon the four false unicorns. To my surprise I discovered one missing.

The pens had not been smashed. The tether ropes had been neatly cut, not torn. The other three looked healthy as ever. But one was gone nonetheless.

At the fort I sought out Ptolemy. I found him in one of the huts clustered below the wall, hard by the squealing, growling animals in their pens. He had daubed his face with some ocher stuff, painting on streaks and spots suggesting a ritual design that was part of whatever religion it was that he followed. The hut was dim, stinking of raw meat and human urine.

With his heel Ptolemy quickly erased strange signs he'd been drawing in the dirt with an ocher-painted stick. I did not accuse him of tampering with the unicorns. I merely reported what I had discovered in the secret valley, then said, "Have you any idea of who might have visited there? Or why?"

"Bedouin slave dealers travel through these parts now and then. Perhaps they took one of the beasts to sell at an Egyptian mart, or even in Damascus."

"If they stole one, why didn't they take all four?"

The exact translation of his reply in Greek was, "I am not prepared to say, Cassius."

Which either meant that he did not know, or that he did know but was literally unready to give me an answer then. For what reason, I could not decide. His gaze was blank, inscrutable. I believed that he did know something, but since the rest of the unicorns were unharmed, I decided not to press him on the point. I departed, thinking he would probably tell me in his own time if he wanted me to know.

Later that same night, I realized he was cleverer than I gave him credit for being. Yet this knowledge was imparted to me in a way that nearly cost me my life.

I was late to enter the dining hall. I had taken a long nap at sundown. All the legionnaires had eaten and gone. Only a few slaves remained, and Locusta and Quintus.

I saluted them in a perfunctory way and took my place upon the couch. A slave slipped a cup onto the ivory taboret alongside. It was strange cup, of porous gray stuff with a swirled, twisted texture.

Locusta stiffened visibly. She darted a glance at Quintus. Being rather drunk, he merely blinked. Suspicion gnawed me.

"What is that strange drinking horn there beside you, Cassius?" Locusta demanded. She rose, to come nearer and examine it. By the light of smoky torches in cressets her gown showed its shabbiness. Her hair was practically white now. In the wake of my suspicion came hideous understanding. A black slave leaned down to pour wine as I answered, "Why, it looks like an ordinary cup, Locusta. Of unusual material but a cup for all that."

Some premonition of danger narrowed her kohled eyelids. She hissed Quintus' name. He sat up, his sword clanking against his thigh. Ruby wine streamed from the slave's jar, fell through space in a glittering stream and dashed into the cup.

The contents of the cup began to foam.

I knew fear then. The evil stuff spilled up and over the cup's rim, trickled down and ate into the ivory of the taboret with little smoking-acid tongues. I was watching some kind of hellish miracle, and my voice cracked.

"I know what it is, Locusta, though I don't know where it came from. A unicorn cup. Fuming and bubbling and—"

I leaped up, overturning the couch. I pulled my dagger out from the fumes from the cup swirled around me, noxious, sickly-sweet. My voice rose to a shout.

"—and full of poison."

CHAPTER XIV

LOCUSTA CAST her eyes down and composed her face. When she glanced at me again a moment later, the jade pupils betrayed nothing. Not guilt. Not even shock. Only the restless crawl of the ringed fingers of her right hand against her thigh gave her away.

Titus Quintus was less sophisticated. He hauled out his sword. I moved back a step. The black slaves ran toward the shadowy corners of the hall.

Quintus whipped his sword down, spilling the cup end over end. The wine sank into the pores of the stone floor, smoking and burning.

Quintus glowered at me. "How long have you known?"

Locusta made a sharp gesture, bangles rattling. "Be silent! He knows nothing."

Drink had loosened Quintus' tongue. "He knows enough to stage this little trick to unmask us. You stupid bitch! You went ahead without consulting me."

"Idiot, *idiot!*" Locusta spat back, still trying to dissemble. "I didn't—"

"You poisoned his wine the way we planned but you didn't so much as warn me! I told you I wanted to be ready when it happened." A loose, uneasy laugh wrenched his mouth. "I can understand your difficulties with the lady, Cassius. She's unpredictable, isn't she?"

White-faced, Locusta struck his cheek. "Gods! You're worse than those black lumps you drive with a whip. I put nothing in the wine. Do you understand what I'm saying? Nothing! *Nothing!*"

A red fire of anger consumed me. I gestured to the spilled and smoking dregs. "It doesn't matter, centurion. What matters is the intent. One way or another, you planned for me to die."

"All right, we did. The suggestion, the plan, was hers." He smiled. "I wasn't unwilling, though."

"What did she offer you in return? Besides the welcome of her dirty body?"

Locusta stalked me, age showing in the hundreds of tiny wrinkles on her face, and in the sagging little folds of flesh hanging along her chin. I wondered how I ever could have touched this mad slut.

She said, "Enjoy your clever jibes, Cassius. Taunt us. Call us names while you still hold the center of the stage. In another moment it'll be taken from you." She pointed to the glittering flat of Quintus' sword. "By that."

The centurion seemed to throw off his drunken lethargy. "I'll tell you what she offered, Cassius, since it's gone this far. The full profits of that collection of caterwauling animals outside, once you were dead. Some cosmetics, a few veils. Locusta thought she could return to Rome safely in the role of my wife. I planned to say I'd been ordered by you to deliver the animals to the Cassian School, the hour you died on a hunting expedition, of a fever. I would collect necessary shipping costs, fees and delivery expenses. We intended to live handsomely on the results of your labor."

The sword lifted, flicking across my chin. I felt a warm trickle of blood run down my throat.

"Now you've spoiled everything, haven't you? Well, I can't permit you to remain alive. Carry tales to the decurion. Actually, I'll enjoy this. You've treated me like filth since the day you arrived."

He drew a breath. "Ready?"

I pulled off amulets and rings to free my dagger hand. "Ready to take you with me."

"Do it slowly, Quintus," Locusta whispered. "I beg you—slowly. I've waited so long. Endured the sickening sight of him, just awaiting this moment."

"That's why you came all this way with me? To kill me?"

Her green eyes laughed, mindless, mad. "Yes."

Quintus unfastened the throat clasp of his short dress cloak. He let the garment fall. To my back I heard sibilant voices. The blacks, frightened. The centurion shouted to them in Greek.

"This is a personal quarrel. The first one of you to stir will die the way this man's going to die."

Pretending to glance down to brush aside the cloak which had fallen by the toe of his boot, he suddenly kicked out hard, sending the cloak flying. Its muffing folds struck me in the face.

I slashed out blindly with the dagger. He cursed, stumbled, and another dining couch crashed over. By that time I had ripped off the cloak.

I faced him, the two of us no further apart than a man is tall. Quintus lifted his sword and drove it at me again.

I didn't dodge fast enough. The point sliced a long cut down my forearm. At once Quintus dashed in, chopping back and forth.

Lunging and ducking to avoid the blade's crisscross sweep, I had a sideways glimpse of a legionnaire at the hall entrance. Gaping, the man was rushing forward to assist the centurion. Locusta motioned him back. The man retreated. He took one look at the sweating faces of the Numidian slaves and fled, shouting an alarm.

Quintus' sword slashed the air above me. Again I ducked. Again. He was puffing, but enjoying the sport.

"Can't—you—reach me—with the—toy knife—Beast-man?"

One dagger throw might finish him, but the knife was not balanced for throwing. I leaped to a table top, then down the other side. Quintus over-extended himself. He rolled his right shoulder ahead of his body, driving the sword out straight to skewer me. I sidestepped, brought the dagger down and through his hand.

The blade cut clean through muscle above his wrist, glanced off bone and embedded in the table. Quintus gave a bellowing scream, jerking like a speared bear. By main force he tore the knife from the table by wrenching his arm. With his left hand he pulled the blade from his maimed flesh and flung it away. The knife sailed through smoky torchlight and clattered against the far wall.

Quintus' right arm hung limp and dripping. He quickly shifted his sword to his left. With lumbering steps he rounded the table.

"No, Cassius. I have no sword arm. The other will do, against nothing."

I raced for the wall and the dagger. He hacked down and across his torso, right to left, with terrible swiftness. The blade sliced my left calf. I tumbled and struck my face on the stones, my breath knocked out.

Pain from the hacked leg shot all through my body, almost throwing me into a faint. Feebly I tried to drag myself toward the dagger I saw gleaming in the shadows at the base of the wall. Oaths, alarms sounded in the fort as the legionnaire summoned others to the struggle. I tried to rise. Quintus was coming up fast behind me.

I couldn't crawl. I couldn't reach the knife in time. A smashing weight drove me back against the stones, making my head whirl with dizziness.

Quintus knelt on me. He shoved his right knee into the small of my back once, then once more. He panted, "The hare's caught. The hare's fairly caught. Wriggle, hare. Wriggle a moment more—"

Locusta screamed, "Don't prolong it, Quintus, Strike!"

Quintus twisted around. "I thought you preferred—"

"I prefer him dead! Kill him, Quintus. *Kill him!*"

The keen of that maniacal voice concealed a rustling near the wall. Quintus pressed me down with his knee while he lifted the sword in his left hand. He touched the point gently to the base of my neck, preparing the last thrust. Then he saw the black man.

The slave had crept along the wall and scooped up my knife. He threw it quick and true. The metal rang on the stones in front of my face. I seized the shaft. The point of Quintus' sword dug into my skin as I wrenched over and rammed the dagger up through the bottom of his chin, to the hilt.

The eyes of the centurion flew open. The sword dropped from his limp fingers. With a hysterical yell I rolled from under him, driven out of my senses by the bright blood gushing like a fountain from between his rigid lips.

I heard the blacks talking gutturally. Down a corridor, soldiers approached. The slaves swung shut the door of the great hall and dropped the bar in place, many of them smiling.

The legionnaires hammered spear butts on the thick door timbers. "Ho! Quintus? Let us in! What's happening in there?"

Dazed, I hunted for Locusta. She stood near the overturned unicorn's cup. Tears made the kohl around her eyes run, streaking her cheeks with black. I said, "Now it's your turn, sweet lady."

She let out a scream of such unearthly fright that I froze. She screamed and kept on screaming, tearing her own hair, rending her garments.

It is an ugly thing to watch a mind die while the body lives. Her mind died then. The last light of sense flickered out in her jade eyes. She began to weep, harder and harder, and befoul herself.

The blacks grew hushed. I couldn't bear to watch her caper there like some ghastly doll, now giggling, now shrieking the vilest obscenities. I averted my face and retched.

When I looked back, an arras behind the dining couches was fluttering. Locusta's wailing died in the distance.

A pool of blood spread out around my right foot. I signaled to the Numidians, and said in Greek, "One of you help me stand. Help me or I can't—"

The room revolved. The paving stones flew up against my face. Quick darkness covered me over.

A dreadful pain numbed my right leg from the hip downward. Human fingers increased the pain.

They pressed, exploring. Then they knotted something tight around my leg, bringing me fully awake with a shriek on my lips.

The hall was as before. Quintus lay open-mouthed, my dagger sticking from the underside of his jaw. All the torches had burned down. Yet the ceiling vaults were suffused with a wavering reddish glare.

The light leaped and danced. Horrified, I realized it came not from within the hall, but from outside. Outcries and sounds of struggle drifted through the slot windows, and curling smoke. A black shape bent over me, binding the calf muscle. Ptolemy.

"Be still," he cautioned. "A moment more and we can go."

"Go where?" I wheezed. "In Mars' name, what's happening outside?"

"When you killed the centurion, that was excuse enough. My people have brought forth spears long hidden in buried pits. By morning there won't be a stone of this fort standing. There. Try to stand. If you cannot, lean on me."

I did as he ordered. I bit down on my lip when my right leg nearly buckled. Ptolemy's chest shone with the sweat of fear as he led me to the arras through which Locusta had vanished.

Out of one low window I glimpsed the courtyard in flames. Black shapes leaped around another fire built in the middle. Other slaves supported two ends of a long pole from which a legionnaire hung trussed, howling as his skin melted and fell in waxy gobs into the fire below.

"Wait, Ptolemy. Since I killed Quintus, why must we run like this? What do we have to fear?"

"Much, Cassius. Your skin is the same color as the centurion's. What you did to him would make a great difference if my people were in the hands of the good devils. But tonight, after many years, the bad devils are loose. Tomorrow they would be sorry for torturing you to death. But tonight, as I say, with blood lust so high, it's not safe to stay. Now you might be safe. In an hour they may be so drunk with killing you wouldn't have a chance."

Unearthly shrieks ripped the air. One of the fortress towers toppled in flaming ruin. Ptolemy hurried me along a damp, dark passageway, saying, "As soon as I learned what happened in the hall, I came to help. The same way you helped me once."

"And the cup?" I panted as we stumbled down narrow stairs. "That was your work?"

"Yes. Careful, now. Take the turn on the right. It's an old passageway that leads out through the wall."

While we rushed on, the dim screams of the slaughter echoing behind us, Ptolemy explained how he'd stolen one oryx from its pen, slain it and fashioned the cup with his own hands. He had put a powder in the cup. Not poison, but a special kind of crushed earth, that foamed and fulminated in contact with any liquid. The powder was supplied by the village wizard.

Ptolemy had concocted the scheme not to place me in danger but to give me a pretext for reporting Quintus to the decurion.

A gust of cool air brushed my face, signifying the tunnel's end. He finished his account quickly.

"All my people knew Quintus and the woman plotted against you. I am not a wise man or I would have realized they would fall upon you when exposed. I didn't plan for Quintus to die or, even worse, for his death to give my people courage enough to dig up the spears."

We reached the mouth of the passage. It opened into a narrow drainage ditch below a deserted section of the fort wall. To my right I saw the precious cage carts, many aflame. Black figures danced around them.

Lions wailed in mortal pain. Monkeys screamed. The burning bars of one cart buckled and three antelope leaped out, their pelts afire, strange moving torches.

The blacks gave chase, slaughtering the animals with spear and sword and club. A lioness tried to escape her cage. The wooden bars snapped under the impact of her thrashing. As she jumped to freedom she impaled herself on the broken stakes.

From above us a legionnaire plummeted off the wall and smashed against the earth. Another body followed. Both men were naked, their heads and genitals gone.

"I can't leave the animals to die," I shouted hysterically. "After all these months of work—"

"Do you want the animals or your life?" I could only shake my head dazedly. Ptolemy seized my arm. "Cassius, wake up or we're both finished! You still have the three unicorns. Weeks ago I hid one empty cage cart and an ox, a ways from here. I never dreamed this night would come so soon when I did it. Hurry now, we must go quickly."

"These are your people, Ptolemy. If you come with me—"

He shook his head, eyes shining sadly in the hellglare. "With the bad devils running loose, I can't go back either. I put myself on your side, the Roman side, helping you. Cassius, I beg you as your friend—no more talk."

"All right," I said feebly. "Which way?"

He led me away from the ditch under the wall. On the crest of the first dune we turned. There before us, the fort blazed up, alight from corner to corner. And all the cage carts were burning too.

Tears streaked Ptolemy's face. A part of him was still primitive. I think he wanted to be with his people in their hour of vengeance. But he said nothing.

Abruptly I picked out a woman's figure fleeing along the parapet from a tower. Men gave chase. The woman's hair was afire, streaming out behind her, redder than it had ever been in life. A spear in her backbone doubled her. Then another. Then two more.

With four spears piercing her body, Locusta fell into the dark, her hair a red banner of her destruction.

Watching her die, I felt nothing.

"Ptolemy? I have seen enough."

We turned our faces to the black night of the desert.

CHAPTER XV

LEAN, FAMISHED and baked nearly as black as my tall Numidian companion, I reached Iol Caesaria after almost thirty days of wandering.

Out of the carnage of the night the fort was destroyed, we had salvaged the trio of oryx antelope. The gray gentle beasts rode placidly in the cage cart Ptolemy had hidden away, and all in all, fared better than we did on the exhausting journey.

We screeched to a stop at the gate of the estate of Cornelius Publius. His manservants started to stone us away as mountebanks. I raised a row. Presently the decurion himself appeared, backed by soldiers. They drove off the crowds that had collected once we reached the city highroad with our marvelous cargo peering from behind thong-and-pole bars.

Publius made us welcome. I slept almost two days, bathed for three hours and gorged myself with food. Publius already knew about the loss of the fort. Legion scouts had reported its destruction and the subsequent fight of all the Numidians. A full cohort had been dispatched into the desert to round up the renegades, a task Publius admitted was hopeless.

Ptolemy smiled in agreement. Publius shook his head sadly time and again as I explained the real cause of the massacre—the malfeasance of Titus Quintus. He grew plum-faced when promising that the lazy first centurion, still idling away his time at a resort somewhere down the shore, would soon reap a whirlwind out of the seeds of his indolence.

My absence from Rome had now lasted about two and a half years. Like a man emerging from the vale of the dead, I listened eagerly to the news of what had been happening. The news, however, was similar to the kind I'd brought Publius—disheartening.

"Nero has all but seized complete power. The Senate has no real authority any longer. Treason trials for those who speak a single word of criticism against the regime have begun. The latest dispatch said that Seneca was requested by Nero to retire. You know what that sort of request means. Comply, or you'll meet some faceless assassin on a dark street. Well, Seneca is completely out of it now. Living in seclusion. Seeing no visitors. The Emperor also managed to rid himself of Octavia at last. He divorced her for barrenness."

"Is Poppaea Sabina the Empress?"

"Aye. Nero married her precisely twelve days after Octavia was banished to Campania. Oh, Cassius, there's no end to the evils of the reign. The Praetorian Prefect, Burrus, is dead. Ostensibly of a mysterious seizure which confounded all the physicians. Probably it was poison. The new Prefect is no bargain, either. A worthless rascal who exploits his position as the most powerful man in Rome."

"Who is it?"

"That ex-criminal Ofonius Tigellinus."

An ominous heaviness clutched my belly. Publius went on.

"Actually there are two Prefects with theoretically equal power. But Faenius Rufus, the former Prefect of the corn supply, is a mere figurehead."

Ptolemy listened patiently to all this, not understanding. I understood all too well. My enemy had reached the acme of power, and would not be happy to see me return.

The decurion also reported that on the island of Albion, which some called Britain, the tribe of Iceni led by their warrior queen, had staged a disastrous revolt against the Legions.

"Fortunately for the sake of our dwindling liberty, the Legions stationed throughout the Empire aren't so enamored of Nero as the Praetorians seem to be. In truth, many of the overseas commanders grumble openly about the lascivious ways of Rome. The drain Nero's excesses make on manpower and money and morale. Thanks to the quick action of one of the generals, Vespasian, the Iceni revolt died a-borning. It also elevated Vespasian to high popularity. Bear his name in mind, Cassius. I hear he's a shrewd customer who appreciates the role the army plays in maintaining the throne. When and if the rotten Julian bloodline ends without issue from Nero—and about time, in my opinion—Vespasian will be a comer."

Later, Ptolemy asked me, "What did all the decurion's talk really mean, Cassius?"

"That evil days have fallen on Rome. And worse ones may be in store so long as Nero lives. Perhaps the evil won't touch us. I'll have high rank when I return."

We saw to it that the three antelope were securely caged. I identified them to all I met as genuine unicorns. I used a sum advanced by Publius to secure passage on a fast ship to Ostia.

As we neared the lovely blue-green coast of Latium, we put in at various ports to discharge cargoes of olives and figs. Word of the unicorns spread inland. Soon great crowds thronged along the beaches, following the ship's progress from afar.

At Ostia I was eager to go ashore as soon as we moored in late afternoon. The captain of the vessel put me off with vague remarks about an inspection of strange animals being required for the sake of public health.

Pacing the deck, I watched a lighter put out from the teeming shore. Shortly the head of the so-called inspector appeared above the rail.

He'd grown older, but the drooping right eyelid and the pearl-hung left ear were all too familiar.

"*Ave*, Cassius!" he greeted, as though we'd never met before. "I am Anicetus, master of the fleet. The regular inspector was detained in town. Here's my certificate of authority to inspect your animal cargo. Now, let's see whether you brought back real unicorns, or only rhinos."

He marched below decks. I followed quickly, not caring for the appearance of the men left behind in the lighter. They were wharf-killers if ever I'd seen one.

In the hold I discovered Anicetus walking round and round the cage, clearly baffled.

"What are these animals?" he demanded. "I've never seen the like before."

"Naturally not," I replied. "They are the beasts the Emperor sent me to Africa to find."

His evil eyelid drooped more than ever. "Unicorns? Come now!"

"That is the name the popular tongue gives them. What their original African name is, I cannot say."

He was visibly upset. "There's a trick somewhere. Where did you locate them?"

"Sir, the Cassian School wouldn't prosper if it revealed trade secrets."

Anicetus snorted. He refused to put his hand in the cage to touch one of the horns as I suggested. I felt he had been ordered to the harbor to prevent my landing. Perhaps Nero thought I might be fool enough to return with rhinos after all.

Anicetus hemmed and hawed about allowing such possible infected creatures ashore. I shouted back, "Infected with what? They're perfectly sound animals. Not a sore or a tick anywhere. I intend to take them into Rome."

"Not until morning," he hedged. "It can't be allowed until then."

"In hell's name why not? I've waited over two years to step on Roman ground again."

He smiled with false cordiality. "Then what's one more night? I must hurry back to the city and present my report. I assure you, Cassius, it will be favorable. On the morrow you have permission to unload. You'll be in Rome by nightfall."

The more I argued, the more adamant he became. At last I gave up. Probably I was too suspicious. The Emperor had un-

doubtedly ordered the bogus inspection to spare himself possible humiliation over some dolt parading rhinos up to the
Palatine.

I drank wine and took my evening meal with the captain of
the ship as the sun sank. I retired to my cabin early, anxious for
sleep and the coming morning.

A raw, ragged shriek of pain dragged me from slumber. "What
the devil—?" I rushed from the cabin clad only in my clout.
Sailors scurried across the deck. The stars glimmered in the
rigging, for it was still the middle of the night. I bumped into
the captain.

"Who cried out?"

"Someone in the hold," he answered sleepily. "I was awakened myself—"

Pushing the sailors out of the way, I hurried to the hold.
Lanterns flickered. A scene of carnage waited there.

One man lay dead, a stranger in shabby seaman's garb. His
belly had been ripped open by a knife. The knife-wielder was
big Ptolemy.

The black was sprawled on the planks, blood pouring from
his ribs where a cut had scored.

He strained up in pain as I bent over him. His black hand
lifted feebly. "Cassius—I tried. I tried well to stop him."

I saw what he meant. In the cage, two of the beasts pawed
fearfully. On the floor, twisted in its own gore and excreta, lay
the third. Its throat had been slashed open.

Tears came unbidden as I bent down beside the big black.

"Who did this, Ptolemy? More than one?"

"No, only—only him, lying there." Though the effort obviously cost him pain, he brought his lips nearer my ear, for his
voice was thin. "Today—I didn't like the looks of that official
or his men. I—have a feeling for people. Today it was a bad
feeling. I came down here with my knife—to sleep. I tried to
stop him—"

"You did stop him, my good friend," I said softly. "The price
wasn't worth it. Rest now. We'll fetch a surgeon. He'll patch

you up soon enough."

His massive black head moved ponderously. "No. I can tell. I'm only sorry I must die so far from my own land. Among white strangers."

His fingers closed over mine. His eyes were full of childlike pain. "But you're no stranger, Cassius. You're my friend, my brother, my—"

He sank back. I held his great black hand until it relaxed after his death-sigh.

I stared at the fine, strong face, tranquil now. I completed his sentence in my mind.

My friend, my brother, my betrayer.

Surely my own success and my wish to rise to riches had taken a heavy toll. Too heavy, I thought.

Furiously I turned upon the captain. "Who is that dead man? A member of the crew?"

"No, sir," he mumbled. "A thief off the Ostia piers, most like. My mate tells me there's a strange skiff moored at the stern. Doubtless the man sneaked aboard. I'll thrash my watchboys for falling asleep, I promise. I don't know what to say about this—"

I looked closely at his rough face. There was no treachery in it. Which was more than I was prepared to say for Anicetus.

Had his inspection, the night's delay and the subsequent arrival of the assassin signified the sly hand of Nero working behind the scenes? I couldn't guess. But I was certain of one thing—I would go straight to the Palatine. I would extract the reward for which good Ptolemy laid down his life.

I snapped at the captain, "You don't know what to say, eh? You careless fool! Fetch a funeral dealer. This man's body is to be conveyed to my home in Rome, the address of which I will shortly provide. I want this cage cleaned out, the body disposed of, and the other two antel—unicorns on the Ostia wharf within an hour. No, not in the morning! To hell with Anicetus and his inspection certificates! At once!"

My shouts prodded him to action. In half the time I'd speci-
fied I stood on the mole while sleepy handlers loaded the cage
aboard a wagon. I climbed up alongside, paid off the help, and
watched the funeral dealer's cart rumble away toward Rome in
the darkness before dawn.

The stars had barely begun to pale. Ostia lay asleep, lightless.
No triumphal processions awaited me on the Via Ostiensis as
the wagon climbed the plain through false dawn.

I talked to the animals now and again, meaningless coos to
soothe them. The air was sharp, cooler than that to which they
were accustomed. Frequently the cart driver made the sign
against the evil eye.

The joke of tricking the Emperor had lost all savor now that
Ptolemy's shroud shone white on the wagon ahead. Vegetable
raisers with their small carts were on their way out of the city.
My driver hailed some of them. They stopped their teams to
gaze in wonder. I was indifferent. What a homecoming!

Death to welcome me. Probably more treachery awaiting
me in my audience with the Emperor. The sight of the familiar
seven hills and the roofs of Rome glittering at the first crack of
daylight showed above the eastern mountains failed to move
me. The only promise the day held out was nightfall. Then,
my mission done, I would call on Serenus and his wife. It would
be painful, but Acte's dear face would not have changed, as so
much else had.

"Beg'ee," sir," the driver wined. "Beg'ee to tell me where we
go with these creatures."

I laughed and huddled deeper in my cloak. "To the Palatine.
To Nero himself."

He gasped and nearly fell from his seat. Then he shook his
head and clucked to his team, convinced I was daft.

By the time we arrived at the gates, the city was waking. As
the daylight increased, crowds gathered and trailed behind the
cart. Here and there someone recognized me and shouted, "*Ave,
Cassius!*"

I stared back in sullen silence. The cart climbed the great hill of the Palatine. It was the smallest of the seven, yet the mightiest, crowned by the great collection of halls, colonnades, palaces, apartments and gardens. Presently I had a company of Praetorians around me. The poor cart driver was nearly out of his wits with astonishment.

We toiled up the Clivus Victoriae, one of the numerous inclined planes built to reach the Imperial buildings at the summit. Ascent of victory indeed! I thought bitterly. Ascent to nothing. Ascent to emptiness. The charm of the eques toga had palled.

But I had sworn a vow. With Ptolemy's murder to spur me, I would claim it. Boldness swept over me suddenly. I was home. I would be rich. I would live a circumspect life and erect a fitting memorial to Ptolemy, who had died for me.

Trumpets hailed our arrival at the entrance to the sprawling Domus Tiberiana. Within the building, a functionary reported, the Emperor was taking his morning bath. He intended to hurry forth to meet his faithful servant Cassius, the man said.

The cart driver helped me uncage the beasts. I tethered them at the entrance to a formal garden. On the garden's far side, under a marble porch, I spied a glitter of gems and ornaments, a party of men rushing along.

White marble walls decorated with gold leaf rose all around. Perfumed fountains splashed. Larks sported in the rising sun. From the summit of the Clivus Victoriae, where the Praetorians had barred the mob with spears, I heard my name being chanted. Across, so it seemed, all the city.

The Emperor appeared on the porch. He hurried over to examine the unicorns, who were blissfully cropping the Imperial turf. I saluted him formally.

Nero appeared older, less regal than before, if he had ever looked regal at all. He wore a morning cloak studded with sapphires. The garment clung damply to the soft folds of his unmanly body. His skin had a gray cast in the sunlight, and his eyes were webbed with the small red lines of indulgence.

As he returned my salute I noticed with a jolt that Tigellinus was among the courtiers who had been in attendance at the Emperor's bath. The Sicilian glared, resplendent in Prefect's armor. I found I could ignore him without a qualm.

"I greet the Emperor," I said loudly. "I bring him the beasts he charged me to find."

Nero threw me a quizzical look. "Frankly Cassius, I'm startled to see you."

"No doubt, sire. The path has been hard, studded with perils."

"And where is your companion?" he asked carefully. "The lady Locusta?"

"Perished, Emperor. In a rebellion of Numidians. There should be a report from your decurion on the matter."

He waved. "I never read reports like that. They leave me no time for pantomimes and such."

Nero walked round and round the two gray beasts. He spent some moments examining the wide plate of forehead horn from which the long spikes sprang. His protuberant eyes slid up to mine, insinuating.

"Truly, Cassius, these are not rhinos. But are they unicorns?"

"Emperor, when I saw them first," I lied carefully, "I judged them to look exactly like unicorns. I brought them back because if unicorns really do exist, these must be the ones."

"And what of the efficacy of the horn cup against poison?" he inquired. "Have you made any tests?"

I hoped I didn't show surprise. What could he possibly know? Nothing, I reasoned. The remark had been casual. I decided not to stir old, cold ashes.

"No, sire, I haven't tested it. I thought you would wish to experiment yourself."

"I shall, I shall indeed." He brushed away perfumed droplets of bath water still clinging to his pale, fatty brow. He frowned. "If I recall aright, Cassius, early reports from the coast said you were returning with three unicorns, not two."

"One took sick and died, Emperor," I replied.

Had he been the motive force behind Anicetus' attempt to foil me? If so, he showed no sign. And my obvious contentment with matters as they stood must have pleased him. He broke into a low chuckle.

"Cassius, I'm delighted to see you're not taking the loss more to heart. Obviously you've had a trying journey. You're very thin."

From behind him, Tigellinus thrust forward. "I demand to know more about Locusta."

Nero giggled. "Always the lover, eh, Prefect? And at such a time! Shame!"

"The matter is contained in the decurion's report," I said, with defiance Tigellinus did not overlook.

The Sicilian's dislike of me was so open and obvious it caused several of the foppish courtiers lounging about to cough and nudge one another in embarrassment. I was afraid Tigellinus might pull some new trick to rob me of my reward, so I hurried on.

"I will be glad to comment upon my wanderings in detail, but at the moment, I would ask the Emperor's leave to claim the boon he promised."

"Oh, yes. That."

The offhand reply made the honor seem as nothing. He laid his pudgy fingers across my left shoulder, meanwhile following a garden songbird with his eyes. He droned away.

"Be it known that I, Nero Caesar Augustus, Princeps and Imperator, do invest and endow this man Cassius—what's your other name?—Cassius Flamma, who is a freed citizen, with the rank of eques, thus entitling him to adorn himself with the ring of gold and the stripe of narrow purple. I enjoin him to recognize that his new rank carries with it not only rights and privileges not afforded lesser men, but also obligations. Henceforth this man shall be addressed by all and sundry as Splendidi Cassius, and shall devote his days to the service and enhancement of his Emperor."

So saying, he took his hand away.

I fell to my knees, because that was the custom. The court-iers cheered and hailed me in bored voices. Only Tigellinus refrained.

Rising, I was surprised when the Emperor said cynically, "See how simple it is, Cassius? The fools in the street think it's some sort of magical rite. Ah, I forgot. You were once one of those—ah, persons—in the street, weren't you?" He beamed. "Now you're one of us. I trust you'll live up to the demands of the rank. Abjure your past in favor of success in the present. Will you?"

While birds sang and fountains tinkled, he thus threatened me with death. If I dared rake up, say, Agrippina's murder, I would be finished. Well, he needn't fear. I was weary of struggles and intrigues.

At the same time I felt oddly deflated. Having risen so far, I felt cheated that there was not more significance to the pro-ceedings. Would there have been for the old Cassius? Or was I the old Cassius still? I sensed not, yet I didn't know exactly how I had changed. Nero addressed me again.

"Well, Splendidi Cassius. I asked you a question."

I bowed my head. "Of course, Emperor. In all things I will obey you."

"Excellent, excellent. In that case your life should be long, honorable and prosperous. One day soon I'll send for you. I want to hear about your adventures, and discuss employing your school at my games. At the moment, though, I have an appointment with the Empress to go over my plans for re-building certain sections of this ugly town upon more pleasing Grecian lines."

He was dismissing me. I saluted and he hurried from the garden, surrounded by his courtiers. Tigellinus threw me a last look to promise that one day we would settle scores.

The Emperor's warning had been clear, if not explicit. My own behavior in the future would spell the difference between a peaceful, secure life and ignominious death. Once again I resolved to ride the flood-swell of Nero's growing status, not struggle against it in any way.

A lackey conducted me to an office where I was detained an hour signing certain documents pertaining to my new rank. Then I descended from the Palatine. Unnoticed, thanks be. The crowds had dispersed.

I might have gone straightaway to purchase a new striped toga. Or I might have gone to the Cassian School to settle accounts with the treacherous Syrax, as I planned to do. Instead, I hired a chair to carry me to the home of Serenus on the Pincian Hill. I found I could not wait till nightfall to make my visit.

The thought of seeing Acte stirred my pulses, even though I knew she was a married woman. To gaze on her would be fulfillment enough.

Where Serenus' house had once stood, desolate black ruins greeted me.

Across the avenue I saw an old gardener. I begged him to tell me about the disaster. He scratched his skull and shrugged.

"A few months back, it was. The house was broken into one night. Looted. Then burned. Rascally thieves! Why, with all the wooden buildings in Rome, it's a wonder the fire didn't spread and cause more damage."

"What happened to Serenus?" I asked, lashed my fear.

"A fine gentleman," sighed the gardener. "Dead. His body was found in the ruins."

"And—his wife? The lady called Acte?"

The gardener hesitated. "Are you a friend of his, sir?"

The words were ashes in my mouth. "I am the eques Cassius Flamma. Answer me."

Hastily he apologized. "Yes, I remember the lady. Lovely. A gentle creature. Your honor, it's assumed she's dead too, since her body was never found. The fire burned a whole day and night. Serenus' remains were barely recognizable. Of course," he added, his eyes watering sympathetically, "the filthy robbers who infest this town are known for carrying off the bodies of poor dead women for unspeakable purposes—"

"Be silent!" I screamed, striking him in the face.

He staggered. "Splendidi, I meant no offense—"

"Splendidi?" I laughed. The wild sound frightened him even more. "Oh, yes. Splendidi indeed. The most splendid of all the damned in Rome."

I left him trembling in his garden. I rushed into the teeming lower streets below the Pincian Hill. Eques Cassius! Splendid Cassius! With death dogging him forever, and a human life the price of every rung of the climb upward.

I would buy my white toga with the narrow purple stripe. I would wear it. But I would know, every remaining moment of my days, that it was an empty honor.

Gaining it, I had lost the one thing in my life that mattered most of all.

Book III

63–64 A.D.
ROME IN FLAMES

CHAPTER XVI

O<small>N THE THIRD</small> day after my return, my temper was sufficiently composed for me to set out for the Cassian School, to
have the very necessary reunion with Syrax.

In the meantime I had reopened my house and seen to the
disposition of Ptolemy's body. I hired tailors to quickly provide me with togas befitting my new rank. At the slave mart I
purchased two stout lads on credit to run my household until
I saw fit to move to larger, more elegant quarters.

One of these slaves I dispatched to Sulla's brother. Deep in
drunkenness and grief on the first night of my homecoming, I
had come up with the idea that possibly Acte might have escaped death in Serenus' house and sought refuge in her former
haunt. The slave came back to say Sulla had not seen Acte
since some time before her marriage, when she left the brothel.
Sulla was certain she was dead.

This heightened my anxiousness for a reckoning with Syrax.
I rode through the streets in a regal litter, runners out ahead
crying, "Make way! Make way for Splendidi Cassius!"

Before we turned in at the Cassian gate, it was evident the
school had prospered. Several adjoining properties had been
purchased and turned into additional dormitories. A much
larger and finer amphitheater had been built to replace the
modest original one. As my bearers put me down, a crowd of
green bestiarii came trotting from their cells to morning prac-

tice. A dusky Egyptian lanista urged them on. The big trainer was capable-looking. He saluted me as an eques. Otherwise I was a stranger to him.

In mounting anger I went to the office. I found Syrax laboring over a letter, scrawling characters in the waxy soot on two hinged wooden tablets. His dark locks shone with some sweetish dressing. Rings decorated his fingers, which now were pudgy. Without seeing his face, it was apparent that he was a great deal heavier, and affluent.

"Is there no one to welcome the owner home?" I said loudly from the door.

His olive head lifted. Surprise and apprehension fleeted across his face a moment, instantly replaced by a merry, mocking smile I knew to be false. Gone was the ferret's cast to his face. His bones were overlaid with the sallow fat of good living. The golden hoop in his ear was his one concession to the past.

"Cassius!" He rushed to embrace me. "I've been looking for you every day."

I shrugged off the cloying touch. "You haven't bothered to send any messages, though."

"Why, I assumed you'd have many affairs that needed attention, and would meet me in your own good time. Come, sit down. We'll have wine. Tell me everything that's happened."

About to clap his hands for a slave, he noticed my stare. "Wine and flattery aren't necessary. Partner." I gave the last word a touch of contempt. "We have other matters to talk about that require a clear head. And, for once, honesty instead of lies." I seized his shoulder. "Explain why you lied about Acte. Why you returned her letters. Bribed the servants in my house to turn her away. Explain before I kill you."

"Cassius, you've lost your mind!" he squealed. He wriggled out of my grip and hurried to the other side of his writing couch. Safe from me, he showed his own anger and envy. "Don't think that just because you're wearing that purple stripe you can treat me like a servant."

"As an eques, partner, I have certain privileges. They include the right to discipline any person of lower rank who offends me."

"Lay one hand on me and I'll—" He bit his lip, masking his rage with another condescending smile. "Cassius, Cassius. Why are we quarreling? I don't see that you have any cause to accuse me of wrongdoing. You told me yourself, that very first night when you swore your vow to Tigellinus, that you wanted success above everything."

"I never meant I'd sanction lying and treachery and—"

"Don't evade me!" he shouted. "You *said* it. Nothing would stand in your way. Nothing. Very well. The girl stood in your way. What I did was prompted by your own words." His eyelids drooped. "Or can't you recall back that far? To the time when you were a common man like the rest of us? Does a high rank fade a man's memory?"

The old trap closed. My anger drained away. "All right, Syrax. I remember."

"Therefore you can't blame me one bit for what I did."

"No," I returned. "I suppose I can't. I can only blame myself."

Syrax was obviously pleased at scoring the point. He ordered wine. What had possessed me to ally myself with this shallow, devious man? An image of the blackened ashes of a great house flitted in my mind, bringing fresh suspicion.

"I trust you know, Syrax, that Acte died with Serenus when robbers overran their house. Further, I trust that's all you know about it."

His face was startled, then ugly. "Will you stoop to accusing me of murder?"

I shrugged. "I only asked a question. How much do you know about it?"

"No more than anyone else! I never saw Acte again after your departure for Africa. Did the sun fry your brains there? You must be mad to even suggest I'd sink to such tactics. And for what? How would it profit me, may I ask? I don't need to rob anyone. We have a going operation here."

He strode to the window. With a flamboyant gesture he indicated the sunlit amphitheater where the pupils were working out with a tame leopard.

"During your absence the Emperor has taken to staging longer and more elaborate games. We're getting our share of his trade. So what need do I have to rob Serenus or you or anyone?"

Deflated, I took a seat and reached for the wine a servant had fetched in.

"None, Syrax. That's obvious. I spoke in anger."

"That's right, you did. But I'm not one to hold a grudge."

And once more he was grinning his old grin, as if a mere quirk of the mouth could wipe out the past. Still, there was no point in haranguing with a man who overcame all obstacles with honeyed words poured out in a torrent. The torrent increased as he drank.

"I want to hear the whole story of what happened in Africa."

"Time for that later. What about the profits here?"

"Thanks to my management, Cassius, the school is on a sounder footing than ever. We have talent far better than any in the early days. Big, strapping brutes. Even if they don't fight, they make fine lion fodder."

"Who are you talking about?"

"The Christians, naturally."

"Christians? The name sounds familiar. But I can't place—"

"That depraved provincial sect from Judea. The one whose prophet was nailed up on a cross as a criminal a few years back."

"Oh yes."

"The members at the moment are mostly Jews, but it's rumored a few Romans have been converted."

"I know nothing about their beliefs or teachings. How do they manage to end up here?"

Syrax chuckled. "Who cares about their beliefs so long as they continue to be sentenced to us? Unlike most other cultists, they refuse to recognize the Roman gods right alongside their own. So they're hailed before the magistrates and ordered to burn incense in honor of the Emperor's genius. Of course they refuse. Posthaste we get a batch of them. That's only one aspect of our success, however. Let me conduct you around the grounds. You'll be proud of what I've accomplished."

Proud? Far from it. I was growing weary of the whole business. But I accompanied him on the tour. He chattered on about how Nero was diverting practically all contracts for bestiarii to the Cassian School.

"The Emperor's favor naturally attracts the attention of many other notables, too. The commissions practically roll in. The old Bestiarius School is struggling to stay in business—one more proof of my devoted attention to our affairs in your absence, I might add. I told you once I have a talent for ingratiating myself with gentlefolk. Even though," he finished with another glance at my toga, "you're the one who wound up with the stripe."

As we climbed into the stands to watch the pupils work out I said, "I'm sorry to hear Fabius isn't prospering. There should be room enough for both schools."

"Agh!" Syrax waved. "Let him flounder. It means more money in our coffers. He wouldn't even have a roof over his head if Xenophon hadn't remained with him."

"The Greek? I thought he'd be free by now. Or dead."

"Just the opposite. Drop by the *Acta Diurna* some time. You'll see Xenophon's name up there constantly. He's the most famous bestiarius in Latium. He's refused the wooden sword five times to continue making money. I made him a handsome offer once. I regret to say he'd have nothing to do with us because of you. He brought up the subject of how you'd cheated him of a garland. He's never forgiven you that, or several other things, I gather."

A memory of the ex-criminal's ugly face haunted me for a moment. For the first time I savored the power implicit in the purple eques stripe.

"Let him try to take revenge. My station and my sword arm are more than a match for him."

We watched the Egyptian lanista give the students pointers on provoking the leopards. I was reluctant to argue any further with Syrax, but one important question remained unanswered.

"What became of Serenus' share in the school?"

"By the terms of his will it passed to his only brother, a rustic who makes his living from a farm outside Rome."

"Serenus never mentioned that he had a brother."

"I understand they were never particularly close. The fellow's not like Serenus at all. He's very countrified. The records of the transfer are kept in the strongrooms of the Probi bank if you care to look them over. Old Probus sends the yokel his share of the profits four times yearly. Otherwise the brother never bothers about the management of the place, except to drop in and gawk whenever he carts a load of leeks into the city." Leaning over, Syrax added confidentially, "You can be sure I skim off a certain amount from the quarterly profits, unknown to him, to increase our fortunes. You don't have any objection to that kind of extra income any more, do you?"

"It's theft, isn't it?"

"Listen to me! That fellow did nothing to contribute to our success. He merely collects—"

"Very well, enough! No more arguing."

"You brought it up," he muttered. Then he brightened. "Notice our new lanista. Name's Ramor. I bought him fresh off the slave block. He has plenty of natural skill."

At the moment the lanista was proving he had natural skill with the whip. He was flaying the hide of a clumsy boy who'd tripped over his own feet and been pawed by the tame leopard. In regular combat the clawing would have produced maiming, or death.

The whipped student wailed in misery. Somehow his cries made me ill. I excused myself.

Syrax stared after me, shaking his head.

Several days later I returned to go over the books and details of a loan for importing new animals from Africa. Importing them was necessary because of the heavy losses we incurred when the trapped beasts died in the burning fort. The brother of Serenus was present in the stands that morning. Syrax introduced us. The fellow, all round-eyed and slow of speech, was the very picture of a rustic. He seemed conversant with Serenus' affairs, though.

In subsequent months I purchased the two houses adjoining mine. With a large expenditure of money I enlarged my property to a size befitting my new station. The summer advanced and I participated in my first review of the equites.

This annual procession, in which each knight was mounted upon a splendid horse, harked back to the days when the equite cavalry had actually defended Rome. Nearly five thousand knights paraded by the Emperor's dais in the Forum, including old dodderers who could barely mount their rented chargers. Attendance was mandatory.

A flurry of excitement was provided when the procession stalled. Nero loudly denounced an impostor by shrieking the timeworn phrase, "Sell your horse!"

The mob hooted and stoned the ignorant rascal. He turned out to be a penniless actor who thought he could increase his fortune by posing as an eques.

The size of my household grew as I added more slaves. The size of my balance in the House of Probi increased in a similar manner. I never entertained, however. I had lost the taste for association with members of the upper classes without ever having acquired it. Perhaps the violence and horror of my experience in Africa had made me eager for seclusion.

At any rate, I left school matters almost completely in the hands of Syrax. He was constantly bustling up and down the

Palatine, arranging to supply various circuses with large comple-
ments of men, as well as the animals which began to arrive
regularly at our Tiber-side wharf.

The magnificent Circus of Nero had been completed across
the Tiber. I attended one performance there, to which only
Senators, equites and their women were invited. I went alone.
The crowd shrieked and applauded loudest when a company
of degenerates, men and women rounded up off the streets,
put on an exhibition of sexual acts. I endured the performance with a queasy stomach. The noisiest ovation came
from Nero's box. The ruby-cheeked Poppaea sat beside him,
growing fat, heavy-breasted and unlovely now that she was
Empress.

The one guest I did invite to my dining table was scarred
old Fabius. He had aged greatly.

While we reclined over dessert, I mentioned my visit to the
Circus of Nero.

"Then you saw the kind of show the public clamors for nowadays, Cassius."

"Yes, I saw it. I was barely able to keep from throwing up.
I'm not a prude, nor even a man of very high morals. But it
strikes me that love-making is a private business, to be privately conducted. It shouldn't be debased by being performed
joylessly in front of thousands."

Fabius wagged a finger. "What the Emperor likes, is performed."

"That doesn't make it right."

"Hush," he said, smiling humorlessly. "Do you want to go
on trial for treason? I tell you, Cassius, I fear for the soul of
Rome, if a city can be said to possess that obscure commodity.
The wind off the Palatine these days is rotten. One day it will
blow to destruction all the things the Republic once stood for.
Liberty, honor, beauty. They're meaningless words any more.
All the Senators and equites—present company excepted—
seem to think about is lining their pockets and indulging their
sexual appetites."

I said nothing. His words depressed me, for I believed he was right. He went on.

"The profession of bestiarius has been cheapened unbelievably too. The number of dead bodies is now the standard for a successful show, not the skill of the animal hunters. And the public hunger for such spectacles grows daily, sanctioned by the Emperor himself. What's to become of us, I wonder?"

The months crept by. I seemed to live in a gray and tasteless limbo. Occasionally I hired some handsome courtesan for a night, but I derived no real pleasure from it.

One rainy morning a few months after the Feast of Saturnalia, a slave arrived at my home with an urgent request that I come to the school at once. I found Syrax stalking back and forth as I entered, clearly overwrought.

"Cassius, we need a new, tough hand to take charge of a worrisome matter."

"What's happened?"

"We're having trouble with one of our best specimens. A fellow just sentenced to us a week ago. I've argued with him. I've pleaded. I've had him whipped. Now I've cut off his food. He still refuses to fight."

"That's an odd attitude for a criminal. Usually they're eager for the chance."

"Not this ox. He's one of those damned Christians." Syrax thumped his fist into his palm. "He'd make a top bestiarius. He's got the build for it. And the looks to attract the Senators' wives. I even changed his name from Marcus to Eros to lend him more appeal. With absolutely no results."

I threw up my hands. "What can I do? If he refuses, he refuses."

"Threaten him. Flaunt your rank. I don't know. I've had no luck. You try. After all, this is your responsibility too."

"Very well," I said reluctantly. "But I hear the Christians don't respond to threats. Even threats of death. Where is he?"

In one of the narrow dormitory cells guarded by two spearmen, I met the young man in question. He had long dark hair, height that nearly matched mine, and a tough, blunt jaw. His eyes were dark and tranquil. No god occupied the niche above the pallet where he stretched out, gazing into space.

I adjusted my toga and coughed. He glanced up. I had expected defiance. I was greeted by calm deference.

"Marcus?"

"The name they have given me is Eros," he said bitterly. "To please their false gods, I suppose."

"I am Cassius Flamma, part owner of this establishment. I understand you refuse to take the training we're obliged to give as part of your sentence."

"Sentence! That sentence was a joke." He turned. Above his clout, ugly suppurating lash marks stood out. "Because I refuse to renounce what I believe, I'm whipped, then starved. Well, if you've come to change my mind, it won't work."

Undoubtedly he deserved another whipping for his quiet insolence. But I rather liked the boldness of his stare. Very few in Rome these days believed in anything more than the value of endless gratification of the senses. Sitting down, I tried to speak moderately.

"Marcus, I understand how you feel."

"How can you, in this profession?"

"I like to feel I have a little sensitivity left. Anyway, I think you do yourself a disservice by refusing to fight. One way or another, you will go to the arena eventually. You'll be dragged there in chains if you won't walk under your own power. Why surrender your life uselessly?"

He said in a quiet voice, "Jesus surrendered his life in Judea. I can do no less."

"Oh, yes, Jesus. Your prophet. I've heard of him."

He replied firmly, "He was more than a prophet. He was God's own son."

"Come now. To which god do you refer? The pantheon's so crowded, it's hard to tell one from another."

"I mean the only one. The one who rules all of us, whether we recognize His power in our lives or not."

I squirmed uncomfortably under his penetrating stare. "I was born a poor man, Marcus. What education I have, I've picked up along the way. I'm not conversant with theological matters. Let's approach the problem from the practical side. Your life will be at stake when you enter the arena. Learn to defend yourself. Others of your cult—"

"Christianity is not a cult. It's a way of life."

I sighed. "Very well. Others of your kind sentenced here have accepted the opportunity to win their freedom. And even made a modest amount of money if they're lucky."

"I'm not interested in freedom or money," he told me. He was not boasting. He merely stated a fact.

"Why are you so stubborn? The rest of your brethren—"

"Yes, they bow down," he cut in quickly. "They accept a sword and they go into the arena to kill animals or each other. But they don't understand what Jesus taught. In return for cruelty, give love. In return for hate, friendship." He lifted one shoulder, an eloquent gesture somehow. "What you do to me doesn't matter. I believe what I believe. Revile me. Starve me. Beat me to death. It makes no difference. The man from Judea was not a man but the son of God. I won't worship your bronze statues alongside Him. If dying unarmed in the circus is the price of faith, I'm ready to pay it."

"Then you'll surely die!" I said, irritated. I rose. "And sooner than you think. Good day."

When I reported my failure to Syrax, he cursed violently and ordered another whipping for the Christian.

I left the school hurriedly. I was disturbed over my anger at the prisoner's behavior. When I thought about it, I realized I'd grown angry because I was embarrassed by the man's conviction. I didn't care a whit for the teachings of his Judean prophet. But the difference between his quiet steadfastness and my own lack of belief in anything except the state of my finances was painfully clear.

Wanting only complete separation from problems of the kind raised by a man like Marcus, I retired to my house and tried to put him out of my mind. I failed. His face appeared in troubled dreams. And as if an unkind fate were deliberately trying to draw me back into trouble, less than a week after my fruitless interview, I became entangled with the Christians again.

I was down on the school wharf late one afternoon at the request of the lanista Ramor. He wanted my opinion on a barge load of leopards newly arrived on approval. He wished to select only the prime ones to train as man-eaters.

While I was pointing out likely specimens, Syrax appeared.

"Ah, Cassius. I heard you were on the premises. There's another of those miserable Christian cultists asking for you."

"You take care of him. I want nothing to do with them."

"I defer to you," Syrax sneered, "since this bearded fool asked for the owner Cassius Flamma. Apparently he considers my station too lowly."

I was sure the slight hadn't been intentional. Because of my record in the arena, I suppose I was more widely known than Syrax. But the jealous way he leaped on the chance remark made me pause. His dark eyes shone unpleasantly as I said, "Who is the man?"

"One of the leading lights of the cult. A rabble-rouser from the provincial city of Tarsus. He's already been in trouble with the authorities. His name's Paulus."

"Where will I find him?"

"In the amphitheater stands."

I nodded and started up the wharf. Syrax got in a last jibe.

"Be careful, partner. Don't get a reputation for sympathizing with these cultists. People will say you've gone soft. But maybe that's not so far wrong. Eh, Cassius?"

I stared back at him sharply. He masked his feelings with the old, meaningless smile, and turned away.

CHAPTER XVII

———⟫●⟪———

I CLIMBED into the stands, empty now that the day's practice was finished. The sand was deserted, whorled by the chill wind of late spring. Against the lowering gray sky a strong, broad-shouldered man was silhouetted, waiting for me. He had long hair shot with gray, and a flowing beard. He wore a simply draped woolen tunic. I judged him to be something more than forty years.

On the upper tier of the stand where he stood quietly, he saluted me, then said in a polite but not obsequious voice, "*Ave,* Splendidi. I am Paulus, a free citizen of Rome."

"What do you want?"

"I've come on a mission of mercy."

I replied sharply, "I'm a busy man, Paulus. Speak plainer. If it has something to do with your cult, I have no time for sermons."

He smiled disarmingly. "Neither does Rome, it seems. Yet I persist."

"Please get to the point of your visit," I said, as rudely as I knew how.

Rudeness did no good. His reply was temperate. "I have come to ask freedom for the young man whom someone has named Eros. His true name is Marcus."

"I know his true name," I retorted. "Also that he is a criminal. Freedom indeed!"

"Isn't it within your power, as an owner of this school, to grant it?"

"You're wasting your time. He was sentenced here, and here he stays."

"Then he'll certainly die," Paulus returned softly. "He'll never fight in the arena. Splendidi, the citizens say you're a man of honor in a profession which is without honor. Do you want Marcus' blood on your hands?"

"All at once I'm the guilty party!" I exclaimed. "I'm not the keeper of those slaves, nor are they mine. I live my life and obey the laws of Rome. The law says Marcus must remain."

Zealous fire blazed in his eye suddenly. He shook a finger at me. "There's the error in your thinking, Splendidi. You *are* my keeper. I am yours. So is each man to the other. The Master taught that. I regret I never heard Him. They nailed Him up long before I had my visions and left my government post in Tarsus to spread His truth, even here to sinful Rome."

I snorted in derision. "Sinful! I've heard about your Christian rites. How men and women mingle together in catacombs near the aqueducts. I understand your chief rite consists of slaying a newborn babe and drinking its blood. I don't see that Marcus would be any worse off in the Circus of Nero than participating in such debased rituals."

Paulus smiled sadly. "Those stories are only that—stories. Tales spread by the Emperor's courtiers. Nero fears us, few and poor though we are." He looked straight into my face, his earnestness making me uneasy. "We will shake the world, Splendidi. Through love and faith, we will topple cruelty and evil and bring His kingdom."

"Enough theology! I dislike your arrogance. Good day."

Gray clouds loomed above us, darkening the noisy streets. Paulus waited a moment more, then shook his head. "Alas, I was told I'd get a different sort of reception from you."

"Then you were misinformed. I'm just like any other Roman."

"Despite what you say, I think otherwise. Your words are harsh, but I wonder if you mean them. One of our number, a slave in the house of the teacher Seneca, told me he'd seen you in conversation with his master long ago, and heard the philosopher speak of you after you'd gone. Seneca said—" A brief, simple gesture that somehow shamed me. "—he said you were a good man."

"Perhaps others have more faith in my nature than I do."

"Perhaps so," Paulus agreed, ignoring my jeering tone. "Will you hear me a moment longer?"

Against my better judgment, I said gruffly that I would. We sat down on the hard stadium benches, with the spring dusk gathering. He described something of the teachings of the Judean, Jesus, whom a Roman procurator named Pilate had crucified between thieves. I remembered details of the story from my childhood. Paulus went on to tell about his strange visions years ago, in which it was revealed to him that there was but one true God, apparently discovered by the Jews but holding sway over Romans and other non-Jews as well. The crucified Jesus, he said, was God's son come to earth. Afire with this truth, Paulus had journeyed to Jerusalem as a missionary, where he had been arrested.

Wryly he told me, "When the people denounced me as a troublemaker, a revolutionary, and demanded my death, I immediately pleaded my Roman citizenship. The procurator Festus was powerless to execute me. I demanded my rights— passage to Rome, to stand trial here for sedition and inciting riots. Which, of course, I did not do. No doubt I put the Empire to great expense and trouble. But I reached Rome, as I wanted. The charges I mentioned were finally dismissed. New ones have been brought against me. I only pray to God I'll have time to preach the truth of Christ here, as I have elsewhere, before the court lawyers get my head on the execution block."

Shivering, I asked, "Facing possible death, you still stay here?"

The man unnerved me with his steady, purposeful manner. He gestured out over the graying hills and squalid tenements. "Here above all is where God is needed most."

"Paulus, if the stories about underground orgies are false, designed to stir popular sentiment against you, tell me the true nature of what you believe."

He did so, though I confess much of his discourse went over my head, including his references to events in the life of his Christus and to a band of twelve men who were apparently the Judean's cohorts. When he concluded I said, "Much of what you say seems similar to the beliefs of the philosopher Seneca."

Paulus shook his head. "No, I can't see there's any connection. He worships the gods of Rome."

"But he lived his life even as you live yours, putting aside personal wants to serve Rome. Until the Emperor dismissed him, that is."

"Then in that sense," Paulus agreed, "he follows the spirit of the Master. As you would be doing, Splendidi, if you saw fit to grant my request and release Marcus into my custody."

A moment of crucial choice had come while we sat talking high up in the gloomy, wind-blown stands. A great black blood-stain showed on the training sand below. I stared and stared at it. Finally I said, "That is my choice, then? Release Marcus or, in your words, accept responsibility for his death? Take his blood on my own hands?"

"Depending on what sort of man you really are, Splendidi, you already know the answer."

I felt a great and deep rage, directed not so much at the itinerant preacher as against my own ill-luck at falling into this trap. I stood up.

"Very well. I may be many things, but I'm no murderer. Go to the barracks and take him, on my authority."

The bearded man gripped my hand. "You've done a fine thing, Splendidi."

"Not because I understand or have any sympathy with your cause, mind you."

"No, but your heart is good. Marcus and I will not forget your generosity."

Gruffly I answered, "Have him out of here promptly. And please don't spread tales about my so-called generosity, or I'll become a laughingstock. I'll have trouble enough explaining to my partners the loss of a prime fighter. Not to mention the handsome profits he'd have brought us."

At the bottom of the steps Paulus turned. Again those burning eyes reached out to me. "You have gained far more than you have lost, Splendidi. I know it. I think you do too. Farewell."

I watched him vault the balustrade of the amphitheater and hurry across the sand to the barracks, displaying more agility and muscle than the Christians were ever credited with by the public. Perhaps what had undone me was his straightforward, honest manliness. Paulus was no weakling, no whining wretch who turned to religion to make up for his own weakness and failure. I suspected he could crack heads with the best, if he ever chose to try.

At once I left for the street gate, walking quickly. I wanted to be gone before my rather rash act was discovered. In a way I was pleased and satisfied by what I had done. I was also refreshingly free of guilt, which astonished me. Just as I neared the outer gate a voice yelled, "Cassius! Wait there! Do you hear? *Wait!*"

Swinging around, I saw Syrax hurrying along a dark gallery. His cheeks were mottled from exertion. His expression was unpleasant.

"I have come from the dormitory," he said angrily. "A guard called me to report your latest order."

"What's done is done. Marcus would not fight in any case."

"He would have fought after we whipped and starved him a while longer!"

"Futile, Syrax. I hold no brief for these Christians. But after talking to that Paulus, it's clear to me that they are determined men. Marcus would only languish and die, if not here, then helplessly in the Circus. I saw no need to be a party to a useless slaughter."

"You don't seem to see the need of many things these days," Syrax snarled.

"Enough! I'm a partner here and my order stands."

"What possesses you lately, Cassius?"

Angering, I said, "Perhaps I've had a bellyful of your deceitful ways."

"Oh-ho!" Malice gleamed in his glance. "So now I'm deceitful, am I? You never objected to my tactics before."

"True. But only lately have I stopped to think of the price we've paid for our success. We've caused countless people misery, driven innocent men to their deaths—"

Syrax drew back a step. He cocked his head insolently. "Who is this speaking? Certainly not Cassius Flamma. Not the man who fought like a devil to win the wood sword. Not the man who opened the most famous beast school in the Empire. Cassius Flamma has died somewhere along the way. Left a weakling for a ghost. A weakling and worse. A coward."

My hands closed to fists. "Be quiet. You've not seen the things I have. The horrors of the time in Africa—"

"I've seen something worse," he cut in. "The decline of a man. This argument has been in the making ever since you returned, Cassius. Now it's plain you've become a sympathizer with traitors to the Emperor. You might as well tell me the rest. Lost your taste for money, too?"

"Gods, you're insufferable!" I shouted. "At what price is money gotten, you twisted fool?"

"Oh," Syrax purred, "and now I'm twisted. Twisted, because I helped you to fame."

"There's more to living than fame and a purse full of coppers and the simpering approval of that gross boy who rules us!" My voice had risen to a shout. My face felt hot. I knew I was provoking him dangerously, yet the words I spoke had been gathering inside me many months, and I could not check them. "My father—a failure, a miserable man who died without a coin to his name—taught me to seek fame, but not at the price of decency. That's what I have forgotten so long, Syrax. It's taken quite a few unsavory things to make me remember. The tricks of that slut Locusta. The way you cheat Serenus' brother so blandly. Your condemning that Christian to death when he had twice the courage of you or I."

My partner opened his mouth to retort, then closed it. He dipped his head, as if to acknowledge my words. Then, that damnable smile crept across his face, eerie in the dimness of the gallery. There was more for me to fear in his calm, cunning grin than all his rantings.

"Cassius, I don't intend to stand here and let you abuse me. One last thing I will say, prompted by your remark about courage. It's you who have lost courage. You who have become the cowering failure. I'm going to give some serious thought to this enterprise. I'm not at all sure I want to remain in business with a stinking milksop."

He gathered spit in his mouth, hawked and blew it against the hem of my toga. Then he spun around and vanished down the gallery, tunic flying, sandals slapping with the rhythm of his rage.

My bearers carried me along through the darkening streets, crying for all and sundry to get out of the path of the illustrious eques Cassius Flamma.

Was I looking at things from the wrong end?

Did I deserve the tongue-lashing Syrax had delivered?

I decided I'd acted correctly in letting Marcus go free. Manumission, while not a frequent occurrence at the arena schools, happened often enough so that my act shouldn't excite too much comment.

Yet why had I done it?

Had I been led down false paths from the beginning? Dazzled by the splendor of Rome that was only a tawdry illusion?

Either I truly was becoming a coward, as Syrax maintained, or else I'd been living wrongly for too many years. Not being a

man of much formal education, I was hard put to explain away
my decision fully, but I knew one thing—I had gained more
satisfaction from the thanks of the cultist Paulus than I had
lost by incurring Syrax's wrath. I realized that Paulus had predicted it would happen thus.

I remembered Acte had once said, the first night we met,
that Rome and its ways might harden my heart. I believed it at
long last. Because now I felt the hardness cracking and crumbling. I had become a different man.

The difficulty was, if I suddenly chose to live a different sort
of life, my past would make it hard to do. More than hard, as
I learned that very same night. Dangerous.

To soak the aches from my bones produced by the damp
spring wind, I took my chair after dinner to an imposing bath
in the Field of Mars. Warm and cold dips lulled and relaxed
me, made me sleepy. On the way home I was only half aware
that my small retinue was passing through a particularly fetid
arcade when the chair set down with a bump. I heard scuf-
fling. Torchlight jigged crazily on the litter curtains. Before I
could jump out, a frightened, frantic voice cried, "Robbers!
Help, get the watch! We're being attacked by—"

Thrusting the curtains aside, I leaped into a confused melee
of shouting men and slaves. One of my retinue was down, his
blood-foaming throat slashed. A knife sailed by my ear. I ducked
and bowled against a bulky man who smelled of leeks and sour
wine. A torch fell to the ground, another. How many brigands
had come out of the night I couldn't see. I had my hands full with
the one trying to close his sweat-stinking fingers on my throat.

I stumbled back as the strangler cursed. "Fights harder than
any fop I ever jumped before. Where's your purse, gentleman?
Let—*agh!*"

Pinned against the chair, I drove my leg between his thighs a
second time. He doubled over. I dug my right thumb in his
eye and jerked, bringing out something wet and lumpish. He
shrieked and reeled back against his companions, eye socket
spraying hot blood.

"Lidor! Frimus! Someone!" I shouted. "Run! Rouse the watch—"

But my slaves were struggling for their lives. I counted at least a dozen robbers. They must have slid from the rooftops and the doorways of shuttered shops. The slaves, lightly armed with staves, whacked heads valiantly. But they had no defense against knives.

Fallen torches burned dim on the pavement, illuminating a tangle of legs. Inside the litter, a thief was ransacking. He'd entered from the other side. I heard him cry in dismay.

"A filthy trick! Nothing here. No gems, not a damned—"

"Nothing but punishment, you scum," I screamed at him, grasping his throat.

His face grew pale, tongue protruding, hands scrabbling at air while he made queer cluckings in his throat. Another thief fell on my back, tried to pull me off. One of the slaves knocked him out of action with his staff. The man on whom I'd fastened a stranglehold found his knife somehow.

It flashed upward between my wrists for my throat. I wrenched aside. The iron tip grazed my cheek, drawing blood. It was a trifling hurt, but it enraged me. I grappled the man down onto the cushions of the litter, nearly broke his arm wrestling away his knife. I held his throat with one hand and raised my other, ready to skewer him.

"The gods defend me," he mumbled, wetting himself out of fear. "The gods take my soul when I die—"

Abruptly, in the place of his slack, evil face. I saw the eyes of Paulus.

"Kill me," the brigand wept. "Don't dangle me. Kill me and have done—"

Cursing, I thrust him bodily out the other side of the litter. "Run. Before I change my mind."

Sobbing in disbelief, he fled. Lights flashed distantly. Men shouted. "Scatter!" a thief yelled. "The vigiles—up to the roofs!"

Quickly as they had come, the death-dealers faded away. They'd killed one slave, a boy named Frimus, barely sixteen. I knelt beside him but it was too late. His throat had been opened ear to ear. The watch raced nearer.

"Bad luck followed us tonight, master," a slave said sadly.

"Bad luck? I suppose. These streets are infamous for thieves. But—"

I said no more. I had only then recalled Syrax's final words to me at the school. He questioned whether he wished to remain my partner.

The convenient timing of the strike by the robbers planted a suspicion I could not ignore no matter how hard I tried.

CHAPTER XVIII

⟶⟫●⟨⟵

THE LADY Paulina told me firmly, "My husband prefers seclusion. He no longer sees visitors."

"I beg you, my lady, at least carry my request to him. It's of great importance."

Rather like a protective hen worrying over one of her brood, the philosopher's wife shook her head. "Cassius, my husband is weary of the world." Her fine face, which I remembered as pretty and composed, showed signs of the same weariness. "For years he put aside private considerations, his desire for the solitude in which to think and write, in order to serve and counsel that young—the Emperor," she amended. "With what result? He was dismissed, humiliated. No, Cassius, I'd only provoke his anger if I spoke to him about you. His orders—"

"My lady," I broke in, "I understand all you say, and I sympathize. But I must ask him a question in confidence. A question I don't dare ask any other man in Rome, for fear it would drift back to the wrong ears. What might happen to me if it did, I can only surmise."

Paulina frowned. "Are you trying to suggest your life is threatened?"

My mouth jerked in a grim smile. I recalled the attack by street thieves, six weeks before. "Yes, my lady. I've waited patiently for Seneca to return from his country estate. If I'm to be turned away now—"

She sighed. "I know it will anger him if I disturb him. But, I will try."

She turned and glided from the atrium. I waited, uneasy in the unnatural quiet of the great house. Seneca had manumitted most of his slaves and barred his doors to clients. I had been forced to make a fearful row outside and practically assault the sole slave who admitted me before the lout would even speak to the philosopher's wife. I paced back and forth, perspiring. The chilly spring was turning to warm summer.

I had not gone near the Cassian School since the day of my quarrel with Syrax. Following the incident with the robbers, no more attempts had been made upon my life. Perhaps the attack had been coincidence. Yet the very fact that nothing had happened merely increased my apprehension, until I found myself starting at the smallest noises in the night.

Paulina returned, smiling in a rather astonished way. "I could hardly believe my ears. He will see you."

As I started quickly away she laid a hand on my arm.

"Please, Splendidi. Don't trouble him overlong. He's a very sad and tired man."

"I will heed your wishes, my lady."

The philosopher was in the peristyle. The curtain had been dropped in place across the roof opening, lending the viridarium beneath a mysterious, clouded look. On a bench in the center of this patch of greensward, Seneca busied with a tablet and stylus. He wore a plain toga which accented his pallor and the age lines upon his face. Beside him was a tray of coarse barley cakes, more befitting an anchorite than a millionaire.

He glanced up, laid the tablet aside. "Welcome, Cassius. Be seated."

"Thank you." I took a place opposite him. "I am sorry to intrude upon your privacy."

"Rules are meant to be broken occasionally. Paulina said it was most important." He put me at ease by extending the barley cakes. "Would you care for one? Such fare suits me better nowadays than the vulgar gluttonies of the Palatine. I understand the Emperor's latest rage is breast of finch in butter and mushrooms. He's so busy diverting himself with new and exotic pleasures that he's lost sight of what's happening in this rotting city."

When I took a cake, he selected one in turn, nibbled a bit of it, then cocked an eye at me. "I see you've taken the narrow stripe. Perhaps you're not in sympathy with my views."

"Strangely enough, sir, though I can't put it so well as you, I feel much the same."

"Then you won't last long as a favorite of Nero. If you ever were foolish enough to want to be one in the first place. Ah, the madness of that boy! Have you seen the new coinage?"

"The denarius with the head of the Emperor capped with a radiating crown? Yes."

"The devalued denarius," he corrected somberly. "Our money grows worthless. So does everything Rome stood for once. And that foolish, spiteful youth still insists upon perpetuating the cult of his personal fame by striking money showing his head with the radiant crown. That crown was formerly reserved for dead Caesars. Men who had demonstrated their greatness. And then there's his scheme for rebuilding Rome to resemble Athens. Not to mention that frightful stupidity with Bassus."

"Do you mean Caesellius Bassus?"

"Aye, the Senator. I knew him well. He has all the wits of a newborn infant. That opinion is only confirmed now that he's told Nero he knows where the legendary treasure of Dido is buried in Africa. Why, that treasure is myth, nothing else. But the Emperor is spending public tax funds so heavily, he must yet spend more to equip Bassus with two thousand slaves to go on his fool's errand in search of nonexistent treasure." Seneca's eyes sparked with sour amusement. "Are you surprised I keep up on things, living alone as I do?"

"Somewhat, yes."

He hesitated, as if debating whether he ought to speak. Then, studying me carefully all the while, he went ahead.

"I do have a few visitors. Generally late at night. Certain disgruntled Senators. One or two highly placed officers of the Legion. We discuss the excesses of the Emperor. And what should be done about them." The glance he threw me was unmistakably a question.

"There is no need to tell me of matters that don't concern me, sir," I said quickly.

"I realize that. However, from the first morning Serenus brought you here, I had the impression you were not quite the hard person you pretended to be. So when I speak in riddles, of treason, conspiracies, I feel I'm on safe ground. We're quite alone. I can easily deny all I've said. Do you find it strange I smile over murder?"

"Murder! I didn't realize—these persons you mentioned wanted to kill—to kill the—"

"Unable to say it, are you?" he broke in, amused. "Yes, that is their intent. It may be merely drunken speculation. But something must be done to rid Rome of this curse. I have never condoned killing. I'm not positive I would do so now. It's a heavy price to pay for the removal of a tyrant. For this reason I have so far refrained from joining the cause of my midnight visitors, except as a partner in discussion." Rapidly he ate another barley cake. "I have said too much already."

"Whatever I hear will go no further," I promised him.

His eyes flashed up, wise and gently cunning. He murmured, "I know, Cassius. That is why I dared speak at all."

Again I wondered at the faith others seemed to have in me, when I had so little in myself. Was the struggle in me so transparent? At any rate, I must have been gaping like a bumpkin. The savant chuckled.

"Don't let me unnerve you with old man's prattling. Paulina told me you came to ask, not listen. Very well. Ask what you will."

"One question only, sir. What do you know about the character of the brother of our dead friend Serenus?"

"Brother?" Seneca returned. "Do you refer to Linus Justus?"

"He was introduced to me as Drusillus. He's the one who owns large farms outside Rome."

"Someone is hoodwinking you, my young friend. Annaeus Serenus had only one brother, younger than he. His name was Linus Justus. He was killed in a skirmish while serving with the Twelfth Legion in Gaul. That was—let me see now—at least ten years ago."

"There were no other brothers, living or dead?"

"None," Seneca answered. "Nor sisters either."

The suspicion I'd harbored these many weeks was suspicion no longer. Shaking with fury, I rose. "Thank you."

"I trust what I've said won't provoke you to any rash act."

At the entrance of the peristyle I halted. "No, sir. But it may well save me from becoming the victim of one."

Though I probably should have remained and done him the courtesy of a full explanation, my heart was so full of wrath I could think of nothing but leaving at once. It was all I could do to murmur a word of thanks to Paulina in the atrium. I intended to drag the whole rotten scheme into the open. Even the monumental treason contemplated by Seneca's friends seemed trifling compared with my own anger.

My bearers carried me straightaway to the Probi banking house. I realized with humiliation that Syrax had gambled upon my indifference to business matters. He had told me I was free to examine the records of the Cassian School kept at the bank, but he'd said it, I recalled, in an offhand way. No doubt he assumed I would accept his word without going to see in person. And I had, fool that I was.

Old Probus himself greeted me when I entered the establishment. Loudly I demanded all the tablets and scrolls pertaining to the Cassian School. Probus discreetly tried to learn the reason for my concern. I said nothing, only repeated my demands.

He ushered me into a private cell reserved for clients of the house. After a brief wait a sharp-eyed clerk began bringing me piles of tablets and scrolls. When he had made his last trip I said, "This is all? I want every last item in your storage vaults."

This is all, Splendidi." The clerk gave me a peculiar look. "Master Probus himself attended me, to see that I brought everything."

"Very well. Kindly draw the drapery and leave me alone."

He retired as bidden. I opened the brass hasp that held the top three tablets together. I began to read, though I had much difficulty with the loquacious legal Latin.

After an hour's search I found what I sought—an obscure reference to the death of Annaeus Serenus, and the statement required by law to record purchase and transfer of his share. The clod fobbed off on me as his brother was no doubt some vagabond actor hired to drop in at the school now and then to maintain the masquerade. The true purchaser of the silent share was clearly listed. Staring at his name, my cheeks grew hot and the pulses in my wrists beat fast.

My partner was Ofonius Tigellinus.

After returning the tablets to the clerk, I rushed at once to the Cassian School. I stormed around the buildings and the amphitheater, shouting for Syrax. No one knew his whereabouts. Very conveniently, I thought. I left a terse, unmistakable message with the clerks, demanding that he come at once to my home as soon as he received my communication.

Then I retired to my house. I took from a chest the long, bright ornamental sword I had worn in the recent equites' parade. Though crusted with gems and fancily finished, it would cut a man down as easily as a plain blade. I set about polishing it while I brooded alone in the tablinium. I kept the sword close by all day.

The house remained quiet, unvisited by messengers, even to nightfall. A yellowish full moon rose, gilding the distant jumble of the Palatine. The evening was unusually still. The streets seemed ghostly, deserted. Many of the most eminent people had followed Nero and his court to Antium for a summer holiday.

I drank a great deal of wine. My temper grew blacker and blacker. I was on the point of taking my sword and going back to the school when a slave scuttled in.

"Master, there's a dirty urchin at the scullery door. He begs to speak with you."

"Lead the way." I carried the sword. No telling what company of murderers might be waiting for me, if Syrax sensed trouble.

But as the slave had reported, it was only a boy with lice in his scraggled hair and fear in his sunken eyes. After checking carefully to see that no one lurked in the sour alley, I stepped outside, out of earshot of the scullery slaves.

"Did the Syrian send you, boy?"

"Yes, Splendidi," he quavered. "For a copper he bade me deliver a message. He knows you wish to meet him. He fears to come here, or to the school."

"Well he might," I muttered.

The boy didn't understand. "He says he is in trouble with the authorities, and in hiding."

"Hiding where?"

"He made me promise not to say."

"Very well. Do you know why he's in trouble?"

"Yes, master. He insulted an influential Senator at the Palatine yesterday. He asks you to fill a purse and come meet him at once."

A trap was being laid. I said quietly, "Where?"

"The only place he thought safe, sir. Beneath the arches outside the Circus Maximus. He plans to leave Rome for several months. That's why he needs money."

I glanced up at the moon, luminous and fair. I might never see it again. I patted the boy's shoulder. "Don't shrink back, lad. See that portly man inside? My steward. He will give you a meal."

The boy cried, "Thank you, Splendidi. May the gods bring you much luck."

I think I smiled, there in the wretched alley outside my home. Were there any gods? If so, I would need their help greatly this night. I knew beyond all doubt that Syrax would be waiting in the maze of the Circus arches with a pack of gutter ruffians behind him, bent on killing me.

I returned to the house for a light cloak and the scabbard for my sword. Over the protests of my slaves, I hurried out alone into the empty streets. Perhaps I would have been wiser to take a flock of helpers. But I had nothing to lose beyond a life grown dull and tasteless. Anger drove me to seek a final reckoning with the cheating Syrian, man to man.

A sultry heat blanketed Rome. The distant shouts of the vigiles sounded listless and weary. I slipped along black thoroughfares, down the hills toward the pillars of the Circus where I had stood for hours as a boy, strengthening my hand by hitting it against the ageless blackened timbers. From towering insulae roundabout rose the voices of the poor, quarrelsome in the summer's night heat. Babies wailed and fretted in the wretched tenement rooms.

All this and more I saw, as if for the last time. Presently I drew up in the shadow of a wall. Directly ahead, the great arched outer wall of the Circus curved away both left and right, a forest of dark nooks in which a man's scream would hardly be heard. Here and there torches guttered, suspended in brackets hammered to the wooden columns.

With quick steps I crossed the street. I slid into concealment behind the nearest column. I searched the dark arcade to the right, saw nothing but pools of reddish torchlight spaced far apart between patches of black.

But when I looked left, I glimpsed a figure six or seven arches down. The man turned his head when I made a noise. A gilt ear hoop flashed.

I stepped out from behind the pillar and began to walk.

As I strode along my belly tightened up. Clammy-warm sweat oozed in the palm of my sword hand. Syrax heard me coming, there at the edge of a pool of torchlight. My sandals rang on the stone. Though I was walking in the heart of Rome, I might have been passing down to the underworld, so eerie and deserted were the passages where crowds jammed on Circus day.

Only the nervous flutter of Syrax's fingers twisting his dark cloak betrayed him. I watched the shadows to his back for signs of hired killers. I saw nothing.

My partner's face glistened with sweat. His lips formed a smile. He was as tense as I, and the smile was an ugly jerk at the corners of his lips.

"There's no purse at your belt," he exclaimed hoarsely. "To flee Rome I need—"

"We can drop the pretenses, Syrax. Your message was transparent. You aren't in trouble with any influential Senator. Only with me."

"Still, you came. Alone."

"To have it out with you. Bring on your cutthroats. I'll give them a go."

"Do you think you can handle soldiers in armor, braggart?" said a voice out of the dark.

Fire glared on burnished breastplates and pointed spear heads. Two Praetorians slid from the shadows behind Syrax, tough, strapping specimens. I paid more attention to the third who appeared. The voice out of shadow fitted a face now—that of the tribune, Gaius Julius.

He saluted mockingly with his blade. "We know a few more techniques of fighting than gutter riffraff. Are you certain you wish to engage us?"

My heartbeat had slowed. Though death could not be far off, I felt oddly tranquil. "Certain, tribune. I wasn't aware my partner had so many exalted friends. I'm ready for you."

Empty bravado. I stood little chance against a trio of professional swords and spears. Syrax was practically capering with pleasure.

"Wait, wait, Cassius! Let's have the whole company first. I think you'll be so surprised by the treat we've prepared, you'll lose all taste for fighting."

He cupped his olive hands about his mouth and called into the dark well of a stair leading up to the high tiers of the Circus:

"Come down now. Bring your prisoner. We have him."

The tribune Julius laughed. Sandals scraped on the stair. Torchfire gleamed along the flat of a knife. The hand that held the knife belonged to Ofonius Tigellinus.

The knife point was pressed against the throat of a shambling creature clad in bloody rags. A woman. Her hair was matted and filthy beyond description. Her step faltered as her captor shoved her along. All at once the knife pricked too deeply. She glanced up, hurt. Her dark eyes reached across the torchlit circle, widening, widening—

Her name came out of my mouth like a madman's shriek. "Acte!"

"Get hold of him, idiots!" Syrax squealed. Julius and the Praetorians lunged.

The sight of her, not a corpse but living, stunned me so much I was an instant late in bringing up my sword. A Praetorian slashed at my wrist with his spear. The sword clattered away.

Julius struck me across the back of the skull with the flat of his blade. I pitched forward on my face.

The two Praetorians hauled me up again. I kicked at their legs, maddened, senseless. A hard iron point jabbed my backbone.

"Writhe all you wish," Julius said. "But you'll drive my sword in when you do."

Syrax slapped me stingingly, twice. The final masks of friendship had dropped, leaving an olive face distorted with hate.

"You fine, clever, strutting peacock! You and your soft coward's guts! You and your eques toga! Did you think that I wouldn't prepare for any eventuality? I knew you'd visit the House of Probus one day. The clerk who brought you the records—" I remembered him, his strange, quizzical glance. "—was handsomely paid by my dear friend and partner

Tigellinus to report, the instant you appeared. I hadn't planned this little meeting so soon. Eventually I intended to get around to it. Dissolve our partnership. But your actions today forced my hand."

He fluttered his fingers at Acte. Her loveliness hidden by grimy rags spotted with dried blood, she hung in the grip of a sweating Tigellinus. Her eyes were glazed with pain. The Praetorians held me tightly while Syrax concluded.

"Take your time, Cassius. Exchange lovesick glances with your little whore. Neither of you will see another sunrise." He tittered. "Partner."

CHAPTER XIX

———⊰⊱———

"Cassius, plead with them. Ask them to spare you."

Acte had spoken, her voice enfeebled, numbed. Her dark eyes shone too brightly, as if she'd lived long in company with fear. She turned her head a little, went on.

"Tigellinus, let him leave Rome. I'll do anything you wish—"

Syrax stamped his foot. "Can't you silence her clacking tongue?"

The Sicilian probed the knife into Acte's neck, making her moan. He addressed Syrax sharply. "Remember whom you're talking to, foreigner."

"And *you* remember the secrets we share."

Tigellinus blinked, bit his lip and kept silent. Syrax turned back to me.

"However, I see no reason why we shouldn't let Cassius in on them. He'll be in no position to tell anyone after he's found floating in the Tiber, the victim of one of those unfortunate nighttime accidents so common in Rome." Syrax moved closer. "I *used* you, idiot. From the start I knew you had too many weaknesses, chief among them your foolish scruples. You tried hard to conceal them beneath a pretense of toughness. But I saw through that. I've hated you from the beginning, Cassius. Did you know that? You're strong. You have a certain clumsy skill in the arena. You can make your way without all the devious stratagems I'm forced to use because of my foreign birth.

But now I'm satisfied that I'm the cleverer of the two of us, despite the way you strut around wearing this rag."

And he tore my toga savagely, ripping a section of the stripe into frayed purple thread. Acte began to cry, softly, hurtfully. Her shoulders wrenched. From far back in the dark along the arches came a strange whinnying noise.

After passing his sword to one of my captors, Julius the tribune hurried away. "Keep quiet with that thing! The vigiles do patrol around here now and then, you know."

In a moment he was back. Syrax said to him, "Are the handlers having difficulty?"

The tribune nodded. "Hurry up with this business. I'm just as anxious as you to watch this clod die, but I don't want to get caught."

I drew a long breath. My head still ached from the tribune's blow. Disarmed, I meant to make a last bid to escape when the time proved right. I had in mind what I would use for a weapon, too. I forced my glance to remain on Tigellinus' mottled face, so as to give nothing away.

Tigellinus drew the knife away from Acte's throat. He watched her carefully a moment. When she continued her soft, frightened sobbing, and gave no sign of struggling, he pushed her to the ground. Then he stood over her.

Bloodied rags fell away, exposing her bruised thighs. Beneath the stained garments she was naked. One breast showed, its whiteness marred by the purple and yellow bruises left by rough hands. I was thankful she could lie huddled and cry so that she needn't watch the jackals on human legs around her. Out of the dark came that weird, high-pitched braying. Angry voices. A clinking, a stamping.

"Cassius, we're all anxious to get on with the main attraction," Tigellinus said. "I'll waste only a few words explaining matters. Like Syrax, I've longed for his moment, since the day you let my favorite, Horus, die. I've never forgiven you Locusta's death, either. I wanted her. I had the rank, the wealth. Yet it was you she picked for a lover."

"What sickness there must be in you," I said wearily. "To ally yourself with the Syrian and go into business only out of revenge."

Syrax waved airily. "Oh, the business was quite another matter. An opportunity for profit that conveniently fitted with Tigellinus' wish to settle with you."

"I am the Praetorian Prefect," Tigellinus broke in, his cheeks puffed out with pride. "Daily I've grown in favor with our illustrious Emperor. When he began demanding bawdy spectacles for private games, I was in a fine position to influence the choice of the school to stage them."

"As I think I told you, Cassius," Syrax carried on, "that dunghead Fabius quarreled with Nero over supplying what he considered to be depraved entertainment. I, on the other hand, have no such qualms. While you were frolicking after unicorns in Numidia, Tigellinus approached me on the subject. Naturally I agreed. Of course I had another partner to consider. He, like Fabius—and you—refused to have anything to do with what the Emperor wanted. So," he concluded blithely, "we were obliged to dissolve that part of the partnership too."

At last the scales were beginning to fall from my eyes. "The robbers who burned the house of Serenus—they were not robbers at all."

"Clever of you," tribune Julius said. "You grow cleverer, in fact, the closer you come to your death. No, they weren't robbers. Just these two fine Praetorians beside you, and myself and a few others. Soldiers can slip through the streets at night unmolested by the watch. We made short work of Serenus, looted his house to make the effect complete. Naturally," he added, with a bow to Tigellinus, "when the Prefect of my branch of the service suggested the mission, I was happy to oblige."

"And you," I said to the Sicilian, "took a share of the school in return for using your influence to secure the hiring of more and more Cassians."

"Brilliant!" Tigellinus cried.

"Anicetus, when I returned—the assassin on shipboard—were they sent by you also?"

"Yes. We thought at first if we slew your unicorns, you would be discredited. Not allowed to land in Latium. The bungler failed. Then Syrax reported you hardly seemed interested in the school. We let matters ride. Until you provoked our action today."

I pointed at Acte sprawled on the ground. "And the girl?"

Tigellinus licked his lips. "A captive in my house, since the night Julius disposed of Serenus. I kept her because she was your favorite, beast-man. She provided me with much pleasure. Not willingly, I admit. Often I've had to tie her down before I used her."

The words blurred, drowned beneath a rising tide of disgust and rage within me. I hung between the two Praetorians awaiting my chance to strike out and kill as many of them as I could before I died. Tigellinus was still speaking, a lewd light in his eggish eyes.

"The real reason I spared her life was to have her present for this moment. So I could take her life before your very eyes. To pay you for taking Locusta from me."

Like the master of the games briskly announcing the next event, Syrax intruded, "I think that settles all questions outstanding, eh, Cassius? Time for our little demonstration. Unnecessary, perhaps. Risky, doing it here. Yet few souls are hardy enough to venture down in these dark places at night. I believe we're safe if we work quickly." He turned, shouted, "The animal!"

Back in the darkness shadows began to stir. Hooves clattered loudly on stone. Men cursed. I had a dim suspicion about what they planned. I rejected it as unthinkable. Yet the evidence of my senses couldn't be denied.

The animal brayed as his handlers tugged his halter and led him out of the dark. The voice of Syrax purred on, as though he were discussing some commonplace subject.

"As you know, Cassius, I've had this little stunt in mind for years. I've labored long and hard to find the secret, which I plan to put to use in the arena as yet another sign of the eminence of the Cassian School. Frankly, it hadn't occurred to me to have a tryout tonight. Tigellinus suggested it. But I think it's fitting. Your last sight on earth."

He swung slowly, his supple fingers indicating the frightened gray animal two coarse-garbed bullies were hauling out of the dark.

"The sight of a jackass mounting your woman."

Red madness clouded my brain. "You slime. You unspeakable *slime*—"

The old, confident smile slipped onto his face. "Always scruples, eh? What a burden they must be. My hours of labor were spent as devotion to the cause of natural science. I've discovered the secret of getting an animal to behave properly with a woman, in the arena or anywhere else, is not the sight of her, which means nothing, but this." He tore away part of Acte's rags. "The scent of blood. Wake her up, Tigellinus. Turn her flat on her back and strip her below the waist. Someone keep watch."

As if Acte realized why the Sicilian was manhandling her, she fought against him. But he was far stronger. His pudgy hands stripped her thighs. One of the Praetorians at my side ran outside the arches to stand guard.

Syrax picked up a bundle of the discarded rags. Laughing, he flung them at the jackass so that they draped across its long wet snout. Acte revived a little, her bruised legs shining naked in the torchglare.

I began to curse and rant, low, steadily. This nightmare was Rome, all Rome, whose rottenness and degeneracy I had once cherished as a shining treasure to be grasped and held. These twisted men and the Emperor would soon make this incredible filth a public spectacle.

The jackass brayed and stamped, growing restive. Suddenly he let out a shrill scream and reared on his hind quarters, his vitals engorged. The last of the scales fell from my eyes.

Acte woke up fully then. Her shriek of mindless fear mingled with the bray of the animal. The handlers could no longer control him. His forehooves pawed the air above Acte's body—

Giving a crazed yell, I struck the Praetorian beside me.

He tried to ram his blade through my ribs. I was already moving, leaping high, wrenching an oily torch from its iron bracket. I flung the torch straight into Syrax's face.

He batted at the flame, fell backward and crashed against the terrified jackass. It reared again, halter lines ripping away from the handlers.

"Go at him!" the tribune Julius howled to his men. "He's unarmed!"

One burly soldier took a firm grip on his spear and rushed me. The other darted in from his street lookout post. I dodged and the driving spear head imbedded in the belly of the soldier charging up. It took a moment for him to realize he'd run straight into death.

He began to caper and foam about the lips, trying to twist the spear from his vitals. I obliged him, kicking him and tugging the shaft loose at the same time.

Even as I whirled around with the weapon, the first Praetorian attacked with his sword. Its blinding arc flashed for my head. Hoofs rang as the mule ran off, the handlers not far behind.

The soldier's sword smashed against the spear I used to parry. The wood snapped and broke. Splinters flew in my face. I rammed the sharp jagged end of the longer piece into the Praetorian's neck.

Fending me off, he dropped his sword. I went after it. Both hands on the haft, I hacked from right to left, chopping him in the calves. He tumbled over with a cry. The killing lust was still raging. A second stroke, delivered with every bit of my strength, swiped clean through his neckbones.

His head sailed away like a ghastly oversized doll's, spraying blood on the nearest column. From the column's base the torch I'd thrown sent up thin tendrils of smoke. I panted for air.

The Praetorian with the spear in his guts was crawling into the darkness, making his death rattle. Of a sudden, sandals whispered behind. I'd forgotten Syrax.

"One way or another, Cassius—"

A phantom out of shadows where smoke curled thick, he flung himself on me, dagger after my throat. I tried to raise the sword. He was too agile. His oily face blurred close to mine, the dagger driven before it, straight for my bowels.

Desperately I threw myself backward, spilling over my own feet. The ferocity of his lunge carried his knife hand on, burying the blade in the pillar. At its base the wood was afire. Syrax's feet tangled in the torch. He fell. His knees crashed down on the burning brand.

He threw his head back and screamed in mortal pain. His tunic blazed up. Tongues of yellow leaped from his garments back to the wooden pillar. In a moment the entire column from base to arch glowed brightly.

Flames spread across the arch to the next column, then across the arcade itself toward the inner wall and the wooden stands above. Syrax's cheeks shone like melted wax as he regained his balance, demented by pain, his whole tunic afire, tendrils of orange starting in his hair. He pulled the dagger out of the wood.

Hate drove him on one faltering step, another. Handling my sword like a spear, I raised it over my head and threw it point first.

Syrax danced high off the paving stones a moment. Then he tumbled back against the flaming pillar and slid down to its base. Chunks of the burned arch began to drop, striking him on the head and shoulders, raining more fire. The skin of his cheeks began to blacken. I had a last ghastly view of that sly face jerking, jerking, as if in a smile—

A sheet of flame leaped up. All that remained of him was the hilt of the sword buried in his belly. The blade was a bright shaft leading into the heart of the fire.

All around, the heat increased. Smoke whirled. Sweat rivered off my body. The wood of the Circus Maximus was ancient and dry, near to rotting in many places. A whole chain of pillars was burning. Fire leaped from one to the next, then the next, like a devil unleashed.

The glare grew unbearable. The wooden stands overhead caught. In a nearby tenement frightened citizens shouted, "Vigiles! Fetch the bucketmen! *The Circus is burning!*"

I plunged down to the next arch, shouting her name.

"Acte! *Acte!*"

The cries were lost among the creaks of smoldering wood and the hiss of sparks. Tigellinus had fled. So had the tribune Julius. And they had taken Acte with them.

I rushed out from beneath the arches. Overhead a section of the stands buckled and dumped flaming debris on the spot where I'd stood a moment before. Half the circumference of the Circus appeared to be blazing, casting a red glaze on the sky. Shouts, screams, the trample of feet sounded from the nearby insulae. Once the flames crossed open ground, the tenements would go up like matchwood, and everyone inside would perish.

Parties of vigiles bawled to one another down dark streets. Their brazen alarm horns blew. Wind fanned my cheeks, hot and growing hotter as the fire fed upon itself.

Again and again I shouted her name. No use.

Then, down one of the tenement thoroughfares radiating from the Circus, I thought I heard my name cried in return.

I raced in that direction. Frantic people swarmed from the buildings, carrying children and piles of belongings. A party of vigiles ran past laden with the familiar water buckets made of rope sealed up with pitch.

Faces, bodies blocked my run up the inclined street. My chest ached. I searched the tangle of frightened humanity for a glimmer of Praetorian armor. People were fighting each other as more and more teemed out of the tenements. Blows rained on me, and curses. Any man strong enough to run away was a weaker man's enemy.

"Clear the path! Coming through!" another patrol of vigiles shouted, knocking men and women out of the way as they ran down to the Circus. At a corner I halted. A poor woman stumbled by, clutching an infant wrapped in rags. She sobbed, "The gods protect us! With this wind blowing, all Rome may burn!"

It seemed so. The sky was a sea of blowing sparks. At the end of the street nearest the Circus, the wall of the first insula in line was afire. The night rang with cries and alarm horns that sounded as far away as the Palatine.

"Cassius? Cassius, where are—"

The shriek was muffled in the thunder of a cart that wheeled round the corner laden with more firemen and their small, futile buckets. Crash after earth-rumbling crash came from the Circus proper. The wooden bleachers gave way, showering off more sparks that sailed through the windy dark like glittering little aerial boats. The sparks set fire to nearby rooftops.

The first insula on the street was now alight from lower floor to top. As I ran on, hunting that voice that had called to me, I saw an infirm old woman limned in a crumbling window on the burning tenement's top story. Even as she implored the hundreds milling below for help they could not give, the timbers under her feet buckled. She sailed into space, howling madly as her body burned and burned.

I ran with the tide of panicked animals that had once been men and women. Those who faltered were trampled. The street rose still more steeply, bending to the left ahead. Just at the point of the bend the last of the row of insulae on my left bulked up against the fire-reddened moon. From that building the scream came again, one of many now, but I knew it was Acte's.

Ruthlessly I thrust a man out of my path, another. I fought around an overturned produce cart and stumbled in a slime of spilled cabbages. Armor gleamed in the firelight outside the insula toward which I was running. Two figures fought with a third.

"Acte, I'm coming. Fight them, Acte, I'm—"

A man lurched against me. I kicked him aside just as the trio of figures vanished within the tenement.

If I had deceived myself, imagined her cries, I still had no choice but to follow. Either Tigellinus and the tribune had her somewhere in that tenement, and had heard my shouts and hoped to escape me in the warren of apartments, or she was lost, and they too, somewhere else in the red pandemonium the night had become.

I plunged inside the black halls of the building.

CHAPTER XX

———>●<———

FEAR-CRAZED men and women washed around me like a human river as I climbed the creaking stairs. The fire's redness through windows was sufficient to light the interior dimly, flinging grotesque shadows on the walls. I seized a woman rushing by.

"A Praetorian and another man, with a woman. Have you seen—?"

"Let go, let go! In another few moments this building will be burning too!" She clawed at my hand, foam on her lips.

"I saw them," a man cried, thrusting by. "The Praetorian's hunting for the roof, the fool. Like she says, this place'll be a pyre." And he proceeded to knock the hysterical woman out of the way and race down the crowded flights to safety.

"Acte, where are you?"

My throat was raw from screaming above the gabble of voices. "Acte—answer!"

I had reached the fourth story and was racing toward the fifth and last, these upper floors all but deserted, when I heard a man's curse, and the moan of a woman.

Firelight seeped through the open doors of the tiny rooms where whole families had dwelled together. I glimpsed the sweaty sheen of Tigellinus' cheeks at the top of the stairs before I saw the rest of his body. A sword glittered in his hand. Acte's face was a white blur in the darkness behind him.

Before I'd gone half up the last flight, Tigellinus began lopping back and forth with the blade, thinking my anger would carry me straight into its path. Suddenly Acte leaped at him.

"Hands off me, you street whore, you!" he howled, slapping at her.

I cleared the last few steps, seized his arm and broke his sword-wrist over my knee.

The Sicilian reeled against the wall. He bounded back, pudgy fingers closing on my neck before I could strike him. My exhaustion, the effect of the fight at the Circus and the long run up the street, had weakened me. I could not get in the swift, sure stroke to kill him.

His breath smelled rotten. His eyes bulged in the dancing red reflections. He backed me against the crumbling stair rail. Under fat, his fingers were metal-hard, and the power born of desperation was in him.

Harder he strangled, throttling sense out of me, harder, *harder*—

Acte tore at his shoulder, his neck ineffectually. My sword hand was behind his back, in an awkward position. I hacked at his left ribs. He darted out of the way but hung on to my throat with that death grip, grunting now, short savage grunts of fury. Leaning his weight against me, he bent me backward to throw me over the rail.

Spots of unnatural light danced in my eyes. At such close range I was unable to work the sword up for a strike. Each time I cut at his hip or his side, he was ready, dancing out of the way. My head swam. One more constriction of his hands, or two—

A door crashed open on the landing. Armor gleamed.

"Tigellinus, it's no use trying the roof. The jump is too wide for—"

"Help me!" he shrieked. "Help me finish him!"

I had a strange, twisted view of the tribune's face as Tigellinus wrenched my head back and forth, back and forth. The

Praetorian seemed too startled to make sense of what was happening.

We'll never get out," he moaned. "We'll never get out."

While Tigellinus' attention was diverted, I brought the sword behind his back again and lashed downward. He stiffened. His left hand loosened an instant. The blade had only nicked his leg, but in that second when his hand relaxed on my throat, I pulled back, then rammed the sword forward and gutted him.

Tigellinus whipped his hands down to stop the blade even as I struck. The twin edges sliced through the palms of his closing hands. The point went into his bowels. He dropped, the last light of sense dulling in his eyes.

Gasping and aching, I left the sword in his belly and stumbled toward Acte.

"Hurry. Down the stairs. The light's bright. The lower floors must have caught already—"

"I can't," she whispered, shuddering. "My legs won't move. I can't go. *Cassius!*"

She was staring beyond me, into the pitchy shadows where the Praetorian had disappeared. I heard a crazed cry, broke away from her, spun just in time to see Julius, somehow jarred out of his daze, lunge at me with the gory sword still leaking droplets of Tigellinus' blood.

I ducked and hit my shoulder against his armored belly. The blade skimmed over my head. I heaved him up. He shouted in terror.

Next thing I knew, I was standing at the stair rail while below, a scream and a crash of wood blended together. He had fallen at least two flights.

Ruddy light danced down there, a mysterious hot well of it in which figures moved like scarlet wraiths. The heat had grown almost unbearable. Acte was crying hysterically. I tried to talk to her, pleaded with her to lean on me and walk. She fought me, scratching.

I was not sure I had strength to make it down to the street myself, let alone with a burden. But I picked her up bodily and slung her over my shoulder and began staggering downward.

When I reached the fourth landing I saw the flames had spread into the first floor and were climbing upward. Faceless men scurried in and out of the apartments, laden with cheap goods. The looters gave me no notice though, bent on their carrion's work. Somehow I managed to lurch down to the second landing with Acte on my shoulder before I remembered the tribune Julius.

Was he dead? Or had he escaped? He knew I'd killed Tigellinus. If he'd fled into the streets, my life was worthless.

I turned and started upward to the landing where I'd seen him fall. A vigile, one of several swarming on the stairs, grappled at my arm.

"Go down, you imbecile! Let your goods burn! Save your life and your wife's while you can."

I did as he commanded. I ran toward the flaming street door with several vigiles following. Just before I stumbled out into the smoke-laden street, I had a glimpse into an open apartment on the main floor to my left hand. The walls of the chamber were afire. Smoke curled along the floor. In the floor's center, a featureless body blackened and smoked. Nearby lay breastplates, a helmet and one greave whose emblems were unmistakable—Praetorian.

Sucking the scorching street air into my lungs, I shifted Acte to my other shoulder. I shoved through the mob, away from the burning building. Julius had apparently made it to the first floor, but a looter had struck him down.

The vigiles were clearing all the insulae hereabouts as the fire advanced. I staggered along wearily, buffeted by people, my hearing so dulled by shrieks and trumpet-blasts and the crackle of flames that the whole scene became meaningless.

Yet some instinct to survive kept me on my feet. The hundreds fleeing became thousands. Companies of fire fighters from as far away as hamlets on the rural plain outside Rome appeared with axes and ladders and their pitifully small buckets. The fire now claimed the sky from horizon to horizon.

By the miracle of some strength I never knew I had, I came to my senses to find myself standing at the gate of my own house.

Dawn grayed the heavens, sultry red and palled with smoke. Acte lay across my shoulder, her face streaked with soot and tears, unconscious.

I reeled inside the house, shouting for the slaves. None answered. They had either rushed out to watch the fire or escaped to freedom.

I climbed with Acte to an upper sleeping room whose door had a bar. Gently I laid her on the stone couch and pulled away the blood-soaked rags. Her bruised breasts stirred ever so slightly. She lived.

For how long she would continue to live, I did not know. Who could say how long any of us would live? The fire covered the entire western section of the city, having moved outward from the Circus Maximus in a huge half-circle. Even on the heights where my house stood, smoke blew thick in the air. I was weary beyond caring.

I barred the door and sank down on my knees beside the couch. I took Acte's limp hand in mine. I rested my cheek against it, feeling the tiny pulse still beating through her skin.

I must stay awake. The fire might sweep on. Looters might invade the house. To take the chance of losing her again was unthinkable. Stay awake. Stay—

I was too weary. I closed my eyes and slept, with Rome in flames beyond my window.

Nine days and nine nights the great fire burned, consuming everything before it.

On the second morning, I later learned, the Emperor raced back from Antium by chariot to personally direct the activities of the thousands of men engaged in wrecking and trenching whole city blocks for firebreaks. All public buildings and Imperial gardens still intact were thrown open to the homeless. Cities of crude huts and tents sprang up all over the Field of Mars. Desolation, despair were everywhere.

Looters ran riot after dark. The wails and lamentations of the homeless never ceased in the streets. Only three of my slaves returned. The rest had run away. It didn't matter. Acte was alive, and revived enough on the second night to say my name a few times and drink a cup of hot wine.

The three remaining slaves were sworn to secrecy about her presence in the house. They readily agreed to keep silent once I showed them the letters of manumission I had written out. They would receive their freedom as soon as it was safe for me to leave the city.

For leave it I must. I had the death of the Praetorian Prefect upon my head, and that of the tribune Julius too.

Hour on end I sat by the couch where Acte slept, comforting her when she roused. I bathed her face and body to remove the accumulated dirt. The bruises on her flesh remained, livid.

The slaves distributed what spare food we had to the needy who came knocking. They brought in reports about new rumors circulating. The rumors said the Emperor himself was responsible for the holocaust which day by day was destroying vast areas of Rome. The rumor-mongers maintained Nero had returned secretly from Antium, set the blaze in the Circus and then retired to the lofty Tower of Maecenas to harp and sing an ode of his own composition entitled "The Sack of Troy." I listened impassively, my guilt like black pain inside me.

That the stories about Nero were given credence I could believe, since they were probably rooted in his well-known wish to raze the city and rebuild it on a Grecian pattern.

On the eighth day, with the fire nearly under control, Acte awakened completely for the first time.

We sat quietly by the window in the barred chamber. Her hair was freshly combed out, and clean. Her bruised body was concealed by a new stola I'd sent a slave to purchase. From our vantage point we could see the wide pits of black ruins. Here and there embers smoldered, but order had been restored. Many great structures had fallen, including the Temples of Jupiter

Stator, Vesta and Diana, the mighty altar of Evander and some buildings on the lower levels of the Palatine. The Forum had been spared, as had the temples and government quarters on the Capitoline.

"That's my work," I said to her. "Desolation. Death. Thousands with everything they owned, destroyed." Through the folds of Acte's gown I held the sweetness of her waist, drawing strength from the gentle press of her body. "I don't remember everything that happened under the arches. But I was the one who took down the first torch."

"Cassius, don't blame yourself. You wouldn't have gone there that night had it not been for the actions of evil men. What happened might have happened in a thousand other ways, from a thousand other chance sparks."

"That's not much comfort. All my life I'll wonder. If Syrax hadn't driven his knife into the pillar, fallen into the fire, might I have put it out in time?"

"Darling, we're done with the past. We're together."

I held her shoulders and kissed her long. "But is the past done with us?"

"Tigellinus died in the insula. So did the tribune. You told me so only a moment ago. There were no other witnesses. And the Prefect's death is the only one that would cause the Emperor any concern. He'll never suspect how it really happened. He'll blame the fire."

My heart hardened again. "He deserved to die. You still haven't told me what happened when he held you a prisoner so long."

She shuddered lightly. In the glow of a wick simmering in the bowl of oil, her dark eyes were haunted.

"I was kept with the slaves. But I was more than a slave. Forced to do things no slave, even the lowest and meanest, would do. I was forced to—"

Abruptly she shook her head. "No. That's done with too. Perhaps one day I'll tell you. One day when we're free of Rome and I—I can speak of it without trembling."

"I haven't thought of where we can go. Perhaps Africa. The decurion Publius once told me the air was much more free there. I didn't believe him. I do now. Of course," I added bitterly, "I'll be running away from my guilt, as well as from everything else."

Acte took my hand in hers and kissed me gently again. "Cassius, why torture yourself? Can you undo what happened in the Circus and afterwards?"

"No. But I wish with all my heart I could."

Acte made no reply. I think she knew, as I did, that if we ever untangled the strands of our lives and found a place where we could live safely and content, I would still waken late at night, out of a dream of flames, and wonder whether I had mocked some unseen god once too often. Wonder whether that god had made me the instrument of his wrath that terrible night when the fire began.

"Do you really think it's unsafe for us to stay in this house, Cassius?"

"Safety is one question, desire another. What Syrax tried to do—what he worked so long and hard to perfect, with the Emperor's blessing—well, if that's the kind of thing Rome stands for now, and condones, I want none of it."

Her brow wrinkled in puzzlement. "What do you mean?"

Astonished, I said, "Don't you remember what happened?"

"When? At the Circus?"

"Yes."

"I remember Tigellinus throwing me on the ground. And some sort of animal whinnying. That's all. Did it have something to do with those awful rags they wrapped around me when they took me from Tigellinus' house? I asked a guard about the purpose of the rags. He laughed."

Grateful relief swept over me. "Yes, Acte. Something to do with that."

"Tell me what."

I shook my head. "If you have things to forget, I do also." I changed the subject. "Our chief worry now is leaving Rome.

I'm reasonably sure you're well enough to travel, though I don't want to risk taking you to a physician to find out. We must move rapidly, yet slowly too. We mustn't arouse anyone's suspicion. We'll make our plans and then one night simply disappear. After that we—Why are you smiling?"

"Because, my darling, I am well. Well enough to travel. Well enough to—to wish for—"

Lout that I am, it took me a moment to understand. But not much longer.

I was fearful of hurting her. But there was hunger in her, as if after all her pain she must find release. Soon we lay together on the couch, the lamp wick out.

Her body was cool and white in the dim reflection of the dying fires, and the bruises did not show. Her breasts were sweet to my tongue, and her lips sweeter. I put my arms around her and possessed her, fully and deeply. She brought me succor from loneliness and despair.

Later, she drifted off to sleep, smiling to herself.

I remained tense and awake, gazing at the fire patterns on the ceiling.

Tigellinus was murdered.

I had done the deed.

Was there anyone left alive who knew?

CHAPTER XXI

THE EVENTS of the following days only strengthened my desire to escape from Rome. It became freshly clear that the Emperor's chief claim to fame lay in the depth of his deceit. And the one joy of the populace had become the practice of public cruelty.

In the wake of the widespread rumors that Nero was responsible for the fire—a fable no sane person believed—scores of slaves and courtiers testified to his presence at Antium on the night in question. The blame was laid on the peculiar Christian sect. Nero denounced the cult in high-pitched screams one morning in the Senate.

By nightfall mass arrests were underway. Groups of Christians were harried through the streets on their way to the courts, pelted with rocks and animal dung by outraged citizens.

The persecution was absurd. Whatever the worth of their beliefs, if the Christians as a group resembled the man Paulus at all, it should have been apparent that wholesale arson was not a method they would choose to cleanse Rome of its alleged wickedness. Yet scapegoats had to be found.

Women and even young children were hauled before magistrates and ordered to burn incense to Nero's genius. When they refused, prison was their lot, followed by a series of hastily arranged games at the Circus of Nero. The Christians were thrust unarmed into the arena to face packs of lions and leop-ards while the crowd jeered.

Though I had in no way become a convert to even a fraction of their beliefs, yet I respected the courage of the Christians. While the rabble ran this way, then that, following each shift of the political wind off the Palatine, the Christians remained steadfast. I remembered that once I too had danced—and gladly—to whatever crazy tune the Princeps chose to play on his lute. The glow of torches burning at night over Nero's Circus across the Tiber depressed me.

While the city's attention was focused on daily outbursts against the cultists, I was able to move here and there about the city virtually unnoticed. I set my three servants free after gaining their promise that they would leave Rome instantly. I visited the Cassian School, which had escaped damage, and put on a show of grief over the loss of my partner. It was as-sumed he'd died like so many others in the fire.

I told the lanista Ramor that after a suitable period of mourn-ing, I would return and try to put the school's affairs in order. Meantime, he would be in charge. He was pleased. He would have been overjoyed, I suspect, had I told him that within days, he would find himself the owner by default of the entire estab-lishment.

At the House of Probi I discreetly withdrew enough cash from my accounts to take Acte and me to Africa and maintain us for a few months. To withdraw more, I felt, would immedi-ately excite suspicion. Of the sharp-eyed clerk who had been in Syrax's pay I saw nothing. Perhaps he was another who had perished in the burning.

In a seedy shop in the Field of Mars, near the acres of ram-shackle huts where the fire refugees lived, I arranged for pas-sage for two persons out of Ostia to Iol Caesaria. I told the pox-cheeked man who handled matters that I was taking a certain married lady away from her husband. Thus my name, which I never gave, and hers, must be protected.

The man laughed and winked in lewd sympathy. Adultery was another subject for fun these days. When I called on him again, he had obtained accommodations on a grain galley leaving Ostia in seven days.

"Seven days!" Acte exclaimed, hugging me. "It'll seem like a lifetime. But once it's over—"

"We shall finally be free," I finished.

We were in the barred chamber, the only room in the house we used, apart from the scullery. The windows elsewhere were shuttered. Cobwebs gathered everywhere. The quiet unnerved me a little.

"I wish we were leaving tonight. I want to be gone from here so badly, my mind invents a hundred different circumstances that will stop us."

Acte smiled and kissed me. "Nothing will stop us, my darling. I feel it."

I held her tightly and told her I hoped this was so. But even when I slept that night, I had wild nightmares in which the shade of Tigellinus rose from the place of the dead to accuse me of murder.

At sunrise there was a loud hammering on the gate. Acte and I waited tensely, hoping it was some tradesman who would go away.

The hammering continued.

Acte's eyes grew fearful. I picked up the sword I kept beside the bed. With false confidence I told her, "Wearing this old tunic, I can pass for a household slave. I'll send whoever it is away." I slid off the gold ring of my eques rank as I left the room.

In the pale first light, a grumpy Imperial herald waited on the doorstep. I rubbed my eyes and mumbled, "Who's rousing a decent household at this ungodly hour?"

"Watch your tongue, slave. And put that sword away. I'm one of three hundred emissaries sent from the Palatine with a proclamation for every eques in Rome."

From under his cloak he produced a heavy scroll adorned with wax seals impressed with the Imperial eagles. "This is the home of—" He consulted the scroll. "—Splendidi Cassius Flamma, is it not?"

"That's correct. But my master has gone to the seashore for a holiday."

"Then you'd better send someone to fetch him. Four days hence, the annual summer review of the equites is to be held in the Forum."

I blinked and feigned stupidity. "How can that be? It was canceled by Imperial order while the fire still raged. I thought the Emperor had dispensed with all ceremonies and rituals because of the chaos in the city."

The herald's eyes narrowed. "For a slave you're certainly conversant with many things."

Hastily I backtracked. "Oh, that's because I'm my master's steward."

"If so, make certain your master is present for the review. The Emperor has also scheduled a new series of games in his Circus immediately following the parade. Details are being posted on the *Acta Diurna* this morning."

His rough face assumed a more tolerant cast. In spite of his splendid attire, he was a slave like I was supposed to be.

"If you want my opinion, friend, I think Nero decided to schedule the parade and these special games to take people's minds off the nasty stories circulating about who started the fire. Well, be sure to pass along the news. The Emperor wants every last eques in attendance, as always. Now I must be off. Let's see, who's next on my list?"

He hurried away down the street. I shut the gate with a cold and heavy hand.

When I told Acte the news, she didn't seem disturbed.

"We'll simply have to leave for Ostia early. Wait there rather than here until the ship sails."

I shook my head. "Impossible."

"Oh, Cassius, no."

"Yes. I must arrange for a horse and ride in the review."

"Why? Among several thousands, you'll never be missed."

"Perhaps. On the other hand, the chief marshal of the parade carefully checks off each eques' name. Not to appear would draw attention to me. If I go I'll be just another face, but my name will be checked off."

As I gathered her into my arms I felt her faint trembling. Indeed, I was a little uneasy too. But I tried not to show it.

"Two or three hours and I'll be done. I can slip away immediately after the parade and join you in Ostia. No one will notice the absence of Cassius Flamma once the review's over, perhaps not for months. Hush, now. No arguments. And no tears."

"I suppose I am being silly, Cassius." She wiped her eyes. "But so many things came between us for so long. I'm afraid something else may—"

"Nothing will happen," I assured her. "Beyond my making certain we'll be safer than ever once we're on that ship."

"Then let me stay with you. Wait for you here during the review."

"No."

"I'll watch from the Forum then."

"No. It's better you go to Ostia. Some of the less savory elements make a practice of breaking into large houses like this one when the city turns out for the parade. And if you went to the Forum, that would be just the time you'd meet some slave from Tigellinus' house. I'd rather have you settled safely at the port. I'll arrange for quarters at an inn. You'll be well protected, I promise."

"I see what you mean. But I think you're being overly cautious."

"Acte, a man is not careless with the treasure he prizes most. He guards it against any eventuality. That's one lesson I've learned from harsh experience."

My words broke her resistance, and she came into my arms eagerly.

Later that day I put on a cloak and went out again. At nightfall a hired litter arrived for her.

The bearers had been led to believe she was some cuckolded noble's wife I was spiriting away. I had dressed her in an expensive stola and many gaudy, if relatively worthless, baubles. Quarters had been secured in Ostia by the same seedy criminal who booked our passage. I'd paid him well. I had no worry that he would betray me, turn my imitation Senator's wife over to wharf thieves to be robbed. In fact I'd made a point of promising that I would search him out and personally wring his neck in such an event.

In the dusky evening light, with torches blowing in the windy street, I took leave of the woman I loved.

"Be careful, darling," she said as she held my hand from the litter.

"There's nothing to worry about, sweetest." I made the fatuous remark loudly, as though I'd been drinking. "Your stupid husband will never even suspect what's happened."

The litter bearers exchanged sly glances and promptly forgot the whole affair. I kissed Acte on the mouth. Her cheek was cold. She smiled, but without heart. The curtains dropped into place. The bearers trotted off down the street, linkboys before and behind, torches flickering. I returned to the empty house.

As the day of the review approached I visited a leading stable to rent my horse. A holiday mood prevailed in the city, despite the ruin left by the fire. On the appointed morning, the parade assembled on the lower slopes of the Palatine.

The high marshal checked off my name without so much as a blink. Trumpets rang. Timbrels thudded. The highest equites, those whose titles were the most ancient, set off toward the Forum riding six abreast. Their ivory togas shone in the bright sunlight. Gems sparkled and ostrich plumes danced on the manes of their mounts.

My place was far back in the procession, on the right-hand side of the rank of six. Luck was with me. The Emperor's podium was erected on our left.

I barely had a glimpse of him as we cantered past, togas whipping in the wind. The Forum rang with the cheers of the hundreds of thousands who jammed every corner to watch. Nero's flushed face was turned toward his painted Empress. Then my horse was past. I was astonished that it had been so quick and simple.

"Cassius Flamma!"

High-pitched and angry, the voice rang out again.

"Cassius Flamma!"

"Ho, that's you, isn't it?" said the spindly old knight riding alongside me.

"Someone must have called from the crowd," I began, chilled. "The Emperor wouldn't—"

"But he's standing!" the old man whispered. "Rein up, you fool. Rein up quickly."

The people nearest us fell silent. The quiet rippled outward and up sloping streets where hundreds clung precariously to the upper stories of gilded government buildings. An assistant parade marshal four ranks ahead spurred back along the line.

"The rest of you hold up. Cassius Flamma? The Emperor summoned you."

The leather reins turned to ice in my hand. The marshal opened a path for me. I jogged left through the rank and back in the direction of the podium.

Behind the Emperor stood a rank of Praetorians in shining armor. Poppaea Sabina watched me with amusement as I reined in before the Imperial stand.

Wind rustled the purple hangings above the Emperor's head as he paced back and forth. My heart thudded so loud inside me I thought all would hear. Beneath my toga wet rivers of sweat streamed down.

But I kept my face like a chunk of wood. The game was still unknown.

"The Emperor has commanded," I said after saluting. "Cassius Flamma attends."

With a snigger he flung out his bejeweled right hand to point at me.

"Cassius Flamma—*sell your horse.*"

The ancient command had the effect of a thunderclap on the mob. Shocked exclamations rippled out like waves on the sea. The leader of the Praetorians behind the throne glanced down the line of his men, as if signaling. I said, "May I know why the Emperor gives that order?"

Evil mirth filled his bulbous eyes. "Because, Cassius Flamma, I do not deem it fitting that our second highest noble order should number among its members—among its members—" He began to stutter then, his lips shining with the spittle of rage. "—among its members the murderer of our—our exalted Praetorian Prefect Ofonius Tigellinus."

The sunlit Forum swam dizzily around me. I tried to brazen it out.

"Emperor, this false accusation—"

From behind the Praetorians, his armor polished to a gold luster, stepped the tribune Gaius Julius.

"The accusation is not false," he said. "I saw you kill him."

The ranked Praetorians swarmed forward, dragged me down from horseback and began raining blows on me while they stripped off the toga with the narrow purple stripe. I was dragged up before the podium. Julius kicked my belly once, hard.

"Vermin! When you pitched me down the stairs, perhaps you thought I died. I did not. I fell one flight and crawled the rest. A pack of looters attacked me. Stripped my helmet and armor after they knocked me down. But just in time, the vigiles arrived and I escaped."

A scene danced in my mind: a blackened body; armor littered in a burning tenement room. The corpse of a looter; not Julius's after all. He had been hiding all these days, waiting for a fitting time to denounce me.

The Emperor thrust the tribune aside, screaming, "I accuse this man Cassius Flamma of the willful murder of Ofonius

Tigellinus. *Arrest him!*"

A hundred thousand throats roared, hatefully crying my name, demands for my death. The Praetorians hustled me away from the podium. I thought suddenly of Acte, waiting and waiting in Ostia.

Waiting now for a man who would never come.

CHAPTER XXII

I was thrust into a sour, dark cell on the lowest level of the Imperial prison. There I heard the Emperor's sentence.

Not instant death at the hands of one of his questionarii, paid torturers and executioners; a last appearance as a bestiarius in his Circus, at the special night games beginning the day after the review.

When the turnkey brought me this word, my hopes rose. Then I realized the hope was false. Clearly Gaius Julius had remained in the background after his brush with death only because he and the Emperor wanted to plan a suitable denunciation and death for me. My appearance was probably meant to be a kind of public execution.

All next day I sat in the gloom, not touching the rotted food the turnkey brought in. A little of my strength returned, and determination too. At least I need not lie down and die like a coward. In whatever event I was scheduled to fight—the turnkey knew, but refused to tell me—I would make as decent a showing as I could before the end came.

I begged the turnkey to help me send a message to Acte. Again he refused.

At nightfall I was taken from the cell, given a cheap clout to wear and thrust inside a wooden cage cart drawn by two mules. Like an animal on exhibit, I was carried through streets where drunken citizens jeered and hurled rocks. I watched impassively from behind the bars. On buildings I saw scrawled in-

scriptions like *Death to Cassius the killer* and *The gods give murderer Cassius the cruel fate he deserves.*

As I stared at the written taunts, I thought a bit on the strange
ways the world worked. How my name had once been scribbled
on walls along with terms of praise. Somehow I preferred what
was written about me now than all the false and empty plaudits of the past.

Nor did I have any hatred for those sneering faces outside
my cart. When I was dead, some new object of the Emperor's
wrath would receive their witless screamed denunciations, and
I would be forgotten. Probably before the next sun rose.

The imposing Circus of Nero glowed with lights. The cart
rattled across a Tiber bridge and creaked down a long tunnel
beneath the stands. The tunnel, by contrast with the array of
torches along the outer walls, seemed unnaturally dark.
Drunken shouts from thousands of spectators rang in the
night. The interior of the amphitheater seemed strangely
black too.

I asked a handler, "Where are the tiers of torches to light up
the sand?"

He chuckled. "Different torches are being used tonight.
Come to think of it, you might enjoy watching before we lock
you up to await your turn on the program."

Under guard, I was taken to the tunnel mouth. A few lanterns gleamed here and there in the stadium, but apart from
those, the packed masses sat in virtual darkness.

Musicians sounded the opening call of the festivities. Lights
were struck in the Emperor's box half way down the right-
hand balustrade. A torch was lighted from the puffs of tinder,
and passed to a man on the sand below the box. He in turn lit
torches in the hands of a dozen slaves grouped around.

The light increased. The crowd surged to its feet, applaud-
ing. The slaves fanned out across the arena. In the glow of the
firebrands, it was possible to suddenly see tall wooden crosses
arranged at intervals around the great oval. On the crosses naked human beings had been nailed up.

At first I refused to believe what I saw. I told myself the black stuff smeared on the feet and legs of the crucified men and women was not what it smelled like. A torch boy reached the cross nearest Nero's box, flung his torch hand high. A young girl of twenty or so hung there. She shrieked when the black pitch smeared on her legs ignited.

All around the amphitheater, a great rosy light sprang up, making the sand bright as day, flashing off the armor of Praetorians in the stands, and off the gilt garland on the head of Nero, who rose to acknowledge the applause. One by one, the human torches blazed up.

"The Christians make splendid illumination, don't they?" the handler asked.

"Lock me up," I snarled. "It makes me sick."

He gave me a boot in the spine. "I hardly think we have to worry about the opinion of a condemned murderer. If the Emperor approves, surely the gods must. Move along!"

Imprisoned in a stone chamber, I pondered over the incredible sight I had seen. Occasional shrieks of pain drifted through the thick walls, mostly women's. At last the door opened again.

"Ready, killer? The Thracians are finished. It's your turn as soon as the sand's cleared."

I was led back to the tunnel opening. Slaves were busy carting off the dead gladiators who had fought in Thracian dress, with small round shields and curved Grecian swords. Other men climbed wood ladders leaning against the crosses. They hacked down blackened bodies, dragged unprotesting new victims up, hammered in the nails and then smeared the Christians with pitch. Nowhere did I see one of the living sacrifices resist.

The charred stink that hung in the air turned my stomach. A guard thrust a long sword in my hand, whispered, "I saw you win the wooden sword. I wish you luck, even though you don't stand a chance. The Praetorians want blood."

"Do you know who I'm going against? A man? Animals?"

"No talking there!" bawled the chief handler. "Get moving, Cassius. Your partner's already come out. See, he's waiting for you by the Imperial box."

A hush had fallen, broken only by the hiss of smoldering pitch and an occasional moan from a woman on one of the crosses. I stepped into the arena. The night erupted with screams of hate.

Rocks and fruit peels and even animal manure showered down on me as I clutched the sword and walked up the sand toward the box where another bestiarius waited. As I marched, I looked into the stands, to show them I wasn't afraid of them or their senseless screaming. The lower tiers were packed with Praetorians, the games being designed to slake the soldiers' hunger for vengeance over the loss of their Prefect. All at once, in the citizens' seats above, two strange faces leaped out.

I recognized the bearded face of Paulus, and beside him, the younger Christian, Marcus. At such a distance I could not see the agony that must be in their eyes as they watched their brethren writhing in silent pain on the crosses. For this I was grateful. Of all the chanting, cursing thousands gathered there that night, only those two were silent as I passed. I smiled to myself, emptily. Two might mourn my death, anyway.

The bestiarius waiting beneath the Emperor's box lifted his sword in salute. I hadn't recognized him because his dark, powerful body displayed many whitened scars, and his hair was streaked with gray.

"*Ave,* Cassius. I've been waiting."

"*Ave,* Xenophon," I said in return.

The Greek turned smartly and lifted his blade to salute the Emperor. Nero was leaning over the rail of his box, amused. I thrust my sword into the air also. Whatever honor I had left demanded the gesture.

"Hail, Caesar," we called together. "We who are about to die salute thee."

Nero gestured. We dropped our swords to our sides. "Hear my command," he said. "Two lions will be loosed. Kill them.

Then each other. One man, or perhaps two beasts will live."
He flung out his arms for silence. The stands nearby quieted.
Though he addressed the noisy Praetorians, his eyes never left
my face. "By my decree, even though the victor be condemned
of a crime, he shall go free if he wins. Beast or human, he shall
be spared in the interests of a good fight."

He dipped his hand to signal the start. A few of the
Praetorians applauded for form's sake. Most didn't even bother,
grumbling openly. They didn't care for the prospect of my going free. Nero sat down, at great pains to show regret that his
decision hadn't been received with utter joy.

Xenophon jogged out toward the center of the arena.
"Cassius, the man who goes free tonight will be one the crowd
will approve, I promise you."

I followed him. He stopped in the sand. Lions snarled and
snapped in a barred cage in the far wall. Xenophon glanced at
me sidewise, adding, "I have enough money and fame to retire
whenever I wish. Nothing would please me more than to take
the wooden sword the night I kill the man I've wanted to kill
for years."

"Then be on your guard, Greek," I said. The old tension
returned. The wooden cage bars creaked up. "I have a chance
to live. I mean to take it."

"Not while there's breath left in me, you—" He finished the
sentence with a string of foul words.

With a guttural growl the first lion padded into the arena.

Deadly quiet fell again. Weird lights sparkled on the sand,
cast by the smoldering bodies on the crosses. The second lion
followed the first. Both stood sniffing the burned air. Both
were males, large, ferocious specimens. Four yellow eyes turned
toward us balefully.

I was no longer the young man I had been when I won
freedom. I wondered how much the rigors of the past years
had slowed me down. The largest lion began walking toward
us.

Sweat trickled along my wrists, making the handle of my sword slippery. The second lion growled again, remaining motionless. We were upwind of them. They caught the scent at last.

Xenophon gave a quick, nervous chuckle, crouched. I moved off to the left of him. The first lion broke into a lope, snarling as it charged.

"Farewell, Cassius," Xenophon called. "This one's all yours."

And with a lithe movement he scooped up a handful of sand and flung it in my face.

The crowd cheered him. Xenophon ran toward the arena's far end, drawing off the second, smaller lion for himself. I scrubbed the sand in my eyes, cursing. I snapped my head up in time to see the long, uncoiling yellow streak of the lion springing.

I hacked at his neck. The edge of my blade glanced harmlessly off his thick hide. The smell of him was hot and putrid as he struck me, his monstrous weight carrying me to the sand. For a terrible instant I stared into his wet red widening mouth, while his hind claws, kicking frantically, lacerated my belly and thighs.

I struck without seeing where I was aiming the sword—and suddenly my fingers were empty.

Empty. The sword gone. Flown from my sweat-slicked palm because the thrust had been too jerky.

The lion went for my throat.

I had no time to think. My knee crashed up into his great writhing belly as he bit into the arm I'd flung across my face. His fangs sank to the bone. Blood gushed, and a scream from my throat.

Again I drove my knee into him, my back near to breaking as I arched up.

The lion tumbled away, scrambled to his feet.

Outraged cries drifted from the stands. "Run, Cassius! Run, lily-liver!"

I rolled over on my face and slid under the lion's belly. I turned my hand to its edge and hit for his vitals, screaming aloud at the jarring impact.

The lion's hind quarters lifted off the ground. He trumpeted his pain. I scrambled from underneath him. He lowered his flowing mane, yellow murder in his eyes.

But when he tried to charge, his hind legs gave way.

He sprawled on his side, whimpering in dumb animal puzzlement. With hair in my face and blood gouting from my useless left forearm, I straddled him, lifted the paralyzed left hind leg out of the way, chopped him twice more in the loins. Then I reached behind me for the glittering sword and rammed it straight through his neck.

The magnificent beast died while I tottered up, everything confusion and dizziness around me. I swung my head from side to side, searching for Xenophon.

Down at the arena's end lay the headless corpse of the other lion. He had finished his animal. He would be coming for me. But where was he?

The blood poured from my arm, washed down my legs in a red torrent. A thousand voices jeered behind me, warning me he was there, and that I was too late.

I spun. My feet tangled. Out of the flickering mist of my dizziness Xenophon towered up, both hands on his sword handle and the blade over his head, aimed for the middle of my skull.

I flung up my own sword, making my right arm rigid as I could. Iron clanged iron. Sparks flew. My sword snapped in half.

I was helpless. Xenophon backed off a couple of paces. Blood leaked from many cuts on his powerful body. He lifted the blade in salute. His cruel eyes shone.

"It appears the winner of the contest is decided."

And he attacked.

White and shimmering, his sword leaped toward my face.

An eternity passed in the heartbeats. I saw my father again. I struggled to remember something. Then I had it, dim from the past—

How he'd learned the trick with the hand from a Numidian gladiator. A gladiator. My father was the one who had put the trick to use on animals.

Xenophon's sword loomed, a split second from my heart.

I dropped to my knees. The point of the blade ripped a trough out of my scalp. I struck him between his legs with the side of my hand.

Over he went, shrieking, stumbling against me. I threw my shoulder to his thighs, dumping him soundly. Then I think I went mad.

The next thing I remember, I was squatting over his body, hacking my hand again and again on the back of his neck. His eyes stared at the sand a few inches from his nose. His head was bent at a peculiar angle. There was no bone within the column of his throat as I hit it, only strange pulpy jelly.

Sobbing for air, I stood up. Taunts, oaths thundered in the stands. But I had won. And the Emperor had made a promise.

I turned and lurched toward the Imperial box. Nero was on his feet, livid. I was conscious of leaving a trail of huge red bloodspots at every step. But I was so deep in death and pain I felt a kind of exultation.

I lifted my head to meet Nero's angered eyes. I wanted to laugh in his face. My right arm was leaden. I brought it up, clenched the fist, raised the hand high.

The mercy sign.

His face dissolved into totally mindless anger an instant. Then it composed. He glanced around the stands. Gaius Julius stormed into the box, stabbing his breastplate with the thumb of his balled right fist, the signal that demanded my death.

"I have sworn—" the Emperor began.

I shook my fist again.

"No!" a Praetorian screamed.

Then a hundred: *"No!"*

Nero Caesar Augustus brought his right arm up from his side. His fingers were extended but his thumb was bent beneath his palm. He had sworn mercy. He hesitated.

The outcries of the Praetorians grew louder. They were on their feet to a man around the mighty amphitheater, stabbing their breasts with their thumbs.

"No! No! No! No! No! No!"

The tribune Julius shouted, "Emperor, he killed our Prefect!"

I shouted up to them, "A vow was made—"

The eyelids of the Emperor drooped sadly. His right shoulder lifted in an exquisite shrug. Almost like a shy youth responding to a maid, he lifted his face and looked out over the noisy crowd.

"No! No! No!"

Once more he shrugged, a pained, uncertain look upon his puffy face. But I was near enough to see a glitter beneath his drooping lids, and at last my heart and my courage broke. This was all staged and arranged in the event of my victory, for without the swords of the Praetorians behind him, the Emperor's power was nil. To surrender me in violation of his own promise would be a gesture of loyalty to the blood-lusting soldiers that none could misinterpret.

"These men," he exclaimed, gesturing to the Praetorians, "are Rome. I—I am only the Emperor."

He gave a quick jerk to his right hand, jabbing the ball of his thumb deep into his soft chest. His mouth formed one word.

"Death."

Pandemonium reigned. Screaming joy, thunderous cheers. The blood running from my arm had been wasted worthlessly. I sank to my knees.

And ten thousand voices chanted, "Death to the murderer! Death! Death! *Death!*"

My mind went dark.

I awakened sometime later during the night, in the cell at the Imperial prison.

A bald physician was bending over me, wrapping my arm with linen. The smell of some tarry unguent was in the air. The turnkey hovered in the background, holding a lantern aloft.

"Ah," said the physician, with emotionless professionalism, "awake, are you? Good. That potion I forced down your throat was efficacious. I'd hate to be held responsible for your failure to appear at your own execution." He tied a last knot and stood back. "Nothing personal, of course."

To the turnkey I said, "When?"

"First light of dawn," he replied with relish. "You're too be marched through the streets to the Forum. Stoned to death there in the manner of criminals."

I labored up from the hard couch, bleary with pain. "I must send a message to Ostia."

The turnkey shook his head. "No, that can't be done."

"I beg you, help me. I'll pay you well. I have much money. I'll write you an order on the House of the Probi that will make you wealthy. Just find me someone to take word to an inn on the coast—"

"No, I'm sorry," he said querulously. "Much as I'd like to, I can't. Strict orders."

Mumbling this, he retired hastily, taking his lantern and leaving me in total darkness. I rested my head on my bandaged aching arm. Only after days of waiting would she perhaps learn how I died.

Soon I grew drowsy. I no longer even had the strength to curse the savage and nameless gods who had destroyed me.

CHAPTER XXIII

$\longrightarrow \Rightarrow \bullet \Leftarrow \longleftarrow$

AT DAWN I was led from the cell to the prison yard.

I moved slowly, deliberately, responding like a dumb animal to the proddings of my guards. In truth I don't think it was a living man who went to his death that morning. I had died the night before, in the arena.

A group of Praetorians waited in the cheerful brightening daylight. The leader stepped forward. He saluted to make his men laugh. Under the burnished helm I saw the face of Gaius Julius.

"*Ave*, Cassius. I trust you slept well. I asked the Emperor's permission to head the detail conducting you to the Forum. I also trust you understand why."

"Perfectly. Get it done with."

"Forward!" he called sharply. His men ringed me and the prison gates creaked open.

Outside a large crowd had already gathered, the inevitable carrion who attended any execution. Their numbers increased as we moved along the twisting streets, Julius smiling and making many jests at my expense.

I intended to offer no resistance when we reached the Forum. All I wanted now was a quick end. The taunts of the mob meant nothing, neither hurting nor provoking me. I closed my mind to the swelling roar of the hundreds streaming along behind the circle of Praetorians. I remembered Acte's lovely face while I still had the chance. Of all those whom I'd known in my wasted life, she was the one person I regretted leaving.

The glittering roofs of an unburned section of the Palatine shone in the distance. The glitter reminded me again that I had worshipped false gods. Only Acte's love had showed me the truth of it. Perhaps this was the price I had to pay for my error.

Several blocks from the Forum, Julius called an order to halt. Another, smaller crowd had gathered just ahead, surrounding a fountain at the intersection. On the fountain's sculptured rim stood a man in a plain robe. His words carried above the mutterings of the pack at my heels.

"—for the ways of God are not evil ways, as your Emperor wishes you to believe, but the ways of righteousness."

"That's treason!" someone cried. I perceived dully that the orator was Paulus.

"Treason to Rome," Paulus called back, "but loyalty to God. I plead with you, citizens. I am one of you, remember, a citizen—turn against the godless ways of this city. Seek the path of righteousness before the evil that flows from the Palatine engulfs you completely."

"Pull that wretch down!" Julius shouted, storming ahead. "Move aside! Let me through!"

Paulus flung out his hand, pointing at Julius.

"See? Even public murder is given a blessing by the debauched creature who rules you. He sends out his killers in the armor of respectability."

"Going to let him get away with that kind of talk, tribune?" a woman screeched from a rooftop. "I say pull him down and kill him!"

Angrily others agreed. Paulus remained standing on the edge of the fountain, however. Suddenly I saw another anxious face below his. That of the young man Marcus.

Paulus seemed unconcerned about bringing the Praetorians' wrath down on himself. He pointed a second time at purple-cheeked Julius, shouting contemptuously, "Look at him preen, that hired brute who conducts a man to his death while making jokes. Is that a specimen of Roman honor? To me it looks more like a specimen of Roman rot."

Wearily I wondered why Paulus was so bent on provoking the soldiers. The tribune's jaw trembled as he yanked out his long sword and waved it at the Christian preacher.

"Stand down and close your filthy mouth."

"I will stand here and proclaim the word of God while I still have strength, assassin."

Julius' temper cracked. The mob shouted for him to strike. He strode forward. The crowd scattered around the fountain. Julius confronted the bearded man.

"You'll stand there and blaspheme against the Emperor?"

"Yes, tribune. The Emperor is no god. The Emperor is an abomination."

"Praetorians!" Julius shrilled. "Half of you forward! Take him! We'll have an extra treat for the people waiting with rocks in the Forum. Two deaths instead of one."

Half the soldiers hastened to obey him. Before they reached the fountain, Paulus shouted down, "To put me to death, tribune, first you'll have to lay hands on me."

And with that he leaped into the crowd.

Marcus knocked several people into the path of the soldiers. Men cursed. The Praetorians milled. Paulus and Marcus were gone down a dim side street, robes flying.

For a moment the tribune was at a loss as to what to do. The mob had gotten out of hand, shrilling for the blood of the preacher as much as for mine. Julius' decision was made for him; the surging crowd around the fountain pushed him and his men down the side street in pursuit. The hundreds behind me thrust forward too, demanding the same thing.

"Watch Cassius, you men back there!" Julius cried, buffeted along. "The rest of you go after the blasphemer."

As if they had a choice. His band of men was hurled along ahead of a living sea of bloodthirsty men and women. The group surrounding me was similarly pushed. In the melee I lost sight of Marcus and his mentor.

Another great crowd swelled the already packed streets at the next intersection. Those people suddenly pressed back against the walls of the buildings. I saw Julius' helm plume dancing above many heads. My guards prodded and kicked me along. "Keep up, lout, keep up."

Standing alone in the center of the intersection ahead, Julius shouted to the men with me, "Take him back! Back to the other street!"

He shouted to no avail. Hundreds jammed in behind us. But the mob ahead of us parted, almost magically, the people shrinking into the shadows to either side of the street. Those behind kept shoving. The Praetorians cursed. I was suddenly toppled forward on my hands and knees, a short sword's stroke from the tribune's legs.

As I clambered up, I heard terrified whispering. Then the whispers melted away to a weird silence. Down another thoroughfare drifted the mutter of the mob waiting in the Forum, a menacing rumble.

Six women clad in white, water jars upon their shoulders, had paused in the middle of the intersection.

The tribune goggled, his face white, sweat-bright, at the Vestal Virgins on their morning journey to the Fountain of Egeria on the Coelian Hill.

Then I understood why Paulus and Marcus had been waiting at the fountain; why they had pelted off down this particular side street when they did. I saw them nowhere about. But far down inside me, a dim red spark of hope, no more than a breath, began to burn.

The scene remained frozen a moment. Sensing he would be cheated, Julius turned his back on the Vestals and raised his sword.

"I'll take the consequences for killing you in front of them, beast-man."

His blade arched up bright in the rising sun. The foremost Vestal stepped forward.

"Tribune! If he is condemned, then he must go free."

Julius hesitated, the sword still over his head. One red impulse and it would kill me—

"Stop him, soldiers! If he kills, it will be an evil omen."

Fickle as the weather, the people in the crowd picked up the cry.

"He must go free!"

"That is the law!"

"Will you defy the gods, tribune?"

"No, don't let him!"

Slowly Julius lowered the sword, trembling. But beaten.

Still, I hardly dared believe, even though I remembered the day when I'd read in the *Acta Diurna* how another criminal had been saved by such an encounter.

I took a step forward. Another.

The Praetorians looked anxiously at their commander. Julius made no move. No soldier stirred either.

One more step. One more.

A wizened oldster made the sign against the evil eye, averted his face. Sword gripped by white knuckles, Julius stared at the cobbles, cursing and cursing under his breath. A muscle in his thick neck stood out like scarlet rope.

The crowd parted. I began to run.

Screaming, struggling, people fought back out of my path. The wind of freedom, of life, was suddenly in my lungs, and the way was open.

From purple shadows beyond the point where the Vestals had paused with their water jars, two men waved as I ran past. I checked, looked back. The dark place where they'd stood beneath the arcade was empty.

Even though they were gone, their faces remained sharp in my mind. Paulus and the young man Marcus, hands upraised in acknowledgment of a debt settled. Even as I had been Marcus' keeper, so, it turned out, they had been mine. They had endangered themselves to lead the soldiers into the familiar path the Vestals took, to save my life.

The Vestals had resumed their procession. People in the crowd began calling the tribune's attention to the fact that the preacher and his companion had vanished. Julius shrieked orders. The soldiers scattered.

But none stopped me.

In the mysterious way that Rome has, the news of my coming traveled ahead. Curious, slack-mouthed people waited as I walked down to the Tiber wharves, no longer hurrying from fear, only from eagerness. I located a river barge and addressed the captain from the quay.

"I am the criminal Cassius who met the Vestals. Take me down to Ostia."

Making the evil eye sign and avoiding my glance, he said, "Get aboard. The sooner you're out of Latium, the better off we'll all be."

I knew Acte would be waiting, and she was. Strange to say, never once did I look backward. The gilt glory of Rome was empty sham beside the glory of having her once more in my arms.

EPILOGUE

Since that fateful morning when I won life out of the jaws of death only because I once showed mercy to a man who possessed neither wealth nor fame, many things have happened to confirm my belief that what was once a splendid nation is now a decaying house, soon to fall.

The preacher Paulus who dared defy the throne was eventually tried and beheaded. And the Emperor discovered the conspiracy Seneca mentioned to me the last time I saw him. The attempt to assassinate Nero never bore fruit. Old Seneca was arrested and ordered to open his own veins with a knife, which he did calmly, so they say, weary of a life of struggle.

But the blood of the Julian Caesars has run out. Five years after Acte and I sailed from Ostia to Africa, the Legions revolted under Galba. Even the Praetorians turned on Nero, sickened by his excesses. The Emperor fell upon his own sword rather than face execution.

In the next year Rome was ruled by a succession of three Emperors, each more incompetent than the last, until finally the general whom the decurion Publius had once spoken about, Vespasian, was hailed to the throne.

A new day of prosperity and freedom was foretold. In truth, I doubt it, though I see things only from afar, from my vantage point here in Iol Caesaria where I found a modest but satisfying job on the staff of kindly Publius.

Rome will not die before my time is done, I imagine. But perhaps the three good sons Acte and I are raising will face the hour of her doom. Or perhaps their sons or their grandsons. In my time, I have borne enough.

Not long past, Acte joined a small congregation of Christians which flourishes here, despite the efforts of Imperial Rome to snuff out the cult. While I am not by nature a religious man, I feel that at least they preach a way of life more honorable than the code by which I lived for a time, before the scales fell from my eyes.

With my dear wife, I am happy as any man can be who is a part of the bewildering, savage, yet often beautiful place which is this world. After much heartbreak, I have found peace at last.

Still in all, I am a Roman. Thus I will take my leave as they do in the city where I was born.

Vale! Good luck to you!

COLOPHON

ARENA is set in Adobe Garamond. Some
of the most widely used typefaces in history are those of the sixteenth-century
type designer Claude Garamond. Robert
Slimbach visited Plantin-Moretus mu-
seum in Antwerp, Belgium, to study the
original Garamond typefaces. These
served as the basis for the Adobe
Garamond romans, the face used for the
body of this book. Chapters are opened
in a bold condensed Century Schoolbook;
chapter opening quotations are set in
Cateano.

Designed and set in the foothills of the
Adirondacks by Syllables using Adobe
software which provided electronic files
used to create plates for printing.